CLARENCF

OR,

A TALE OF OUR OWN TIMES.

BY THE
AUTHOR OF "HOPE LESLIE," &c &c

" Return, return, and in thy heart engraven keep my love,
The lesser wealth, the lighter load—small blame betides the poor."
BISHOP HEBER

IN TWO VOLUMES

VOL. I.

Southern District of New York, to wit.

BE IT REMEMBERED, That on the seventeenth day of March, in the fifty-fourth year of the Independence of the United States of America, A. D. 1830, CARY & LEA, of the said district, have deposited in this office the title of a book, the right whereof they claim as proprietors, in the words following, to wit:

"Clarence; or a Tale of our own Times. By the Author of 'Hope Leslie,' &c. &c.

' Return, return, and in thy heart engraven keep my lore,
   The lesser wealth, the lighter load—small blame betides thee poor.'
                                                    BISHOP HEBER.

In two Volumes."

In conformity to the Act of the Congress of the United States, entitled, "An Act for the encouragement of learning, by securing the copies of Maps, Charts, and Books, to the authors and proprietors of such copies, during the time therein mentioned." And also, to an Act, entitled, "An Act, supplementary to an Act, entitled, An Act for the encouragement of learning, by securing the copies of Maps, Charts, and Books, to the authors and proprietors of such copies, during the time therein mentioned, and extending the benefits thereof to the arts of designing, engraving, and etching historical and other prints."

                                    FREDERICK J. BETTS.
                    Clerk of the Southern District of New York.

Sleight & Robinson, Printers, New York

DEDICATION

To my Brothers—my best friends, the following pages are inscribed, as a tribute of affection, by

THEIR AUTHOR.

PREFACE.

We had intended to affix a precise date to the following narrative, when we seasonably recollected the prudent counsel of my Uncle Toby! "Leave out the date entirely, Trim," quoth my Uncle Toby—"leave it out entirely Trim, a story passes very well without these niceties, unless one is pretty sure of 'em!" "Sure of 'em!" said the corporal, shaking his head.

The reader will be pleased to suppose the events of our story to have occurred at any period within the present century, and will have the indulgence to pardon sundry anachronisms, particularly the liberty the author has taken in anticipating the masquerade of 1829.

CLARENCE;

OR,

A TALE OF OUR OWN TIMES.

———

CHAPTER I.

"Dis moi un peu, ne trouves tu pas, comme moi, quelque chose du ciel, quelque effet du destin, dans l'aventure inopinée de notre connoissance ?"

MOLIÈRE.

It was one of the brightest and most beautiful days of February. Winter had graciously yielded to the melting influence of the soft breezes from the Indian's paradise—the sweet southwest. The atmosphere was a pure transparency, a perfect ether; and *Broadway*, the thronged thoroughfare through which the full tide of human existence pours, the pride of the metropolis of our western world, presented its gayest and most brilliant aspect.

Nature does not often embellish a city; but here, she has her ensigns, her glorious waving pennons in the trees that decorate the park, and the entrance to the hospital, and mantle with filial reverence around St. Paul's and Trinity churches. A sud-

den change from intense cold to rain, and then
again to frost, changes and successions not uncommon in our inconstant climate, had encircled the
trees, their branches, and even the slightest twigs that
bent and crackled under the little snowbird, with a
brilliant incrustation of ice, and hung them with
countless crystals—nature's jewels—how poor in
the comparison a monarch's regalia !

The chaste drapery of summer is most beautiful ;
but there was something in all this gorgeousness,
this ostentatious brilliancy, that harmonized well
with the art and glare of a city. It seemed that
nature, for once, touched with the frailty of her
sex, and determined to outshine them all, had don-
ned her jewelled robe, and come forth in all her
queenly decorations in the very temple of art and
fashion ; for this is the temple of these divinities, and
on certain hours of every auspicious day is abandoned to the rites of their worshippers.

But the day has its successive scenes, as life its
seven ages. The morning opens with servants
sweeping the pavements—the pale seamstress hastening to her daily toil—the tormented dyspeptic
sallying forth to his joyless morning ride—the cry
of the brisk milkman—the jolly baker and the
sonorous sweep—the shop-boy fantastically arranging the tempting show, that is to present to the
second sight of many a belle her own sweet person,
arrayed in Flandin's garnitures, Marquand's jewels,
Goguet's flowers, and (oh tempora! oh mores!) Ma-
nuel's ' ornamental hair work of every description.'

Then comes the business hour—the merchant,
full of projects, hopes, and fears, hastening to his

counting house—the clerk to his desk—the lawyer to the courts—the children to their schools, and country ladies to their shopping.

Then come forth the gay and idle, and Broadway presents a scene as bustling, as varied, and as brilliant, as an oriental fair. There, are graceful belles, arrayed in the light costume of Paris, playing off their coquetries on their attendant beaux—accurately apparelled Quakers— a knot of dandies, walking pattern-cards, faithful living personifications of their prototypes in the tailor's window—dignified, self-complacent matrons—idle starers at beauties, and beauties willing to be stared at—blanketed Indian chiefs from the Winnebagoes, Choctaws, and Cherokees, walking straight forward, as if they were following an enemy's trail in their own forests—girls and boys escaped from school thraldom—young students with their backs turned on college and professors—merry children clustering round a toy-shop —servants loaded with luxuries for the evening party, jostling milliners' girls with bandboxes—a bare headed Greek boy with a troop of shouting urchins at his heels—a party of jocund sailors from the 'farthest Ind'—a family groupe of Alsace peasants—and, not the least jolly or enviable of all this multifarious multitude, the company of Irish orangemen stationed before St. Paul's, their attention divided between the passers-by, their possible customers, and the national jibes and jokes of their associates.

It was on such a day as we have described, and through such a throng, that one lonely being was threading his way, who felt the desolateness of that deepest of all solitudes—the solitude of a crowd—the loneliness of the tomb amidst abounding life. He was a stranger. No one of all that multitude, high or humble, saluted him; no familiar eye rested on him. He was not old, but the frosts of age were on his head, and his cheek was indented with furrows of 'long thought and dried up tears.' There was not one of all the gay and reckless, confident in happiness, and secure in prosperity, that could sympathize with the sullen, disappointed, and wretched aspect of the stranger; but the beggar as he passed him forgot his studied attitude and mock misery, and the mourner in her elaborate weeds threw a compassionate glance at him. The stranger neither asked nor looked for compassion. Though his dress indicated poverty, there was that in his demeanour that would have repressed inquiry, and seemed to disdain charity. Something like a scornful smile played on his features, a smile of derision, of hostility with a species that could be thus occupied and amused; such a smile as a show of monkeys might extort.

A knot of ladies stopped his way for a moment. "Was you at Mrs. Layton's last night?" asked one of the fair ones. "Indeed was I—something quite out of the common way, I assure you. Nothing but Italian sung—nothing but waltzes danced." "Do you know poor Mrs. Bruce is just gone?" "Poor thing! is she?—Where did you get your Marabouts?"—"Is not that hat ravishing?"—"Do you know Roscoe's furniture is to be sold to-morrow?"—"Julia, look, what a sweet trimming!"—

" My ! let that old man pass."—For an instant the
gaze of the pretty chatterers was fixed on the ashen
countenance of the stranger, and there was something in the expression of his large sunken eye, as
its sarcastic glance met theirs, that arrested their
attention and steps. But they passed on, and their
thoughts reverted to trimmings, parties, and Marabouts.

The stranger pursued his way slowly and pen-
sively as far as Trinity-church, and then crossing
Broadway turned into Wall-street, where he eyed
the bustling multitude of merchants, merchants'
clerks, brokers, and all the servants, ministers, and
followers of fortune, with even a more bitter mental
satire than the butterfly world of Broadway. As
he reached the corner of William-street, his attention
was attracted by a beautiful boy who stood at a
fruit-stall stationed there, trafficking with an ill-
favored old woman for a couple of oranges. The
love of childhood is a tie to our species that even
misanthropy cannot dissolve. Perhaps it was this
bond of nature that strained over the stranger's
heart; or there might have been something in the
aspect of the boy that touched a spring of memory ;
a faint colour tinged his livid cheek, and the veins
in his bony forehead swelled. The boy, unconscious
of this observation, completed his bargain, and
bounded away, and the stranger perceiving that he
in turn had become the object of notice to some
loiterers about the stall, purchased an apple and
passed on. In taking a penny from his pocket,
he dropped his handkerchief. The old woman
saw it, and unobserved, contrived by a skilful sweep

of her cloak to sequester it, and at a convenient opportunity transferred it to her pocket, saying to herself as she did so, " It is as fine as a spider's web, a pretty article for the like of him truly ; it's reasonable that my right to it is as good as his," and with this comment entered on the records of conscience, she very quietly appropriated it.

In the mean time the stranger pursued his way down William-street, and the little boy, who, for some reason had retraced his steps, was running in the same direction, tossing up his oranges, and amusing himself with the effort to keep both in the air at the same moment.

Intent on his sport, he heedlessly ran against the stranger, dropped his oranges, knocked the man's cane from his hand, and nearly occasioned his falling. Something very like a curse rose to his lips. The boy picked up the cane and gently replaced it, saying at the same time, with such unaffected earnestness, " I am *very* sorry, sir," that softened by his manner, and perceiving it was the same child who had before attracted his attention, he replied, " Never mind, boy ; pick up your oranges." He did so, and looking again at the stranger, who to his unpractised eye seemed old and poor, he said modestly, " Will you take one, sir ?"

" No, no, boy."

" Do take one."

" No, thank ye, child."

" I had much rather you would than not ; I don't really want but one myself."

" No, no ; God bless ye."

By this time they had reached an old Dutch domicil, with a gable end to the street, one of the few monuments that remain of the original settlers of our good city.

The steps or (to use the vernacular word) the *stoop* had just been nicely scoured: the boy perceiving the stranger breathed painfully, and moved with difficulty, sprang forward to open the door. The sound of the lifted latch brought out an old woman who appeared by the shrill tones of authority and wrath that issued from her lips, at the sight of the boy's muddy footsteps on the clean boards, to be the " executive" of the establishment.

She stood with a scrubbing brush in her uplifted hand, and the boy started back, as if he expected farther and more painful demonstrations of her anger. " Stay, stay, my child," said the stranger, " and sit down on that bench," and then turning to the old woman, " hold your foul tongue," he said, " and let the lad alone."

" Leave him be! It's my own house and my own tongue, and neither you nor any other man can master it."

" God knows that's true," replied the stranger, and without wasting any farther efforts on the confessedly impossible, he very unceremoniously extended his cane, and poked the woman's garments within the door, so as to enable him to shut it in her face, which he effected without delay. Perhaps the boy laughed from instinctive sympathy with the power of the superior sex ; he certainly laughed most heartily at its timely demonstration, and shouted again and again, " Cracky! cracky!" an exclamation that the young urchins of our city often send up, equivalent to "a palpable hit, my Lord !"

The saturnine features of the stranger relaxed, and from that moment there was a tacit compact between him and his young friend, who seemed the only link that connected him with his kind. He received even his pity with complacency, for he felt that the pity of a child was tolerable, because 'without any mixture of blame or counsel.'

. The boy's father, Mr. Carroll, was clerk in an insurance office opposite the stranger's lodgings. Frank came daily to his father's office, and as he passed and repassed the stranger's door, he stopped with some good humored greeting, or to share with him his fruit, cakes, or candy. His bonbons were received with manifest pleasure, but never eaten, at least in Frank's presence, and when he inquired the reason of this extraordinary abstemiousness, his friend would answer, "I keep them to console me, Frank, when you are away."

Mr. Carroll's desk was stationed at his office-window, and his eye often involuntarily glanced from his books to his boy, whose benevolent friendship for the forlorn stranger, he secretly watched, and promoted, by permitting him to loiter in his society, and by daily largesses of pennies.

What draught is so delicious to a parent as a child's virtue ? What spectacle so beautiful to man as the aspect of childhood ? childhood flushed with health and happiness; its buoyant step, its loud laugh, and joyous shout; its little bark still riding in its secure and guarded haven; its interminable perspective of an ever brightening future ? And in-

fancy—who has not looked with prophetic eye on
the fair face of infancy, the dawn of never ending
existence, and seen in vision the temptations, the
struggles, the griefs, the joys, that awaited the unconscious little being? Who has not contemplated
the placid minute frame, enveloping such capacities
for suffering, and not longed to withhold it from its
fearful voyage? Peaceful infancy! must those
senses that now convey to thee but the intimations
of thy new existence, become the avenues of all good
and evil? Must these pulses which now beat so
softly, harmoniously, throb with passion? Must this
clear eye be dimmed with tears? this soft cheek,
this smooth brow be furrowed with care and sorrow?
Even so; for the destiny of humanity is thine, with
its joys and its triumphs. Enfolded in this minute
frame are the capacities of an angel. Go forth
then, labor, struggle, and knowledge shall fill thy
mind with light of thine own—endure, and resist,
and from the fires of temptation shall rise and soar
to heaven, the only phœnix—virtue.

CHAPTER II.

"Vous avez de l'argent caché."

L'AVARE.

THE stranger with whom Frank Carroll had contracted so intimate an acquaintance was known to
his hostess, and to Frank, and with them only did
he appear to have any communication, by the name
of Flavel. Frank was satisfied with finding that he was
always glad to see him, interested in his little wants,
attentive to his prattle, and reluctant to part with
him ; and his Dutch hostess being regularly paid
the pittance of his board, felt no·farther curiosity in
his conduct or history.

This remarkable exemption of Dame Quackenboss from one of the ruling passions of her sex, was
more strikingly illustrated towards another lodger,
who had, for ten successive years, rented her miserable garret. All she knew of this man was, that
his name was Smith, that he was employed in copy-
ing papers for lawyers, that he thus earned his subsistence, that he practised the most rigid economy (as
she suspected) and accumulated money. Economy
was a cardinal virtue in the eye of Mistress Quackenboss—*the* virtue, par excellence, and she reverenced
Smith as its personification. Every one has a beau-
ideal, and Smith was hers. To him alone was she
ever known to defer her own convenience. He was
allowed, whenever he wished it, a quiet place in her
chimney-corner, where he was wont to warm his

benumbed fingers and toes, while he heated on her coals the contents of a tin cup, that served him for tea-kettle, shaving-cup, gruel-pot, and in short was his only culinary utensil.

The indulgence of a fire in his own apartment was limited to those periods of intense cold when it was essential to the preservation of life, and then it was supported by the faggots and coal-cinders, which in the evening he picked up in the streets. His apparel was in accordance with this severe frugality. For ten years he had worn the same coat, hat, neckcloth, and waistcoat, and he still preserved their whole and decent appearance, from his "prudent way," as his landlady called it, of dispensing with their use altogether when he was in-doors, and substituting in their stead, in summer, a cotton, and in winter, a well patched red baize-gown. Our inventory of his wardrobe extends no farther. He did his own washing within the walls of his little attic, and they told no tales. That they could have betrayed secrets was evident from the extreme caution with which he always locked the door of his apartment, whether he was in or out of it. This was the occasion of a semi-annual altercation with his landlady, who very reluctantly conceded to him his right to an exemption from her house-cleaning. With this exception, he was the subject of her unvarying respect and commendation. "A saving and a thrifty body was John Smit," she was wont to say; "and if there were more like him in our city we should not have to pay for an alms-house and a bridewell, beside having the Dominies preaching the money out of our pockets for an Orphan-Asylum."

She magnified his virtue by contrasting him with
Mr. Flavel. "No wonder," she said, "that *he*
had come to the fag-end of his money. Every day
he left sugar enough in his cup, and victuals on his
plate to serve John Smit a week. And such loads
of clothes as he put out to wash—a clean holland
shirt every day—it was enough to make a body's
heart ache! and clean linen on his bed *twice* a week.
True, he paid for it—but she could not abide the
waste, how long would his money last at that rate?"
Thus she passed in review the common habits of a
gentleman, in which Mr. Flavel indulged, though
in the main he seemed to observe a strict frugality.
She usually concluded her criticisms with a bitter
vituperation of Mr. Flavel's and Frank's friendship.
"What business had he to bring that rampaging
boy there, slamming the door, and tracking the
entry; in all the ten years John Smit had lived in
the house, he had never had one track after him."
She kept up a sort of thinking aloud, an incessant
muttering like the low growl of a mastiff in his
dreams, and this last remark was repeated for the
hundreth time, as she passed by Mr. Flavel's door
on her way to Smith's room, and with a harsher emphasis than usual, from her seeing some dark traces
of poor Frank's footsteps, and hearing his voice in
a merry key in Mr. Flavel's apartment.

Smith had appeared to be declining in health for
some months—for several weeks he had rarely left
the house, and for the last week Dame Quackenboss had not once seen him. She remembered the
last time he came to her kitchen was late in the
evening—that he was then trembling excessively,—

obliged to sit down for some minutes, and that when she had lighted his lamp for him, he supplicated her, in the quivering voice of a sick or frightened child, to carry it for him as far as his chamber door. She had imputed his agitation to physical exhaustion, and all unused as she was to such manifestations of pity, she had, on the following morning, deposited some soup and herb tea at his door, with the proper intimations of her charity. Smith's emotion was, in truth, owing to a cause known only to himself, and far different from that naturally assigned by Mrs. Quackenboss.

He had come in that night as usual with his little bundle of sticks and shavings, and was groping his way up-stairs with his cat-like inaudible tread, when Mr. Flavel with a lighted lamp in his hand, wrapped in his white dressing-gown, and looking more ghastly than usual, passed from his room across the entry to the parlor, and after remaining there for a moment, returned, without perceiving Smith, who remained riveted to the spot where Mr. Flavel had first struck his sight. To Smith's excited imagination, he appeared a spirit from the dead, and a spirit invested with a form and features of all human shapes, to him the most terrible.

From that night he had never left his room, and his landlady deemed it prudent to defer no longer investigating his condition, lest it should be betrayed in the mode Hamlet suggested for the discovery of Polonius. She found his door, as she expected, locked. She knocked and called—there was no answer. She screamed, but in vain; not the faintest sound, or sign of life, was returned;

and concluding the poor man was dead, and with the usual vulgar fear of encountering the spectacle of death alone, she hastily descended the stairs, and communicating her apprehensions to Mr. Flavel, she begged he would stand by, while she forced open the door. He attended her, followed by Frank. The weak fastenings gave way at once to her forcible pressure, and they all entered the apartment so long and so sedulously concealed. Smith was living, but insensible, and apparently in a deep lethargy. Nothing could be more miserable and squalid than the room, its furniture, and tenant. He lay on a cot-bed, tucked so close under the inclining ceiling, that he seemed hardly to have breathing space. There was no linen on his bed, and his coverings were made of shreds and patches, which he had himself sewn together. A little pine-table, with an ink-stand carefully corked, crossed by two pens worn to the stump, and as carefully wiped, stood by his bed-side. A broken basin, mug, tea-cup, and plate, bought at a china-shop for a few pennies—a single chair, the bottom of which he had curiously repaired with list, and a small box-stove, comprised his furniture. His thread-bare garments were hanging around the room. A six-penny loaf, half-eaten and mouldy, a dried herring, and a few grains of rice rolled in a paper, and tied, lay on the table.

Quiescent as the landlady's curiosity had hitherto been, it was now called into action by what usually proves a sedative—the means of present gratification. After a glance at the sick man, she made a rapid survey of the room, and holding up both

hands, exclaimed, "John Smit's a fool! and that's
what I did not take him for—lock his door indeed!
he might as well bolt and bar a drum-head—a pretty
spot of work, truly, to have to wrench off a good
lock to break our way into this tomb, where there's
nothing after all but his old carcass!—Ah! what's
this?" A new object struck her eye, and stooping
down she attempted to draw from beneath the bed
an iron box; she could not move it; her predilection was confirmed; her long cherished faith in
Smith's worldly wisdom re-established, and looking
up with an indescribable expression of satisfaction
and triumph, and laughing outright, for the first
time for many a year, she exclaimed, "Johny a'n't
a fool but!"

Her look appealed to Mr. Flavel. He did not
notice it. Frank enforced it by taking hold of his
arm, and saying, "See, see, Mr. Flavel!" But
Mr. Flavel saw but one object. His eyes were
riveted to Smith. For a moment he gazed intently, and then uttered his thoughts unconsciously
and in a half suffocated tone—"Good God!—It
cannot be—and yet how like! He removed
the black and matted lock from Smith's forehead.
It was wrinkled and furrowed. "Seven and twenty
years might do this—No, no, it is impossible."—
He turned away and covered his eyes, and then
again turned towards the dying man, and exclaimed
vehemently, "It is—it is—it must be he!" and
putting his lips down to the dull ear, he shrieked in
a voice of agony. "Savil! Savil!" The poor
wretch made a convulsive struggle, half opened his
eyes, and looked mistily on Mr. Flavel. A slight

shudder passed over his frame, and he sunk again
into his deathlike sleep.

The landlady now interposed, and rudely seizing
Mr. Flavel's arm, " Clear out!" she said, "what
right have you to be tormenting him?"   Mr. Flavel
shook her from him, and again bending over Smith,
he murmured, " No, no, it cannot be—I was wild
to hope it—and if it were—oh God!"   He turned
away abruptly, and said hastily, "Come, Frank—
come down stairs with me.   Frank followed him,
and when he was again in his own room, he took
the boy in his arms, and wept aloud.   Frank gazed
at him in silence..   To a child there is something
unnatural and appalling in the tears of a man, but
the benignant tenderness of the boy, however,
soon surmounted every other feeling.   He wiped
away Mr. Flavel's tears, and caressed and soothed
him; and then whispering, as if he were afraid to
speak aloud on a subject that had called forth so
much emotion, " had I not best," he asked, " run
and beg Dr. Eustace to come and see that man?"

" Dr. Eustace!—who is he?"

" Our doctor—mother's doctor—the best doctor
in New York!"

" God bless you—yes—why did not I think of
it?—tell him I beg him to come instantly.   No,
say nothing of me—here Frank—say nothing to
any one, not to your father even, of what you have
seen to-day—but this doctor will not come to this
poor devil—what shall we do?—I have money
enough to pay him for half a dozen visits—tell him
so, Frank."

" Dr. Eustace does not care for the money, sir;"

said Frank, as he ran off, with all possible haste, on his benevolent errand.

"Poor boy," thought Mr. Flavel, "you must yet learn that there are no disinterested services in this world!" The doctor arrived in a few moments, but not before Mr. Flavel had disciplined himself into perfect self-command. As the doctor came from Smith's room, Mr. Flavel stopped him in the entry, and inquired if the poor man were still alive. The doctor said "yes," and that he thought it possible he might be revived for a short time, as he had probably fallen into his present state from extreme exhaustion and helplessness.

"You hear what the doctor says," said Mr. Flavel to the landlady, who was also listening to the doctor's report—"do your utmost—if the man dies now, he dies from your neglect."

The landlady put in her protest, and a just one, but Mr. Flavel did not stay to listen to it.

Either his reproach, or the thought of the strong box, which, it had already occurred to dame Quackenboss, might, in default of heirs at law, escheat to the mistress of the tenement, roused all her energies. She prepared a warm bath, and did every thing else the physician required, in the shortest possible time. The warm bath and powerful stimulants produced such an effect on the patient, that the stupor gradually subsided, and when the physician saw him in the evening, he was restored to consciousness. This the doctor told Mr. Flavel, and said at the same time, "the man must have died but for the assistance given him to-day—the discovery of his situation was quite providential."

"Providential!" echoed Mr. Flavel in a sarcastic tone, "the same *Providence* has interposed that left the poor wretch pining in desertion, and exposed to the accidents of starvation and death!"

"Yes, Sir," replied the physician, "the same Providence. I suspect, if we could read this man's history, we should find that he is now enduring the penalty which the wise government of Providence has affixed to certain offences. I infer from all I can learn from your landlady and from my own observation, that this Smith is a miser, and that he is dying of self-inflicted hardships, which have induced a premature old age. I do not believe he is more than fifty."

"Fifty! good God!" exclaimed Mr. Flavel, in a voice so startling that Dr. Eustace turned on him a look of surprise and inquiry; but he instantly recovered his self-possession, and added, "are you skilled? are you accurate, doctor, in your observation of ages?—The man seemed to me much older."

"I am not infallible," replied the doctor, "but my profession naturally leads me to make nice observations on the subject. I perceive in this man indications of vigor quite incompatible with advanced age in his present circumstances. The first thing he did when he recovered a glimmering of consciousness, was to look for a key which was under him in the bed—he grasped it and held it firmly clenched in his hand—so firmly that it would have been difficult to have wrested it from him. A painter could hardly have invented a better illustration of miserliness than the apartment of this poor wretch—the iron chest peeping from beneath his bed, and its key still tenaciously held by the famished, dying creature. My blood ran cold as I looked at him. This evening his reason is stronger, and I have persuaded him, as the fear of dropping the key increased his restlessness, to let me attach it to a cord and fasten it around his body."

"Do you think him then quite rational this evening?"

"Perfectly—perfectly himself, I fancy. I proposed to send a nurse to him, but he protested most vehemently against it, repeating again and again that he was a 'poor man—a poor man—nurses were extortionate.' I told him I would defray the expense for a night or two, for I thought I should sleep better if I had not left him to die alone, but he still remonstrated, saying that 'a nurse would burn a light all night; would eat up all he had; would keep a fire;'—and on the whole I thought so violent an interruption of his usual habits might do him more harm than good."

"He is then entirely alone?"

"Yes, but nothing can make any material difference in his condition. This is but a temporary revival. The man must die in the course of a day or two." The conversation was now turned from Smith, but Dr. Eustace still prolonged his visit. He found Mr. Flavel far more stimulating to his curiosity, than the poor mendicant miser. He had a variety of knowledge, a keenness of perception, a lucid and striking mode of expressing his thoughts, and withal, a vein of deep and bitter misanthropy, that indicated a man of marked character and singular experience. The doctor's pro-

fessional interest, too, was awakened. He saw Mr.
Flavel was suffering from severe physical derange-
ment, and he hinted to him the necessity of some
medical application, which Mr. Flavel declined, in-
timating at the same time, his complete infidelity in
the science of medicine. The doctor soon after
took his leave, with a somewhat abated estimation
of his new acquaintance's sagacity. Few men,
however liberal, can bear to have their profession
disparaged.

At his usual hour Mr. Flavel retired to bed, but
not to sleep—the strange and strong emotions of the
morning had been soon subdued, and his subsequent
reflection had convinced him they must be ground-
less. These reflections were in daylight, when
reason bears sway; but alone, in the stillness, darkness, and deep retirement of the night, his imagination resumed its ascendancy. That face, so well
known, so well remembered, so changed, and yet
the same, haunted him. The bare possibility that
it was the same, had awakened passions that he had
believed dead within him. He passed in review the
last few weeks of his life. He was himself changed
—he no longer 'dwelt in despair.' His soul had
revived to kindly influences. The instrument, that
he believed broken and ruined, and that had sent
forth nothing but discord and wild sounds, had
responded music to the touch of nature—to the
breath of sympathy. "What was it in this boy,
whom he had so recently known, that had melted
his frozen affections? what, in his mild tender eye,
that pierced to the very depths of his soul?" His
thoughts again reverted to the strange agitations of

the morning—and again, the electric flash of hope
darted athwart his mind. He started from his bed.
"Are these the mysterious intimations of Providence?—*Providence!* If such a power exists, it
has been to me oppressive—obdurate. Have I not
ceased to dread it?—to believe it? Still the web
of nursery superstition clings about me. I had
dreams last night of the long dead—forgiven—forgotten—forgotten! Singular, that such dreams
should be followed by this strange event! Am I
doating? I must still this throbbing heart. I will
see him again, though the opened wound should
bleed to death!" Thus deciding, and obeying an
impulse of inextinguishable hope, Mr. Flavel took
his lamp, wrapped his dressing gown about him,
and cautiously ascended to Smith's apartment. He
found the room in darkness. He closed the door
after him and advanced to the foot of the bed.
The sick man was in a sweet slumber, but the sudden light of the lamp falling directly across his
face awakened him. At first he seemed confused,
doubtful whether he still dreamed, or whether the
apparition before him were a reality or a spectre,
but in an instant the blood mounted into his pallid
face, and he made an effort to shriek for help. The
sound died on his powerless lips—drops of sweat
burst out on his forehead—he stretched out his arm
as if to repel the figure, and articulated in the lowest
whisper—" Not yet! I am not dead yet! oh don't
come yet!"

"Fool!—madman!—What do you take me for?
I am a living man—speak, speak to me once more."
The affrighted wretch was confounded with a min-

gled horror of the dead, and dread of the living—
the terrors of both worlds were before him—his eyes
were glued to Mr. Flavel, and his features seemed
stiffening in death. "Oh, speak to me!" reiterated
Mr. Flavel, agonized with the apprehension that he
was already past utterance. "Speak one word—
am I deceived?—or are you John Savil?"

"*Clarence!*" murmured the dying man.

Flavel staggered back and sunk into the chair—
a deadly faintness came over him, but in one instant
more the tide of life rushed back, and he darted to
the bed, crying, "'Tell me, is he living?"

The poor wretch made an effort to reply, but the
accents died on his lips—there was a choaking
rattling in his throat—he attempted to sign with his
hand, but the weight of death was on it, and he
could not move a finger—he fixed his eye on Flavel
—its eager glance spoke—but was there life or
death in its language?—who should interpret it?

Flavel bent over him in torturing, breathless
expectation. The faint hue of life faded from his
lips. There was a slight convulsion in his throat,
and his eyes closed. Mr. Flavel rushed to the door
and called aloud, again and again, for help—no
one answered—no one heard him.

Again he returned to the bed and laid his hand
on the dying man's heart. It was still feebly beating. "There is yet a spark of life," he thought.
"It may be possible once more to revive him."
A bottle of spirits of hartshorn was standing on
the table; he dashed it over his face, bosom, and
hands. Smith gasped, and unclosed his eyes. Mr.

Flavel administered a powerful stimulant—the effect seemed miraculous—the mysterious energies of nature were quickened—consciousness returned—and after repeated efforts, he articulated, "he lives—wait."

Mr. Flavel pressed both his hands on his own heart, which seemed as if it would leap from his bosom; and warned by the effect of his first impetuosity, he attempted to be calm, and to say deliberately, "Savil, I'll forgive you every thing, if you'll rouse your powers to tell me all you know." He again offered the medicinal draught.

The dying man received it passively, and shortly after said, "I am too far gone to tell it!"

"God help me!" exclaimed Flavel, in utter despair.

"It is all written," murmured Smith.

"Written!—where?"

"Oh! do not speak so loud to me. It is all written; when I'm gone, you'll find it."

"Where?—tell me where!"

"In my iron box."

What the physician had said of the box and key flashed upon Mr. Flavel's mind; he instantly dragged the box from beneath the bed, threw open the blankets, and tore the key from the skeleton body.

The ruling passion, strong in death, nerved Smith with supernatural strength. He raised himself in the bed—"Oh, don't take my money," he cried—"there is not much—'tis but such a little while I want it—it is my all. Oh, there's somebody coming—they'll see it—they'll see it—Oh, shut the box!"

Mr. Flavel did not hear him ; he heard nothing, saw nothing but a manuscript, which he seized, and dropping the lid and turning the key, he threw it on the bed, and left the apartment, without seeing the tears of joy that streamed from the miser's eyes, as, sinking back, he breathed out his last breath, muttering, " My money is safe !"

CHAPTER III.

Come and sit down by me!
My solitude is solitude no more.   MANFRED.

"Who is this Mr. Flavel, Frank, that you make
such an ado about?" asked Mrs. Carroll, as she
was adjusting a napkin over a cold partridge which
her son had begged for his friend.

"Who? why, mother, you know—the person
who lives in William-street."

"Ah, that I know very well; but he is only a
lodger there: where does he come from?"

"I am sure, mother, I do not know."

"What countryman is he? You must know that,
Frank."

"An American, I believe; he speaks just as we
do;—no, I guess he's English; he speaks shorter,
and cuts off his words just in that crusty way that
father says is English."

"Does he never say any thing about himself?"

"No, never. Oh, yes! I remember the day I
carried him some of those superb peaches cousin
Anne sent us, he said I was the only person in the
world that ever thought of him; and he said it in a
choking kind of way, as if he could scarcely help
crying."

"Does he seem extremely poor?"

"Yes—oh, no; not so very poor—I never think
of his being poor when I am with him, any more
than if he were a gentleman."

"Is he well looking?"

"Yes, mother; at least I like his looks very much

now; but when I first saw him, I thought him such a fright! He has very large black eyes, and they are so sunken in his head, that they looked all black to me; his hair is a dark brown, like father's excepting where it is gray; and his skin looks like some of the old shrivelled parchment in father's office; and he is very tall, and so thin that it seems as if his bones might rattle; and he has turns of breathing like a cracked whistle. But for all, mother, I like his looks; and one thing I know, I had rather be with him, than with any body else."

Making all due allowance for the juvenile superlatives of Frank's description, Mrs. Carroll was at a loss to understand what attraction there could be in the stranger to counteract the first impression of such a figure as her son had depicted. After a moment's pause, "Does Mr. Flavel give you any thing, Frank?" she asked.

"Mother! he has nothing in the world to give; that he very often says to me."

"What can make you like him so much, Frank?"

"Because I do, mother. Now don't say that's no reason; just give me the partridge, and let me go."

"Not quite so fast, if you please, Mr. Frank? You surely can tell me, if you will, what it is that attaches you to this stranger? Does he talk to you, —does he tell you stories?"

"Not very often. He has told me of some shipwrecks, and of the Obi men in the West Indies."

"It's extremely odd you should care so much about him; what can the charm be?"

"I am sure I do not know, mother; only he is always glad to see me, and he seems to love me, and he has not any body else to care for him."

Mrs. Carroll smiled, kissed her boy, and added to the partridge she had arranged, a small jar of jelly, and Frank ran off, happy in the indulgence of his affection, without being compelled to give a reason for it. When he arrived at the little Dutch domicil, a hackney coach was standing before the door; and as Frank put his hand on the latch, the coachman called after him, " Here, my lad, tell the folks in there to make haste; it's bad enough to wait for my betters, without being kept standing for the alms-house gentry."

The sound of Frank's first step in the entry was usually greeted by a welcoming call from Mr. Flavel; but no kind tone saluted him now, and alarmed by an unusual turmoil in his friend's apartment, he hastened forward to his door, which stood a little ajar, and there he remained riveted to the threshold, by the scene that presented itself. Mr. Flavel lay extended on the bed, his eyes closed, and his head awkwardly propped with chairs and pillows; his hostess was bustling about him, and at the moment arranging a neckcloth around his throat, while two strapping blacks stood at the foot of the bed awaiting the conclusion of her operations to convey him to the coach. He appeared entirely unconscious, till an involuntary exclamation of " Oh, dear!" burst from little Frank's lips. He then languidly opened his eyes, and attempted to speak; but failing, he made a violent muscular effort, and succeeded in beckoning the child to him, took his hand, and laid it first on his heart, and then to his lips. Frank burst into tears. " Stand away, boy," cried Mrs. Quackenboss, rudely pushing Frank, " stand away, the men can't wait."

Frank maintained his ground : " Wait for what : what are you going to do with Mr. Flavel ?"

" What am I going to do with him! send him to the alms-house, to be sure."

" Oh ! don't send him to the alms-house."

" And what for not to the alms-house ?"

" Because—because he is so very sick, and the alms-house is such a strange place for him to go to. Oh don't—don't send him there."

" Pshaw, boy ! stand away—I tell you there's no time to be lost."

" Let him stay one minute then, while I can run over the way, and speak to my father about him."

" No, no, child, what's the use ?" replied the old woman. But when Mr. Flavel again attempted to speak and failed, and tears gushed from his eyes, still intently fixed on Frank, her obduracy was softened and perhaps a superstitious feeling awakened. " It's an ugly sight to see the like of him this way," she said, " go but, boy, and be quickly back again."

Frank ran, found his father, and touched his heart with the communication of his benevolent grief. " Well, my son," he said, " what do you wish me to do ?"

Frank hesitated ; his instinct taught him that the proposition his heart dictated was rather quixotic, but his father's moistened eye and sweet smile encouraged him, and when Mr. Carroll added, " speak out, Frank, what shall I do ?" he boldly answered, " take him home, to our house, sir."

" My dear boy ! you do not consider."

" No, father, I know it—there's no time to con-sider ; the men are waiting to take him to the

alms-house. The alms-house is not fit for Mr.
Flavel, father ; and besides, I can never go there to
see him. Oh, don't consider—do come and look at
him."

Nature inspired the truth of philosophy, the
senses are the most direct avenues-to the heart, and
Frank Carroll felt that the sight of his friend would
best plead his cause ; and he deemed it half gained
when his father took up his hat and returned with
him. As they entered the apartment together, Mr.
Flavel, whose eye, ever since Frank left the room,
had been turned towards the door in eager expectation, rose almost upright on the bed, stretched his
hand out to Mr. Carroll, drew him to the bed-side,
and perused his face with an expression of intelligent
and most mysterious earnestness. He then sunk
back quite exhausted, and articulated a few words,
but so faintly that they were not audible.

Mr. Carroll was confounded. He first thought
the stranger must be delirious ; but after a moment's more consideration he was assured of his
sanity, and he felt that there was something in his
appearance that accounted for Frank's interest, and
justified it. It was the ruin of a noble temple.
Humiliating as the circumstances were that surrounded him, there was still an air of refinement
about him that confirmed Frank's opinion that the
alms-house "was not a fit place for him," and when,
a moment after, the old man fondly laid his hand
on Frank's head, and the tears again gushed from
his eyes, the boy turned to his father as if the appeal were irresistible, saying, " There, sir, you will
take him home with us, won't you ?"

To tell the truth, Mr. Carroll's heart was scarcely less susceptible than his son's, and he only hesitated from dread of a certain domestic tribunal, before which some justification of an extraordinary and inconvenient charity would be necessary. Therefore, while the hackman was hallooing at the door, the blacks were muttering their impatience, and the old woman kept a sort of under barking, he proceeded to make an investigation of the subject.

He took the old woman aside : " Who is this Mr. Flavel ?" he asked.

" The Lord knows."

" How long has he lodged here ?"

" Six weeks."

" Has he paid you his board regularly ?

" What for should I keep him if he had not ?"

" Then I am to understand he has ?"

" Yes, yes; and in good hard money too ; for I can't read their paper trash."

" And how do you know that he has not money to pay any farther expenses you may incur for him ?"

" How do I know ?—how should I know, but by finding out ? When I came in the room to make his fire this morning, he laid in a stiff fit, and I made an overhaul of his pockets and trunk, and nothing could I find but a trifle of change."

" Has he not clothes enough to secure you ?"

" Yes, he has lots of clothes ; but who wants dead men's clothes to be *spooked* all their lives; and besides, a lone woman, like I am, what should I do with a man's clothes ?"

" You can sell them to the pawn-brokers."

"No, no; its bad luck to meddle or make with *daut* clothes. Come Tony," she continued turning to the black men, "take hold; and Jupe, as you go by the 'ready made coffin' store, call and tell them to send a coffin for Mr. Smit. The body is short, and narrow at the shoulders; let them send an under sized one, that will come at a low price; for poor Mr. Smit would not like waste in his burying.— Come, boys, up with him."

"Oh, father!" exclaimed Frank, in a voice of the most pathetic entreaty.

"Stop, fellows!" cried Mr. Carroll, and then turning again to the surly woman, "keep Mr. Flavel for the present," he said, "spare no attention. I will send a nurse and physician here, and see that all your charges are paid."

"No, no; there's one death in the house already, and he'd soon make another—the place will get a bad name—let him quit."

Mr. Carroll perceived that her dogged resolution was not to be moved, he was disgusted at her brutal coarseness, and not sorry to be in some sort compelled to the decision which his heart first prompted, he asked Mr. Flavel if he thought he could bear to be carried on a litter to Barclay-street. For a moment Mr. Flavel made no sign of reply; but pressed his hand on his head as if his feelings were too intense to be borne. Then again taking Mr. Carroll's hand in both his, he murmured "Yes."

Every expression, every movement heightened Mr. Carroll's interest in Flavel, and strengthened his resolution to serve him. He ordered the blacks to go immediately to the hospital for a litter, and himself hurried home to prepare his wife for the reception of her unexpected and extraordinary guest. This was a delicate business; but he executed it with as much skill as the time admitted. Mrs. Carroll, though kind-hearted and complying to a reasonable degree, never lost sight of the 'appearance of the thing,' nor was she ever insensible to the exactions and sacrifices that render many forms of charity so costly. She heard her husband through, and then exclaimed, "What have you been about, Carroll! You may as well turn the house into an alms-house at once. I don't know what people will think of us! You and Frank are just alike! There's some excuse for him; but really, Carroll, I think you might have some consideration. What are we to do with the man?"

"Whatever you please, my dear Sarah, it can be but for a very little while. If he lives, I will get lodgings for him. I had not the heart to refuse Frank."

"Frank should be a little more considerate; but men and boys are all alike. I never knew one of them have the least consideration. They just determine what they desire must be done, and there's an end of their trouble. A sick *man* is so disagreeable to take care of, and who is to do it here? You surely would not have me nurse him; and as to Barbara and Tempy, they have their hands full already."

"I have already thought of this trouble, my dear wife, and have obviated it. On my way home I met Conolly; he applied to me to recommend him to a place as nurse, or waiter; I have directed him to

come immediately here; he is perfectly competent
to all the extra labour necessary, and as to the rest,
my dear Sarah, no creature beneath your roof will
ever suffer for attention or kindness."

Mrs. Carroll smiled, in spite of her vexation, at
this well-timed, and in truth, well-deserved compliment; and when Frank at the next moment bounded
in, looking beautiful with the flush of exercise and
the beaming of his gratified spirit through his lovely
face, and springing into his father's arms embraced
and thanked him, and kissed his mother, and expressed the joy of his full heart by jumping
about the room, clapping his hands, and other
noisy demonstrations; Mrs. Carroll went with as
much alacrity to make the preparatory arrangements, as if the charity were according to the accepted forms of this virtue, and as if it had origi-
nated with herself.

Before an attic room, which was most suitable to
the condition of the expected guest, could be prepared, he arrived; and Mrs. Carroll alarmed by his
pale and exhausted appearance, which seemed to her
to portend immediate death, threw open the door of
her neat spare-room and thus instated the poor sick
stranger in the possession of the best bed and most
luxurious apartment of her frugal establishment.

Mrs. Carroll had a worrying vein, but the serene
temper, superior qualities, and affectionate devotion
of her husband duly tempered the heat and prevented its rising to the curdling point.

There were a good many annoyances in this benevolent enterprise that none but a housewife as precise as Mrs. Carroll could rightly appreciate. "Any
other time," she thought, "she should not have cared

about it, but the room was just white-washed and the curtains were so uncommonly white, and though the chimney smoked the least in the world, it did smoke, and every thing would get as yellow as saffron, and it was such a pity to have so much racing over the new stair-carpet—if she only had not given away the old one—and Tempy would get no time for the street-door brasses, and nothing did try her so much as dirty brasses; and in short, though every inconvenience seemed to her peculiar to this particular case, her good dispositions finally triumphed over them all, and her sick guest was as scrupulously attended as if he had derived his claim from a more imposing source than his wants.

CHAPTER IV.

"'Tis nature's worship—felt—confess'd
Far as the life which warms the breast !-
The sturdy savage midst his clan
The rudest portraiture of man,
In trackless woods and boundless plains,
Where everlasting wildness reigns,
Owns the still throb—the secret start—
The hidden impulse of the heart."   BYRON

A few days of skilful medical attendance from
Dr. Eustace, the care of a tolerable nurse, and the
kindest devotion of the whole Carroll family, worked
miracles on Mr. Flavel's exhausted frame.

He seemed no stranger to the little comforts
and modest luxuries he now enjoyed. No 'Christopher Sly' awaking from his dreams, but as if he
might have been both 'Honor' and 'Lord' all the
days of his life. But, though the refinements of
Mrs. Carroll's *spare-room* did not produce any
marked sensation, the kindness of the family did;
no look or word escaped his notice; never was man
more sensible—more alive to the charities of life.
Dr. Eustace said he appeared as much changed
since the first time he had seen him, as if an evil
spirit had been driven from his breast to give place
to the ministry of good angels.

"Do you mean to pay a compliment to my children, Doctor?" asked Mr. Carroll, to whom the
Doctor had addressed his remark.

"No; not to them exclusively. I think your

influence, Carroll, on Mr. Flavel is more striking
than theirs—than Frank's even—though he doats on
Frank; but I have noticed that you excite an obvious emotion whenever you come into his room; and
once or twice I have been feeling his pulse when you
were coming up stairs, and feeble as they were, the
sound of your approaching footsteps has quickened
them even to throbbing."

"It's very odd," said Mrs. Carroll, "if he really
feels so much, that he never speaks of it; not that I
care about it at all, you know; but I think it is but
civil, when one is receiving all sorts of favors, to
express some gratitude for them."

"I am sure he feels it, and feels it deeply," replied Doctor Eustace. "He betrayed so much
emotion yesterday in speaking of your husband,
that I thought it prudent to leave the room; and to-
day he begged me, in case he should suddenly lose
his speech or faculties, to request Mr. Carroll to
keep him under his roof while he lived. He knew,
he said, that Carroll's means were too limited to
allow him to indulge his generous dispositions, and
he wished him to be informed, that he had sufficient
funds in the hands of the Barings to indemnify him
for any expenses he might incur. He has made
some memorandums, to that effect I presume, to be
given to you in case of his sudden death."

"That is just what I should have expected," exclaimed Mrs. Carroll, "true John Bull, keeping up
a show of independence to the last gasp; as if a
few dollars were a compensation for all this trouble
in a gentleman's family. Now, my dear husband
don't look so solemn; is it not a little provoking,

considering all our trouble, to say nothing of expense ?''

" Yes, dear ; a *little* provoking."

" Oh! nothing ever provokes you. I should not think any thing of doing it for a friend, but for a stranger it is quite a different affair."

" Few would scruple doing for a friend, Sarah, all you have done for Mr. Flavel, but I know few beside you that would have done it for a stranger."

Mrs. Carroll was mollified by her husband's praise. She knew she in part deserved it, and she was too honest to put in a disclaimer. " I know, Charles," she said, " that I am not half so generous as you are;" that was true ; "but I have really done what I could for the old gentleman ; gentleman he certainly is; that *is* a satisfaction ; poor man, I do feel for him. Yesterday, doctor, after you told me that a recurrence of the fits might carry him off at any moment, I thought it my duty to hint to him the importance of seeing a clergyman, and I proposed to him to send for Mr. Stanhope. He replied very coldly that he wished to avoid all unnecessary excitement. *Unnecessary!* said I. My dear madam, said he, do not give yourself any uneasiness on my account. I must take my chance. Quackery cannot help me."

" He has, no doubt, had a singular experience," said Mr. Carroll, " and has probably peculiar religious views, but I trust, better than these expressions indicate. When I went into his room last evening, Frank was reading the bible to him, and Gertrude stood ready with her prayer book, to read the prayers for the sick. He had, it seems, re-

quested this. His face was covered with his handkerchief, and I left them to their celestial ministry.
Mr. Flavel has probably lived in a corrupt state of
society and has become distrustful of religious
teachers—has involved them all in a sweeping prejudice against the priestly office. Such a man's de-
votional feelings would have nothing to resist in the
ministry of children. He would yield himself to
their simplicity and truth, and feel their accordance
with the elements of Christian instruction. I feel
an inexpressible interest in him, and I cannot but
hope that the light of religion has, with healing on
its beams, penetrated his heart."

"That is hoping against hope, Charles; if he has
any such feelings as you imagine, why, for pity's
sake, does not he express them?"

"There are various modes of expression; his
present tranquillity may be one. There are persons
so reserved, so fastidious, that they never speak of
their religious feelings."

"Well—that's what I call being more nice than
wise," replied Mrs. Carroll, "especially when one,
like Mr. Flavel, has done with the world."

Mr. Carroll made no reply. His wife's mind
was of a different texture from his, and the sensation her remarks sometimes produced was similar to
that endured by a person of an exquisite musical
ear from a discordant note. He said something of
not having seen Mr. Flavel since dinner, and went
to his apartment. He was sitting up in his bed and
looking better than usual. Frank sat on one side
of him, abstracting the skins from a bunch of fine
grapes, and giving them to the invalid. His little

sister, Gertrude, on the other, reading aloud.
"Where did you get your grapes, Frank?" asked
his father.

"Cousin Anne Raymond gave them to me, but
I would not have taken them if I had not thought
to myself, they would be good for Mr. Flavel."

"Why not, my son?"

"Because cousin Anne is such a queer woman.
I wish I had not any rich cousins; or, at least, I
wish mother would not make me go and see them.
I am glad we are not rich, father."

"Riches do not, of course, Frank, make people
like your cousin Anne; but how has she offended
you?"

"In the first place, I met her in the entry, and
without even saying, 'how do you do,' she asked
me if I had scraped my shoes."

"There was surely no harm in that."

"I know that, sir; but then she might have
looked first, as you would have done. Mother told
me before I left home, about cousin Anne's famous
carpets, and charged me to scrape my feet, and I
had. Blame her new carpets! I wish I had soiled
them."

"My son!"

"Well father, I was too provoked with her;
there was ever so much fine company in the parlor,
and I went to get myself a chair, and they were all
looking at me, and I stumbled, I don't know how,
but at any rate I broke the leg of the chair, and
cousin Anne laughed out loud, and said to one of
the gentlemen, 'I expected it,' and then she whispered to me, 'always wait for a servant to hand

you a chair, my dear;' and then she ordered the man to give me some cake—I was determined I would not take any if I died for it, and one of the ladies said, the young man is quite right, it is too *rich* for him."

Mr. Carroll laughed at the boy's simplicity. "Frank," he said, "she meant too *rich* to be wholesome."

"I don't know what she meant, sir, but I hate the very word rich. Soon after, when most of her visiters were gone, she said, 'so Frank, your mother has a famous new hat—where did she get it?' I told her it was a present from aunt Selden; 'I thought so,' said she, 'I thought she would hardly buy such an expensive hat.' I hope mother will never wear it again—I wish she would not wear any fine presents."

"I wish so too, Frank; but was this all that our cousin said?"

"No, not all; but I will tell you the rest some other time, sir." The rest, which Frank's delicacy suppressed, was in relation to his father's singular guest. Mrs. Raymond made many inquiries about him; said it was absurd to take in a man of that sort. It was making an alms-house of your house at once; and beside, it was an enormous expense; but, as to that, it seemed to her, that poor people never thought of expense; to be sure, benevolence, and sentiment, and all that, were very fine things, but for her part, she did not see how people that had but fifteen hundred dollars a year could afford to indulge them.' This scornful railing was not, of course, addressed to Frank, but spoken, as if he had neither ears nor understanding, to another rich supercilious cousin. This, conspiring with the mortifying incidents of the morning visit, filled the generous boy's bosom with a contempt of riches that all the stoicism of all the schools could not have inspired. When he, afterwards, related this supplement to his cousin's conversation, Mr. Carroll's only reply was, "It is true, my dear boy, that our income admits few luxuries—but the luxury of giving shall be the last that we deny ourselves."

But we must return to the little circle around the invalid's bed, which was soon enlarged, by the addition of Mrs. Carroll, and the following conversation ensued, and seemed naturally to arise from what had preceded.

"Suppose for a moment, Frank," said Mr. Flavel, "that one of the good genii of your fairy tales were to offer to make your father rich, would you accept the offer?"

"No, no; not if he must be like other rich people."

"What say you, my little Gertrude?"

"Not if he were to be at all different from what he is."

"I am not in much danger," said the delighted father, "of sighing after fortune while I possess you, my children."

"Then," said Mr. Flavel, whose countenance seemed to have caught the illumination of Carroll's, "you do not desire fortune?"

"No, I do not; at least I have no desire for it that in the least impairs my contentment. Every day's observation strengthens my conviction that mediocrity of fortune is most favorable to virtue, and of course to happiness."

" And you would not accept of fortune if it were offered to you ?"

" Ah, that I do not say; money is the representative of power—of the most enviable of all power, that of doing good. I have my castles in the air as well as other men—my dreams of the possible happiness to be derived from using and dispensing wealth."

" And you flatter yourself that with the acquisition of wealth you should retain the dispositions that spring naturally from the bosom of virtuous mediocrity ?"

" Surely, Mr. Flavel, some men have resisted the corrupting influence of money, and have used it for high and beneficent purposes. At any rate, if I flatter myself, the delusion is quite innocent, and in no danger of being dispelled. It is scarcely among the possible casualties of life, that I should possess wealth ; my decent clerkship only affords moderate compensation to constant labor. I have not a known relative in the world, and I never gamble in lotteries"—

" Life is a lottery, my dear friend," replied Mr. Flavel; " your virtue may yet be proved."

" Heaven grant it !" sighed Mrs. Carroll.

" Then you do not share your husband's philoso-phic indifference to wealth, Mrs. Carroll ?"

" Wealth, that is out of the question; I do not care for wealth, but I confess that I should like a competency—I should like a little more than we

have; my husband works from morning till night
for a mere pittance."

"Why should not I? Labor is no evil."

"Pshaw! Mr. Carroll, I know that; but then
one does like to get some compensation for it. You
seem to forget the children are growing up, and
want the advantages of education—"

"Pardon me, that I never forget; but the essen-
tials of a good education are within our reach, and
as to accomplishments, they are luxuries that may
be dispensed with, and for which I, certainly, would
not sacrifice the moral influences of our modest
competence."

"I do not see, Charles, that moral influences
need to be sacrificed. If you were as rich as Crœ-
sus, you would be careful to instil good principles
into your children."

"Perhaps so; but I have more confidence in the
influence of circumstances favorable to the formation of character, than in direct instruction. The
most energetic, self-denying, and disinterested persons I have ever known, have been made so by the
force of necessity. Mr. Flavel, you must have seen
a good deal of the world—are you not of my opinion?"

"My opinions," replied Mr. Flavel, with a sigh,
" have been moulded by peculiar circumstances, and
scarcely admit of any general application. Mrs.
Carroll has given honorable reasons for coveting
more ample means; she may have others equally
strong"—he looked inquiringly at Mrs. Carroll, as
if anxious she should speak her whole mind on the
subject, and she frankly replied, " Certainly, I have

other reasons ; I should like to be able to live in a better house—to have more servants and furniture—in short, to live genteelly." Mr. Flavel's countenance for a moment resumed its sarcastic expression, and Mr. Carroll rose and walked to the window; but Mrs. Carroll, without observing either, continued, " By living genteelly, I mean merely, being able to move in good society, on equal terms."

" Is cousin Anne *good society?*" asked little Frank.

" Yes, my son," replied his father ; " all your mother's connections are good society."

If there was satire in the tone of Mr. Carroll's voice, it passed unnoticed by his wife, who said, with the most perfect self-complacency, " Yes, that's true ; my family has always been in the very first society, and it is natural that I should wish my children to associate with my relatives."

" Perfectly natural, my dear wife, but perfectly impossible, since wealth is the only passport to this good society, at least, the only means of procuring a family ticket of admission."

" Well, that's just what I say, just what I desire riches for; but then," she continued, with a little petulance in her manner, " if you had not been so particular, Mr. Carroll, we might have kept on visiting terms with some of our connections. We have been repeatedly invited to uncle Henry's and cousin William's."

" Yes, we might have been guests on sufferance, and have gone to weddings and funerals at sundry other uncles and cousins, but I was too proud, Sarah, to permit you to receive your rights as favors."

"There is such a thing, Mr. Carroll, as being too proud for one's own interest; and for our dear children's interest, I think we should sacrifice a little of our pride."

"It can never be for the interest of our children," replied Mr. Carroll, with decision, "that they should sacrifice their independence of character for the sake of associating with those to whom the mere accidents of life have assigned a superior—no, I am wrong—a different station. I have no ambition that my children should move in fashionable society; I do not believe that in any country it includes the most elevated and virtuous class; certainly not in our city, where the aristocracy of wealth is the only efficient aristocracy. No, I thank God that there is a barrier between us and the fashionable world; that we cannot approach it near enough to be dazzled by its glare: for like the reptile that fascinates its victims by the emission of a brilliant mist, so the polite world is encircled by a halo fatally dazzling to common senses." Mr. Carroll spoke with less qualification, and more earnestness than was warranted by his more deliberate opinion; but he was particularly annoyed at this moment by the display of his wife's ruling passion.

"It does not signify talking, Mr. Carroll," she replied; "you and I can never agree on this subject."

"Not exactly, perhaps, but we do not materially disagree. Indeed, if the old rule hold good, and actions speak louder than words, you have already given the strongest opinion on my side, by allying

yourself to a poor dog, who you well knew could
not sustain you in the fashionable world."

. Mrs. Carroll felt awkwardly, and was glad to be
relieved by a summons to the parlor, where she
found the ' cousin Anne,' from whose gossiping
scrutiny the insignificance of her humble condition
did not exempt her.   While Mrs. Carroll was par-
rying her ingenious cross-examination relative to
her guest, her husband continued the conversation
with him: "Fortunately in our country," he said,
" there are no real, no permanent distinctions, but
those that are created by talent, education, and virtue.   These fashionable people, who most pride
themselves on their prerogative of exclusiveness,
feel the extreme precariousness of the tenure by
which they hold their privileges.   A sudden reverse
of fortune, one of the most common accidents of a
commercial city, plunges them into irretrievable obscurity and insignificance ; for to them all that portion of the world that is not shone upon by the sun
of fashion, is a region of shadows and darkness.
Perhaps I overrate the disadvantages and temptations that follow in the train of wealth; but if my
estimate of them increases my own fund of contentment, my mistake is at least useful to myself.   The
fox was the true philosopher; it is better to believe that
the grapes which we cannot reach are sour, than to
disrelish our own food by dwelling on their sweetness.
But, Mr. Flavel, I beg ten thousand pardons for my
prosing.   I have wearied you with all this common-
place on the commonest of all moral topics."

" No, not in the least ; it is a common topic, because one of universal interest.   No, my dear

friend, your sentiments delight me. I find myself
in a new region. I feel like one awakened from a
confused, distressful dream. Life has been a dream
to me ; strange, eventful, suffering."

His voice faltered, and Conolly, his nurse, entering at the moment, and observing his agitation,
whispered to Mr. Carroll that he had best remove
the children, for he believed the old gentleman was
going in his fits. The children were accordingly
dismissed, and a cordial administered, though Mr.
Flavel protested it was unnecessary, for he felt
stronger than he had done for some time, and
lowering his voice, he requested Mr. Carroll to
send Conolly away, and direct him to remain below
till called for. "I must be alone with you," he
said, "I must not, I cannot delay this longer."

Conolly was dismissed and not recalled till after
the lapse of an hour, when the bell was rung repeatedly and so violently that the whole family, in
excessive alarm, ran up to the sick chamber. Mr.
Flavel was in violent convulsions in Mr. Carroll's
arms, who was himself bereft of all presence of mind.
He gave hurried and contradictory orders. He sent
for Dr. Eustace, and on his appearing, appealed to
him, as if happiness and life itself were at stake, to
use all his art to restore Mr. Flavel to consciousness. For twenty-four hours he never left his bed-
side—scarcely turned his eyes from him; but at
the first intimation that he was recovering his senses,
he quitted him, retired to his own room for a few
moments, then came out and took some refreshment,
and returned with a calm exterior to his bed-side.
Still the unsubdued and intense emotions of his

mind were evident in his knit brow, flushed cheek, and trembling nerves. He could not be persuaded to leave Mr. Flavel for a moment, day nor night. He would not suffer any one else to render him the slightest service, and he watched him with a mother's devotion—a devotion that triumphs over all the wants and weakness of nature.

CHAPTER V.

" When just is seized some valued prize.
And duties press, and tender ties
Forbid the soul from earth to rise,
How awful then it is to die !"   Mrs. Barbauld.

WEARY days and nights succeeded. To all Mr.
Carroll's family it seemed as if he were spell-bound.
His color faded, his eye was red and heavy; he
had forgotten his business, his family, every thing
but one single object of intense anxiety and care.
His altered deportment gave rise to strange and
perplexed conjectures ; but curious glances and
obscure intimations alike passed by him as if he
were deaf and blind. Dr. Eustace said in reply to
his anxious demand of his medical opinion, " If Mr.
Flavel has quieted his mind by the communication
he has made to you, he may again have an interval
of consciousness. The mind has an inexplicable
influence on the body, even when to us it appears
perfectly inert." Mr. Carroll made no answer.
Nor, when Conolly's curiosity flashed out in such
exclamations as that " Sure, and its well for him,
any way, that he's made a clear breast of it," did
he reply word or look to the insinuation. He per-
severed in his obstinate silence even when Mrs.
Carroll, impatient at this new exclusion from conjugal confidence, said, " I am sure I don't wish any
one to tell me any thing about it ; but your silence,
Charles, does wear my spirits out ; where there is

mystery, there is always something wrong. I had misgivings from the first; you must do me the justice to remember that. A great risk it was to take in such a singular stranger. I always thought so, you know. We could not tell but he had committed some great crime. Dear! it makes my blood run cold to think what sort of a person we may have been harboring." All this was said, and passively endured, while Mr. Carroll was swallowing his hasty breakfast. He moved abruptly from the table, and, as usual, hurried to Mr. Flavel's apartment.

Frank was startled by his mother's suggestions. He dropped his knife and fork, and signed to his sister to follow him out of the room. "Oh, Gertrude," he said, "do you believe Mr. Flavel is a bad man!"

"No, Frank, I know he is not."

"How do you know it?"

"Why perfectly well. He does not seem so."

Gertrude certainly had given an insufficient reason for the faith, that was in her; and it had little effect in allaying Frank's apprehensions; and impelled by them he ventured, though he knew it was forbidden ground, to steal into Mr. Flavel's room. His father was at his constant station at the bedside. Frank drew near softly, took Mr. Flavel's hand, looked at him intently, and then hiding his face on his father's breast, he sobbed out, " He has not committed any crime, has he, father ?"

Mr. Carroll disengaged himself from his son, and locked the door. " My dear child," he said, " I am fearful, but I must trust you. While the breath of life is in him you shall know."

·' Know what, father? Oh, don't stop."

" You shall know whom you have brought to me." He stopped, almost choaked by his emotion.

" Oh! tell me—tell me, sir."

" My father!"

Frank was confounded; he scarcely comprehended the words; his mind was still fixed on his first inquiry. " But has he committed any crime?" he repeated.

" My dear boy, I do not know; I only know he is my father."

" Father—father," repeated Frank, as if the words did not yet convey a distinct idea to his mind, but as he uttered them they penetrated Mr. Flavel's dull sense, he languidly unclosed his eyes, and looked up with something like returning intelligence, but it seemed the mere glimmering of the dying spark; his eyelids fell, and he was again perfectly unconscious.

Mr. Carroll shuddered at his own imprudence. He knew that Mr. Flavel's life hung by a single thread. Till now he had resolutely acted on this conviction, and had now been betrayed by a coercive sympathy with his child. He summoned Conolly, and taking Frank into his own apartment, impressed on him the importance of keeping the secret for the present, and Frank's subsequent discretion proved what self-government even a child may attain.

Doctor Eustace, at his next visit, announced a slight improvement in his patient, which was followed by a gradual amendment. This, the Doctor said, could not last; the powers of nature were exhausted. Of this, Mr. Flavel was himself perfectly aware, and said, with his characteristic firmness, " if it is in the power of your art, Doctor, suspend the last stroke for a little time."

Medical skill did its utmost; happy circumstances shed their balmy influence on the hurt mind; and the mercy of Heaven interposed to protract the flickering flame of life. Mr. Flavel's countenance assumed an expression of serenity, and when his eye met Carroll's, it beamed forth a bright and tender intelligence, that seemed almost supernatural. As his strength permitted, he had short and private interviews with him, during which he communicated his history. We shall recount it in his own words, without specifying each particular interruption.

" Do not expect, my son," he said, " minute particulars. I scarcely dare to think of past events. I dare not recall the feelings they excited; you will sufficiently comprehend them by their ravages.

"My father was a gentleman of Pembrokeshire, in England. At his death his whole property, a large entailed estate, went to my eldest and only brother——Francis Clarence.—— We never loved each other; he had no magnanimity of temper to reconcile me to the injustice of fortune. He was a calculating sensualist, governed by one object and motive, his own interest. I was naturally of a generous and open temper. Our paths diverged. He entered the fashionable and political world. I drudged contentedly in mercantile business for an humble living. He married a woman of rank and fortune. I a beautiful unportioned girl. Her name was Mary Temple. It is now almost thirty years since I have pronounced that name, save in my dreams. She was your mother. I have forgiven her.

"You were born at a cottage near Clifton. When I first took you in my arms, I was conscious of a controlling religious emotion; I fell on my knees and dedicated you to Heaven; I now believe my prayer was heard.

" I must not stir the embers of unholy passions; an evil spirit entered my paradise; I was persuaded that it was imbecile and ignoble passively to bear the yoke of a lowly fortune; and to permit my lovely wife to remain in obscurity. Favor and patronage were offered, and a road to certain wealth opened to me in a lucrative business in the West Indies. My wife and child could not be exposed to a tropical climate, they were to be left to my *brother's protection*. My *brother* was my tempter. Oh! the folly of foregoing the certain enjoyment of the best gifts of Heaven in pursuit of riches—at best a perilous possession, and when the foundations of human happiness are gone, virtue and domestic affection, a scourge, a curse! Two years passed; my wife's letters, the only solace of my exile, became infrequent. Some rumors reached my ear. I embarked for England. My brother and wife were in France!—— Be calm, my son—I can bear no agitation——I followed them—I found them living in luxury in Paris. I broke into their apartment; I aimed a loaded pistol at my wife; my brother wrested it from me; we fought; I left him dying ; returned to England, got possession of you, and re-embarked for Jamaica."

Here, in spite of the force Carroll had put on his feelings, " My mother ?" escaped from his lips.

" Your mother ; she died long since in misery and penitence."

" In penitence ; thank God for that."

" I returned with a desperate vigor to my business ; by degrees, my son, you won me back to life ; but I had horrid passions ; passions, that never slumbered nor slept, tormenting my soul, and I was not to be trusted with the training of a spirit destined for heaven. When you were five years old, your health drooped. The physicians prescribed a change of climate. I had a clerk, John Savil, a patient, and as I thought faithful drudge. He was going to England on business for me, and was to return directly. I intrusted you to his care, and also a large sum of money to be remitted to England. This money was the price of the sordid wretch's virtue. While the English ship in which he was embarked lay in the harbor, awaiting the serving of the tide, he escaped with you, in a small boat, to an American vessel. During the night a hurricane arose. All night, wild with apprehension, I paced the beach. The morning dawned ; the sun shone out, but I could neither be persuaded nor compelled from the shore, till the news was brought in by a pilot-boat, that the English ship was capsized and that every soul on board had perished.

" I was then first seized with epileptic fits ; the effect of exposure to a vertical sun, combined with

my grief and despair. This malady has since re-
curred at every violent excitement of my feelings.
The wretch who robbed me of my only treasure was
the same whom I discovered at my lodgings in
William-street; the miser. In my trunk you will
find a manuscript I obtained from him. It contains
the particulars and explanation of his crime, and
the fullest proof that you are my son. This discovery brought on a return of my disease, which had
well nigh ended my suffering life, when Frank
brought you to me. God only knows how I survived that moment of intense joy.

" But I must return to those years which have worn
so deep their furrows. Time seared, without healing my wounds. I resumed my business; all other
interests were now merged in a passion for the acquisition of property. I seemed endued with a ma-
gic that turned all I touched to gold. I never mis-
took this success for happiness; no, the sweet fountains of happiness were converted to bitterness. Memory was cursed and hope blasted; I was not sordid,
but I loved the excitement of a great game, it was
a relief to my feverish mind.

" After a while, I formed one of those liasons
common in those islands, where man is as careless
of the moral as the physical rights of his fellow-
creatures. 'Eli Clairon was the daughter of a French
merchant; she had been educated in France, and
added to rare beauty and the fascinations of a versatile character, the refinements of polished life.
Though tinged with African blood, I would have
married her, but I was then still bound by legal ties.
Her mother, whose ruling passion was a love of ex-

pense, to which I gave unlimited indulgence, connived at our intimacy, till the arrival of 'Eli's father from France. He had contracted there an advantageous matrimonial alliance for her. I was absent from her in the upper country. She was forced on board a vessel, in spite of her pleadings and protestations. The first accounts from the ship brought the intelligence that she had refused all sustenance, and thrown herself into the sea.

"O my son, did not the curse of Heaven fall on every thing I loved? I believed so. 'Eli left a son; I resolved never again to see him—never again to bind myself with cords which I had a too just presentiment would be torn away, to leave bleeding, festering wounds. I supplied the child's pecuniary wants, through his grandmother. She contrived afterwards to introduce him, without exciting my suspicion, among the slaves of my family. He was a creature of rare talent, and soon insinuated himself into my affections. It was his custom to sit on a cushion at my feet after dinner, and sing me to sleep. There was a Spaniard, a villain, whom I had detected, and held up to public scorn. The wretch found his way to my apartment when I was taking my evening repose. I was awakened by a scream from Marcelline. He threw himself on my bosom, and received through his shoulder the thrust of the Spaniard's dirk. The assassin escaped. I folded the boy in my arms; I believed him to be dying; he believed it too, and fondly clinging to me, exctaimed, 'I am glad of it—I am glad of it—I have saved my *father's* life!'

"From that moment he recovered the rights of nature, and became the object of my doating fondness; but no flower could spring up in my path but a blight was on it. My temper was poisoned; I had become jealous and distrustful. Poor Marcelline was facile in his temper, and was sometimes the tool of his sordid grandmother, to extract money from me. I was often unjust to the boy. Oh! how bitterly I cursed the wealth, that made me uncertain of the truth of my boy's affection!

"Marcelline was passionate in his attachments, guileless, unsuspicious, the easy victim of the artifices of bolder minds. At sixteen, he was seduced into an affair in which his reputation and life were at hazard. He believed he owed his salvation to the interference of a young Englishman. In the excess of his gratitude, and at the risk of disgrace with me, he disclosed the whole affair to me, and claimed my favor for the stranger, who proved to be my nephew, Winstead Clarence. My soul recoiled from him; he was the image of my brother: but for Marcelline's sake, I stifled my feelings, permitted Winstead to become a member of my family, and thus was myself the passive instrument of my poor boy's destruction.

"I have not strength for further details. Young Clarence was no doubt moved to his infernal machinations by the hope of ruining Marcelline in my favor, and, as my heir at law, succeeding to my fortune. My broken constitution stimulated his cupidity. Practised as I was in the world, his arts deceived me. My poor boy was a far easier victim. He destroyed our mutual confidence. While, to me, he appeared the mentor of my son, he was decoying him into scenes of dissipation and vice; and while, to Marcelline, he seemed his friend and advocate, he magnified the poor fellow's real faults, and imputed to him duplicity and deliberate ingratitude. Incited by Winstead, Marcelline gamed deeply; and on the brink of ruin, he confessed to me his losses, and entreated pardon and relief. I spurned him from me. He was stung to the heart. Winstead seized the favorable moment, to aggravate his resentment and despair. He retired to his own apartment, and inflicted on himself a mortal wound. I heard the report of the pistol, and flew to him. He survived a few hours. We passed them in mutual explanations, and mutual forgiveness. Thus did I trample under my feet the sweet flower that had shed a transient fragrance in my desolate path!

"I once again saw Winstead Clarence; I invoked curses on his head. I now most solemnly revoke those curses.

"As soon as I could adjust my affairs, I left the West Indies for ever, execrating them as the peculiar temple of that sordid divinity, on whose altar, from their discovery to the present day, whatever is most precious, youth, health, and virtue, have been sacrificed.

"My brother was dead; but Winstead Clarence had returned to England: and I abjured my native land, and came to the United States, where I was soon known to be a man of great riches, and precarious health. I was, or fancied myself to be, the object of sordid attentions, a natural prey to be hunted down by mean spirits. My petulance was patiently

endured; my misanthropy forgiven; I was told
I was quite too young to abandon the thoughts of
marriage, and scores of discreet widows and estima-
ble maidens were commended to my favor. Literary institutions were recommended to my patronage, and emissaries from benevolent societies opened
their channels to my meritorious gifts. Wearied
with solicitations, and disgusted with interested attentions, I determined to come to New York, where
I was yet unknown.

"Scorning the consequence of wealth, and indifferent to its luxuries, I assumed the exterior of poverty; and the better to secure my incognito, I hired a
lodging at the old Dutch woman's, where I remained
in unviolated solitude till my meeting with Frank
stimulated once more to action, that inextinguishable thirst of happiness which can alone be obtained
through the ministry of the affections. Frank's
striking resemblance to you at the period when I lost
you revived my parental love—a deathless affection.
He seemed to me an angel moving on the troubled
waters of my life. I sedulously concealed my real
condition from him, even after I had determined to
bestow on him the perilous gift of my fortune. I
distrusted myself—I dreaded awaking those horrid
jealousies that had embittered my life—I wished to
be sure that he loved me for myself alone.

"You may now conceive my emotion when I discovered that my son lived—was near me—was the
father of Frank Carroll—when you saved me from
being sent to the alms-house, an accident to which
I had exposed myself by my carelessness in not pre-
paring for the exigency that occurred. But you

cannot comprehend—who can, but He who breathed into me this sentient spirit, who knows the whole train of events that have borne it to the brink of eternal ruin—who but He, the All-Seeing One, can comprehend my feelings when I found myself beneath my child's roof: when I found what I believed did not exist—a disinterested man, and him my son! when I received disinterested kindness, and from my children!

" Forgive me, my son, for so long concealing the truth from you; it was not merely to strengthen my convictions of your worth, but I deferred emotions that I doubted my strength to endure. When I am gone, you will find yourself the heir of a rich inheritance; it may make you a more useful—I fear it will not a happier man.

" In my wrongs and sufferings, my son, you must find the solution, I do not say the expiation, of my doubts of an overruling Providence—my disbelief of the immortality of that nature which seemed to me abandoned to contend with the elements of sin and suffering, finally to be wrecked on a shoreless ocean. Believe me, human life, without religious faith, *is* a deep mystery.

" But, my dear father," said Mr. Carroll " you have now the light of that faith ; you now look back on the dark passages of life without distrust, and forward with hope ?"

" Yes, yes, my son; my griefs had their appointed mission ; the furnace was kindled to purify; it was my sin if it consumed. But how shall I express my sense of that mercy that guided me to this hour of peace and joy, by those dark passages through which

I blindly blundered! My son, there is an exaltation of feeling in this full trust, this tranquil resignation, this deep gratitude, that bears to the depths of my soul the assurance of immortality. I now for the first time feel a capacity of happiness, over which death has no power—it is itself immortal life, and I long to pass the boundary of that world whence these glorious intimations come.

"My beloved son, do not wish to protract my exhausted being. I should but linger, not live; tomorrow, if I am permitted to survive till then, I will press your children to my bosom and give them my farewell blessing. Kneel by me, my son, and let us send up together an offering of faith and thanksgiving to God."

During the following evening, Mr. Carroll communicated the secret to Dr. Eustace and his family. The doctor commended his prudence in so long withholding it, sympathized with his sorrow, and congratulated him on his prospects. Mr. Carroll shrunk from his congratulations. The wealth that had been attended by such misery to Mr. Flavel, and must come to him by the death of his parent, seemed to him a doubtful good.

Nothing could be more confused than Mrs. Carroll's sensations. She was half resentful that the precious secret had so long been detained from her; and quite overjoyed to find it what it was. She was afraid some attention to Mr. Flavel might have been omitted, and from the first he had appeared to her such an interesting person!—such a perfect gentleman!—and then there was a deep, unhinted feeling of relief at finding out at last that her husband—her dear husband, was of genteel extraction.

From his children Mr. Carroll received the solace of true sympathy. " Is Mr. Flavel our grandfather ?" said Gertrude, " and must he die ?" Frank remained constantly in a closet adjoining the sick room, listening and looking, when he might look, without being perceived. Doctor Eustace made his morning visit at an earlier hour than usual. He found his patient had declined so rapidly during the night, that life was nearly extinct.

" Tell me truly, my good friend," he said to the doctor, " how long you think I may live ?"

" Your life is fast ebbing, my dear sir."

" Then, my son, call your wife and children : let me call them mine before I die."

They were summoned, and came immediately. Mrs. Carroll's heart was really touched ; she said nothing, but knelt at the bed-side. The children did not restrain their sorrow ; Frank sprang on the bed, kissed Mr. Flavel's cheek, and poured his tears over it. Mr. Carroll would have removed him, but his father signed to him to let him remain. "Frank, my sweet child," he said, " God sent you to me ; you saved me from dying alone, unknown, and in ignorance of my treasures—you brought me to my long lost son !"

Here Conolly, the Irish nurse, who was sitting behind Mr. Flavel supporting him in an upright position, gave involuntary expression to his pleasure at the solution of the riddle that had wrought his curiosity to the highest pitch. " Sure," he said, " and it's what I thought, he's his own son's father, sure is he !"

This exclamation was unheeded by the parties in the strong excitement of the moment, but afterwards they had ample reason to recall it.

"My children, my children;" continued Mr. Flavel, "live to God; I have lived without Him; the world has been a desert to me; I die with the hope of his forgiveness; God bless you, my children; kiss me, my son; where are you, Frank? I see you; farewell!" His voice had become fainter at every sentence, and died away at the last word. Still his eye, bright and intelligent, dwelt on his son, till after a few moments he closed it for ever.

A deep silence ensued; Mr. Carroll remained kneeling beside his father; his eyes were raised, and his lips quivering. But who can give utterance to the thoughts that crowd on the mind at the death of the beloved;—when aching memory flashes her light over the past, and faith pours on the soul her glorious revelations; when the spirit from its high station surveys and feels the whole of human destiny!

CHAPTER VI.

"That there is falsehood in his looks
I must and will deny:
They say their master is a knave,
And sure they do not lie."

BURNS.

"At this moment I must think for you," said Dr. Eustace to Mr. Carroll, after the family had withdrawn from the chamber of death; "of course you will wish to avoid for the present the public disclosure of the circumstance recently developed?"

"Certainly."

"Then lay what restrictions you please on Mrs. Carroll and the children, I will take care that Conolly does not gossip." Accordingly the funeral rites were performed in a private and quiet manner. The clergyman, and the few necessary assistants were struck with the grief of the family being disproportioned to the event; 'but,' said they, 'death is always an affecting circumstance, and the Carrolls are tender-hearted.'

On the morning after the funeral Mrs. Carroll was washing the breakfast-things, her head busy with various thoughts. To some she gave utterance and suppressed others, pretty much after the following manner: "Charles, my dear, I think we had best give Conolly Mr. Flavel's—la! how can I always forget—our dear father's clothes; I believe it is customary in England for people of fortune to do so."

"Give Conolly what consideration you please,

Sarah, but leave my father's personal effects undisturbed."

Mrs. Carroll nodded assent, "I do wonder," she continued, "what cousin Anne will say now! she did ridicule our taking in a *pauper*, as she called him, beyond every thing"—to herself, "I did keep it as secret as possible, but we shall be rewarded openly! what a mercy Charles never suspected his riches; if he had, he would just have sent him to lodgings;" aloud, "Only think, dear, the children the other day in Mr. Flavel's—how can I!—our father's room, asked me to send them to dancing school; I told them I could not afford it; he smiled, I little thought for what—dear souls! they shall go now as soon as it is proper"—to herself, "*can't afford it*—thank heaven, I have done for ever with that hateful, vulgar phrase." "By the way, Charles, I saw in the Evening Post, that the Roscoes' house is to be sold next week; it would just suit us."

"The Roscoes' house; my dear wife, the Roscoes have been my best, at one time, my only friends; I could not be happy where I was continually reminded of their reverse of fortune."

"Oh, well; I do not care about that house in particular; there are others that would suit me quite as well; but I hope you will attend to it at once; this house is so excessively small and inconvenient." Mr. Carroll assured his wife that she must suppress her new-born sensibility to the discomforts of her dwelling; "for his own part," he said, "he had no heart for immediate change. His mind was occupied with sad reflections, softened, he trusted, by gratitude for singular mercies. Besides, it was necessary, and he rejoiced it was so, before he could receive any portion of his father's property, that his claim to it should be admitted in England, where it was vested; he wished, therefore, that Mrs. Carroll would not at present make the slightest variation in their mode of life. She submitted, but not without betraying her reluctance, by saying, she wondered what forms of business were for, they were too provoking, too stupid, and so utterly unnecessary!

Mr. Carroll made no farther secret of the change in his prospects. He assumed the name of Clarence, and forwarded the necessary documents to England. In other respects he kept on the even tenor of his way.

About six months after a certain John Rider, Esq., a lawyer better known for his professional success in the mayor's court than for his distinction before any higher tribunal, joined a knot of Irishmen who were hovering round a grocery-door, and earnestly debating some question that had kindled their combustible passions. It appeared they were at the moment particularly jealous of the interference of an officer of the law, for one and all darted at him looks of impatient inquiry and fierce defiance. The leader of the gang advanced with a half articulated curse. He was pulled back by one of his companions. " Be civil, man," he said, " it's his honor, Lawyer Rider; he'll ne'er be the one to scald his mouth with other folks' broth,"

" Ah, Conolly, is that you ?"

" Indeed is it, your honor ; was it me your honor was wanting ?"

"Yes; I have been to your house, and Biddy told me I should probably find you here."

" And what for was she sending your honor to the grocer's ? She might better have guided you any way else to find me."

" To seek you, may be, Conolly, but not to find you."

" Ah, your honor's caught me there ; but I'll tache the old woman."

Rider perceived from Conolly's flushed cheek, that he was in a humor to demonstrate some domestic problems that might not be agreeable to a spectator, and therefore instead of accompanying him to his own room, to transact some private business he had with him, he proposed to him to walk up the street. Conolly assented, saying to his companions as he left them, " Stay a bit, lads, and I'll spake to Lawyer Rider about it."

" About what is that, Conolly ?"

" Is it that your honor has not heard about Jemmy McBride and Dr. Eustace ?" The doctor's name was followed by an imprecation that expressed but too plainly, ' Jemmy and the whole Irish nation versus the doctor.'

" I have heard something of this unlucky affair, but you may tell me more, Conolly."

" Indeed can I; for wasn't I there while his knife was yet red with the blood of him ? and wasn't Jem my father's own brother's son ?"

" But Conolly, you do not believe the doctor had any thing to do with McBride's death ?"

" That I do not say. But I believe, by my soul I do, the doctors have more to do with death than life, the heretics in particular, saving your honor's presence. Any way, Jemmy McBride died in his hands, and the very time he had said the poor fellow was mending; but that was all to keep the priest away. Never a confession did Jem make; never a bit prayer was said over him, nor the holy sign put on him; nor, Mr. Rider, as true as my name's Pat Conolly, was there a light lighted for his soul to pass by. The next night the doctor told Jemmy's wife, a poor innocent cratur that knew no better, that he was going to examine the body to look after the disease a bit; and so she, God forgive her, gives him a light, and he goes in the room and makes fast the door. But you see, the old woman, Jem's wife's mother, looked through the key-hole, and she saw him at his devil's work, and she ran, wild-like, to the neighbors, and there were a dozen of us at Roy McPhelan's, that were thinking to keep poor Jemmy's wake that night, and we made a rush of it, and forced the door, and there stood he over poor Jem, and such cutting and slashing, och! my heart bleeds to think of it; indeed does it, and poor Jemmy's soul tormented the while; for it's sure, your honor, his soul was there looking on his body handled that way by a heretic. Roy seized his knife, and would have had the life of him, but Jem's wife set up such a howling, and she held Roy's arm, and made us all stand back while she said the doctor had shown kindness to her and hers, and we should first kill her before a hair of him should be the worse for it. And then he calls to me, and he says, 'Conolly,' for he knew me, it's six months past when I was nurse to one Flavel, and he says, ' Co-

nolly, my friend,' (the devil a bit friend to the like of
him!) 'Conolly,' he says, 'you'll get yourselves
into trouble at this mad rate. Go, like honest men,
and make your complaint of me, and let the law
take its course.' And there was one McInster
among us, who is but half an Irishman, for his
grandmother was full Scotch, and he's always for
keeping the sword in the scabbard, and he would
be for persuading us to the law, and while we were
all giving our advice, in a breath like, Jemmy's
wife whips the doctor through a side door, down a
back passage; and once at the street-door, he made
a bird's flight of it. But we'll have our revenge. A
hundred oaths are sworn to it."

"Don't be rash, Conolly. Have you consulted
a lawyer?"

"That have we, Mr. Rider, and he says there's
no law for us, and sure is it the laws are made for
cowards, and we'll stand by ourselves."

"Listen to my advice, Conolly, you know I
am a friend to the Irish—you know how hard I
worked for you all in Billy McGill's business."

"Ay, your honor, sure you did make black
white there. Did not I say you was a lawyer,
every hair of you?"

Rider was compelled to swallow Conolly's compliment, equivocal as it was, and he replied, "I do
indeed know something of the law, and believe me,
it will be the worse for you all if you take any violent measures. The doctor, though a young man,
is well known, and has many friends in the city.
That Mr. Carroll, or Clarence as he calls himself,
at whose house you first knew him, is ready to up-

hold him in every thing. You have not heard, perhaps, Conolly, that the old man you nursed left a grand fortune ?"

"Lord help us ! no. I have been out of the city ever since the old gentleman's funeral, till Easter Sunday, the very day poor Jemmy died."

"I suppose you know that this Carroll claims to be son to the old gentleman ?"

"Ay, sure, did not I hear him with my own ears call him so ?"

"Just state to me, Conolly, precisely what you recollect about this matter."

"Some other time, your honor, the fellows are waiting for me now."

"Heaven and earth, man ! you must not put it off; it's a matter of the first importance, and here's something to make all right with your friends."

Conolly pocketed the douceur, smirking, and saying, "Sure I'll do my best to pleasure you Mr. Rider; but my head's all in a snarl with Jemmy and this d——d doctor."

"Begin and you will soon get it clear—you were some time at Carroll's ?"

"That was I, and for a time it was all plain sailing, though the old gentleman used to mutter so in his sleep, and look at Mr. Carroll so through and through like, that I thought there was more on his mind than we knew of; and, I was sure from the first he was no poor body, for he had the ways of a gentleman entirely, and you know they are as different as fish and flesh."

"Yes, yes, Conolly, go on, we all know he was a gentleman."

" And you know too, may be, that he had epileptics.
Well one day after they had had a long nonsense
talk about riches, Mr. Carroll sent us all out of the
room to stay till he rung, and sure he did ring, dis-
tracted like ; when we came in the room the old gentleman was in fits, and Mr. Carroll was not much
better ; and from that time he was an altered man ;
he had been kind before, but now it was quite entirely a different thing. It was plain, his life was
bound up in the old gentleman's. I had nothing
worth speaking of to do any more, he gave him all
his medicines, and his eyes was never off him day or
night, and they would often be alone together. I
had my own thoughts, for there was something in
their looks, I need not describe it to ye, Mr. Rider,
for if you've had either father or son you know what
it is."

For an instant the current of Rider's feelings
turned, it was but an instant, and he said, " Yes, I
understand you, go on."

▶ " I have not far to go, for the fire burned too bright
to burn long. It was but two or three days after
that he found himself to be just on the launch, and
he told Mr. Carroll to call in the family, and then it
all came out just as I expected, your honor. He
called them all his children, and Mr. Carroll ' my
son' again and again, and talked to the child, that's
Frank Carroll, about being his grandfather. I could
tell you just the words if you please."

" No, they are of no consequence."

" Then, your honor, there's not much more to
tell. They all cried of course you know, and I
cried too, and that's what I have not done before,

since I quitted home. He spoke but few words,
but they were rightly said as if he'd had them from
the priest's lips, and then he just sunk away like an
infant falling asleep."

Rider hesitated for a few moments; Conolly's
statement was particularly hostile to his wishes, and
the course to be pursued required some delibe-
ration; "These epileptic fits," he said, "are very
apt to derange the mind—the doctors tell me they
always weaken it."

"Sure they lie then;" and here followed an exe-
cration of the whole faculty; "I've seen men die,
many a one, both at home and here in America,
and never did I see one behave himself to the very
last, in a more discreet, regular, gentale-like manner, than this Mr. Flavel; I don't know how he
lived, but he died like a gentleman, any way."

"I must strike another key," thought Rider;
"Conolly," he said, "it is not worth while to dilly-
dally about this matter any longer; I know I may
confide in you. This Mr. Flavel, or rather Clarence, had an own brother's son in England, whom
he hated, and had wronged. If he died without
children, and without a will, his nephew would, of
course, be his natural heir. Now, is it not possible, that, feeling very grateful to this Carroll, he
might consent to pass him off for his son; just to
call him so, you know?"

"No, no, Mr. Rider; he did not die like a man
that was going off with a lie in his mouth."

"Perhaps you don't consider the whole, Conolly;
it was an innocent deceit—stop, hear me out—Carroll, who, besides getting the fortune, would gladly

wipe off the disgrace of having been an alms-house slip, might beguile him on; Eustace combined with him, at least I suspect so, and," he added, cautiously looking about him, "if he keeps the fortune, one thing is sure, the doctor will have a good slice of it; he will swear through thick and thin, every thing Carroll wants."

"Och! the villain! what will he swear?"

"That the man was of perfect and sound mind; Conolly, this is a hard case and we must try every expedient—every way to get justice done; now if you will stand by us—my client is generous, and he has authorized me to spare neither pains nor money to get witnesses for him—name a particular sum, my good fellow."

"For what? tell me what I am to do just."

"Why, in the first place, you are to right your cause with this doctor; he's more than suspected already of leaguing with Carroll, and if your testimony goes against his, he can't live in the city."

"Ah; that would pleasure me!"

"And if three or four hundred dollars—?"

"Three, or four! *four!* I have one hundred already, and that would just make up the sum, and fetch them all over; the old man, and Peggy, and Roy, and Davy, and Pat, and just set them down gentalely in New York—but tell me how deep in, it is you want me to go?"

"That we must consider; if we could prove the old gentleman was not in his right mind."

"No, no, Mr. Rider, I would not like that; it's ill luck dishonoring the dead that way."

Rider, like a careful angler, had prepared various

baits for his hook. One refused, he tried another; " Well, my good fellow, if you cannot on your conscience say, that you think the old gentleman was a little out, may you not have been mistaken in thinking you heard those words, grandfather, son, father? hey, Conolly?"

"You mane, Mr. Rider," said Conolly with an indescribable leer, "whether I can't quite entirely forget them; that is to say, swear I never heard them at all?"

Rider, hardened as he was, felt his cheeks tingle at this sudden and clear exposition of his meaning; "Why, Conolly, on my honor," he said, "I believe that my client has the right of the case, and we are sometimes forced, you know, to go a crooked path to get to the right spot. Those words might have dropped from the old man accidentally, just as he was going out of the world, and then Carroll and the doctor between them might have contrived the rest. The doctor is as cunning as the devil himself; you know how he hoodwinked your cousin's wife—a scandalous affair that was—and yet I don't know how you are to right yourselves; we have no law for you, Conolly, and you know our people don't like club-law."

"D—n the law; the law was made for villains; I beg your pardon, Mr. Rider. Its true I can't sleep till we're revenged on the doctor—four hundred dollars ye say, Mr. Rider? It would be heaven's mercy to the poor souls that's starving at home. What is it ye'll have me forget?" Conolly's conscience had by this time become as confused as his mind. The opportunity of gratifying his resentments against the doctor, and of obtaining the means of bringing to this land of plenty, this full sheaf, his lean and famished brethren at home, overpowered his weak principles, and his real good feeling, and he listened to Rider's lucid and impressive instructions in relation to the testimony he was to deliver, with strict attention and with reiterated promises to abide by them. Rider did not forget to make Conolly fully sensible of the importance of keeping the purport of their interview a profound secret, and then giving him a farther earnest of future favors, he bade him good night. As Conolly's 'God bless his honor,' and 'long life to him,' died away on the lawyer's ear, he was entering a plea in arrest of judgment before the tribunal of conscience. 'After all,' he thought, 'if I have saved Eustace's life from these violent devils, I have done more good than harm; another man might have let them go on; certain it is, Eustace once out of the way, the property would have been ours;' his thoughts diverged a little—' ours?—yes, I may say *ours*; five thousand pounds if I gain it; one should work hard for such a fee!'

Mr. Rider's client had found a fit instrument to manage his cause; a most unworthy member of that profession which from Cicero's day to our own times, has called forth the genius, the ardor, the self-sacrificing zeal of the noblest minds of every age.

CHAPTER VII.

"Are you good men and true?"
MUCH ADO ABOUT NOTHING.

MR. CLARENCE, (we shall hereafter call this gentleman by his rightful name,) as has been stated, transmitted to his deceased father's agents in England,
such documents as he deemed necessary to establish
his claim.   They were admitted as sufficient, and
satisfactory, and the property, amounting to about
ninety thousand pounds sterling, was transferred to
his account, and transmitted to him.

Mr. Winstead Clarence was, at the same time,
apprized of the death of his uncle, and of the fact
that the property, which in case of his uncle's death
without a will, devolved on him as his nearest
blood-relative, was intercepted by an American,
claiming to be Edmund Clarence' son.   This, Mr.
Winstead Clarence declared, and perhaps believed to be, an incredible story.   His lawyer
examined the papers, and was of opinion that the
claim might be contested, but as the ability of
the English agents to respond for so large an
amount of property was doubtful, he advised that
the suit should be commenced against the pretended
heir, and prosecuted in the American courts.   Accordingly, Mr. Winstead Clarence wrote to John
Rider, Esq., to institute a suit, and instructed him to
rest its merits on the ground of collusion between
Mr. Carroll and the doctor; and to procure *adequate testimony at any cost.* As a sort of insurance

on the cause, he promised Rider, in case of success,
five thousand pounds. He had formerly had some
acquaintance with Rider in the West Indies, and had
had occasion to admire the professional ingenuity
with which he had there managed a very suspicious
business.

Whatever confidence Rider might have had in
his own talent, he was too well aware of his questionable standing at the bar, to assume the exclusive conduct of the suit; he therefore associated
with himself a counsellor of the highest reputation
for integrity as well as talent; taking care, of course,
in his statement of the case to this gentleman, to re-
present Conolly as a *bona fide* witness.

The facility with which lawyers persuade themselves of the righteousness of a cause in which they
have embarked, is often alleged as a proof of the
tendency of the profession to obscure a man's
original perception of right and wrong. Perhaps
no class of men have a deeper sense, or a more ar-
dent love of justice, but they are of all men best acquainted with the uncertainty of human testimony,
and most conversant with the dark phases of human
character. In the case in question, the honorable
counsellor was persuaded that Mr. Clarence had
been guilty of deliberate villany. Had he not been
so, nothing would have tempted him to attack and
undermine, by the power of his eloquence, the character of an innocent and high-minded man.

The cause produced a considerable sensation. It
not only involved a large amount of property,
but the reputation of individuals which had been
hitherto unquestioned. Mrs. Clarence' relationship
with some of the most distinguished families in the

city, was, at the dawn of her prosperity, remembered,
and the cause became a topic in fashionable circles.
The trial before one of the Judges of the Supreme
Court, then holding The Sittings, was announced
in the morning papers.   At an early hour the court
room was crowded to overflowing, and notwithstanding the opinion of certain of our English friends,
that the decorum of judicial proceedings can only
be secured by the necromantic presence of gowns
and wigs, the most silent and respectful attention was given to the proceedings.   Mr. Clarence
sustained himself through the whole cause with unvarying dignity.   Nor even when it assumed an unexpected and most threatening aspect, did he manifest any emotion.   His manly calmness contrasted
well with the disinterested enthusiasm of a young
friend, who never quitted his side during the trial.
This youth, Gerald Roscoe, with the fervid feeling
of fifteen, confident in his friend's right, and indignant that it should be contested or delayed,
expressed his feelings with the unreservedness natural
to his age ; sometimes by involuntary exclamations,
and then as unequivocally by the flashings of one of
the darkest and most brilliant eyes through which
the soul ever spoke.

Rider's assistant counsel opened the cause for the
plaintiff, and in his behalf appealed to the jury, as
the natural guardians of the rights of a stranger, a foreigner, and an absent party.   He then
proceeded to state, that he rested the cause of
his client on two points, which he expected to
establish : first, that in default of heirs of the
body, he was heir at law and next of kin to the
late Edmund Clarence, Esquire, who had died in-

testate; and secondly, he pledged himself to prove
fraud on the part of the defendant, a collusion between him and his witnesses, by which he had obtained possession of, and still illegally detained the
property which by the verdict of the jury could alone
be restored to the rightful claimant. He should state
what he could support by adequate testimony if necessary, but what he presumed would not be contro-
verted, viz. that the deceased, Edmund Clarence,
after having resided in a sister city for some
months, and his condition having been well known
there, had come to the city of New York, where,
for reasons irrelevant to the present case, he had assumed the name of Flavel, concealed his real consequence and fortune under the garb of poverty, and
lived in mean and obscure lodgings. That during
this time he had made an accidental acquaintance
with the child of the defendant; that their acquaintance and intercourse had been watched and promoted by the defendant; that all this time Mr.
Clarence' health was manifestly declining, under
the encroachments of a most threatening malady; that during a frightful attack of this constitutional malady, he was removed to the house of
the defendant, still personally an utter stranger to
him; that there, with seeming good reason, but certainly most unfortunately for the cause of his client, he
was secluded from the observation of all but the family of the defendant, his family physician, (a most
intimate friend,) and a *male nurse*.

That Mr. Clarence survived his removal to the
house of the defendant about three weeks; that immediately after his decease, the defendant had for-

warded to England documents containing evidence
of his consanguinity and claim to the property of
the deceased. The evidence of this newly discovered relationship was supported by a written
declaration, assumed to have been wrested from
a dying miser by Mr. Clarence, and by him given
to the defendant—by the testimony of the child of
the defendant—and by the dying declaration of Mr.
Clarence, attested by Dr. Eustace.

He then proceeded to say he should rest the cause
of his client on the powerful, and to him he must
confess irresistible deduction from circumstances,
and on the direct testimony of a single witness. This
witness was the nurse to whom he had already alluded. In the documents sent to England no mention had been made of this man, though he presumed
it would not be denied that he was present when the
deceased gave utterance to those startling declara-
tions, which Dr. Eustace had so fully vouched.
This nurse had gone from the defendant's service to
his own humble walk of life, and had never received
any communication from the defendant; and had first
heard of the present controversy when summoned by
the plaintiff's counsel to appear as a witness on the
trial. He therefore begged the gentlemen would
listen attentively to his testimony, and would give it
the weight it deserved, as coming from a man who
could not possibly have any motive for disguising,
or perverting, or withholding the truth.

Nothing could exceed the astonishment of Mr.
Carroll, his counsel, and his friends, when Conolly
was named as a witness on the part of the plaintiff;
they exchanged looks of inquiry and alarm, and as

Conolly brushed past them to take his station
at the witness' stand, Doctor Eustace, who had
a grudge against his whole nation, half ejaculated,
"The d——d Irishman!" The words reached
Conolly's ear, and nerved his half-shrinking resolution; and once having girded on the battle-sword,
he was determined with true blood to fight out the
cause, right or wrong.

After some prefatory and unimportant interroga-
tories, the counsel for the plaintiff asked Conolly to
state how he came into the service of the deceased
Mr. Clarence. "You see, gentlemen," he said, "I
was just leaving service next door to Mr. Carroll's,
a big house it is, where they keep more servants
than they pay; and so they were going to hold back
my dues, and I thought to myself I could not go
astray to take a bit of advice of Mr. Carroll; and
said he to me, ' Conolly, is it that you're going
to leave the place?' Indeed, sir, and that am I not,
said I, for I've left it already. And he seemed right
glad of it, and said he'd a bit of a job for me—a sick
man to nurse—and if I would come straight away
to his house, he would spake to my employer, and
he was a very fine gentleman, and sure he was he
would pay me. ' Och! Mr. Carroll,' said I, ' it
takes more nor a gentleman to know a gentleman.
They don't scruple showing their hands dirty to us
servants—God forgive me, for myself calling me so
here in America.' "

Conolly was interrupted, and told to go straight
to the point. "Well, your honor, I did go straight
to the gentleman's chamber; for gentleman I saw he
was, and no poor body, with the first glance of my eye."

"How long did he live?"

"Somewhere between three and four weeks, your honor; but that was nothing to signify, for Mr. Carroll paid me the full month's wages, like a free-hearted gentleman as he is, any way."

"How was Mr. Clarence treated by Mr. Carroll and his family?"

"Trated, your honor! As a good subject would trate the king, or a good Christian the Pope. He'd every thing that money could buy for him, and all that hands could do for him, and Mr. Carroll and his boy, that's Frank Carroll, were by his bed both day and night, sure were they."

"Did Mr. Clarence, a short time previous to his death, have a confidential, that is to say, a private conversation with Mr. Carroll?"

"Yes, your honor, that did he, and I dont belie him in saying so. It was just three days before he died, and the family had all been about him, and they'd had a flummery talk about riches, and Mr. Carroll spoke as if he cared nothing at all about them, and by the same token ye may know he's neither rich nor poor, for it's they that have got more than they want that set store by riches, and we that's poor that are tempted to sell our souls for them— God forgive us!"

"Spare your reflections, my good friend, and tell us what happened after this private conversation?"

"Well, your honor, when the bell rang distracted-like we all ran up together; the poor old gentleman was in his fits again, and he'd been making a clean breast of it, and it seemed a heavy unloading

he'd had—it had like to have brought him to his
death struggle."

"But he revived, and was himself again after
this ?"

"Yes was he, but weak and death-like."

"Did you perceive any change in Mr. Carroll's
manner ?"

"That did we ; as the doctor will remember for
he said to me, 'Conolly,' said he, 'I am afraid Mr.
Carroll will go astray of his reason, for he's quite
entirely an altered man, and so was he—his eye was
down-cast, and his cheek flame-like, and I thought
it was watching and wearying with the old gentleman, and I tried to get him to take rest, but not a
word would he hear of it ; he never left him for one
minute day nor night, and for the most tune he kept
us all clear of the room, till the morning the doctor
told the old gentleman he'd but scant breathing-time
left, and he asked to see the family, and especially
the boy, that's Frank Carroll, to thank them for all
their kindness to him ; and they all come in, and the
boy was on the bed by him and kissed the poor old
gentleman and cried over him, and then he took the
hand of each of them and he gave his blessing to
each and all, and he says to me, 'God bless you
Pat,' said he; and that was the last word he spoke.
I think, your honor, he called me Pat for shortness'
sake, and knowing it was all one to me ; for when
I first came to his service, Conolly bothered him, and
I told him if it plased him better, he might call me
Pat McCormic, for McCormic was my father's name
and Pat my godfather gave me ; but McCormic
bothered him still worse than Conolly, and then I

told him if it were asier, to call me 'Pat Ford,' for that was my grandfather's name, that rared me, and the boys at home called me that just, and it's only since I came to America that I took the name of my mother's brother, which is Conolly."

Here Conolly was interrupted, and told that the court had no concern whatever with his cognomens.

Conolly's excursiveness was doubtless partly owing to his natural garrulity, but quite as much to his desire to get through his testimony as to the last scene with the least possible quantum of lying. He had a common superstitious feeling about the superior obligation to tell the truth of the dying, and he would have preferred traducing Mr. Clarence' whole life to misrepresenting his death-bed.— In reply to some farther questions that were put to him, as to Mr. Carroll's deportment after Clarence' death, he testified to his having been closeted a long time with the doctor.

The plaintiff's counsel then having signified, with an air of complete satisfaction and even triumph, that they had completed their examination, Mr. Carroll's counsel cross-examined the witness, acutely and ingeniously, but without eliciting the truth. There was a strange mixture in Conolly's mind, of malignant resentment towards the doctor, and good will to Mr. Clarence ; of determination to secure the price of his falsehood, and of desire not to aggravate the injury he inflicted ; a compound of good-heartedness and absence of all principle, and that mixture of simplicity and cunning, that characterizes his excitable and imaginative nation.

During his cross-examination he was questioned in relation to his exclamation when the fact of Mr. Clarence' relationship to the Carrolls first flashed across his mind. He denied it entirely; denied ever having heard a word indicating such a fact from any person whatever, till he was summoned to the trial.

Mr. Carroll's counsel then ably stated his grounds of defence, which, as they are already well known, it will not be necessary to recapitulate.

Doctor Eustace, as witness in behalf of the defendant, was next examined. His calm philosophic countenance, strongly contrasted with the sanguine complexion, large open lips, low forehead, bushy hair, and little, keen, restless gray eye of Conolly, at another time would have commanded respect and confidence.

But now, watchful and distrustful eyes were fixed on him, and by some he was even regarded as deposing in his own cause. Next to the misery of conscious guilt, to a delicate mind, is the suffering of being suspected by honorable persons. Doctor Eustace was embarrassed; there was neither simplicity nor clearness in his testimony, and though he never contradicted himself, yet there was a want of directness, and of self-possession, that darkened the cloud gathering over him and his friend.

Frank Carroll was the next witness offered in behalf of the defendant. His face was the very mirror of truth. Her seal was stamped on his clear, open brow. His whole aspect was beautiful, artless, and engaging, and after a single glance at him, the

plaintiff's counsel objected to the admission of his
testimony. He contended that a child of eleven
years was too young to be disenthralled from his
father's authority—certainly was too flexible a
material to resist his influence—that he would
be merely the passive medium of his dicta-
tions. His objections were strenuously opposed
by the opposite counsel, and overruled by the
court, and Frank was directed to take his station.
He was intimidated by a discussion which he did
not perfectly comprehend, and not aware of the im-
port of his evidence to his father, and occupied only
with a wish to shrink from public notice, he entreated
Mr. Clarence, so loud as to be overheard. to excuse
him, and permit him to go home. His father endea-
voured to inspirit him, but finding his efforts inef-
fectual, he sternly bade him go to the assigned
stand. He obeyed with trembling and hesitation.

After a few unimportant preliminary questions,
to which he replied in scarcely audible monosylla-
bles, he was asked to state all that he could recollect of Mr. Clarence' death-bed scene. It requires
far more presence of mind to tell a story than to answer questions. Poor Frank was abashed. His
manly spirit quailed; he tried to gather courage;
he looked up and looked around; every eye was
fixed on him, and it seemed to him as if every man
were an Argus. His lips quivered, his crimsoned
cheeks deepened to fever heat, and when the judge in
a voice of solemn authority bade him proceed, he
burst into tears.

His father now interposed, and sternly commanded him to speak. The voice of his offended father was more terrible than even the eyes and ears of the staring and listening crowd, and he at last told his story, but with down-cast eyes, hesitation, and blundering.

He was asked to relate all he remembered of Mr. Clarence' visit to the miser's room, when he (Frank) was with him. He did so; but he could not be sure of any particulars. He was sure Mr. Clarence was very much agitated; but when cross-examined, he was not at all sure but it might have been the expression of sympathy at the extreme misery of the famished, dying old man. He thought he recollected Mr. Clarence pronouncing the name of Savil; but on the cross-examination he was not sure he had not first heard that name from his father. On the whole his testimony appeared, even to Mr. Carroll's firmest friends, confused and suspicious. A fatality seemed to attend his cause. When it was opened, there was not, on the part of the defendant's friends, a doubt of its favorable issue; but the most confident among them now began to fear the result, and many there were who secretly asked themselves if it were not possible they had been deceived in him. His counsel, in this threatening position of affairs, offered to bring forward any number of witnesses to the hitherto unimpeached integrity of his, and of Doctor Eustace' character. The plaintiff's counsel said they would concede that point to the fullest extent it could be required.

Nothing then remained but to present before the court the miser's manuscript. This was objected to as an isolated, unattested document, and, of course, null and impotent in the present cause. The judge, however, remarked that it might throw some light on the impeached testimony of the defendant's witnesses, and he overruled the objections of the plaintiff's counsel.

The document was accordingly read as follows: "I, Guy Seymour, formerly of England, since an inhabitant of Jamaica, and now of the city of New York, United States, do declare that this writing contains the truth and nothing but the truth, so help me God. Twenty-seven years ago this 5th day of August, A. D. 181–, I was sent from the island of Jamaica by Edmund Clarence, Esq. with the sum of $10,000, which by me was to be remitted to England; and with his only son, Charles Clarence, who was sent on the voyage for the benefit of his health. The devil tempted me to abscond with the money. I took the child too to guard against discovery. I left the vessel in which I had embarked in the evening, hoping I should not be missed till it was at sea, and they would believe I had returned to shore with my charge. I got on board an American vessel. When I arrived in New York I heard the English vessel was lost. Therefore no inquiry was made about me. I put the child to a decent lodging. The woman imposed on me, and made me pay a cruel price for his board, charges for washing besides. On the 25th day of the following January, being A. D. 181–, I took him to the city almshouse. He was then five years old. I marked his age and the name I had given him, Charles Carroll, on a card, and sewed it to his sleeve. I did not lose sight of the boy. One year after he was taken from the alms-house by one Roscoe, and has since got well up in the world. I now declare, that when I die he shall be heir to all I possess: eight thousand dollars in my strong box, besides one half-jo, one Spanish dollar, three English pennies, and a silver sixpence, all contained in my knit purse, which my grandmother (a saving body she was, God bless her!) knit for me when I was eight years old. When she gave it to me, 'Johnny, son'y,' said she, 'mind ye well these words I have knit into your purse, and ye'll live to be a rich man.' The words are there yet, ' a penny saved is a penny gained,'—betimes I think the devil branded them on my soul. I put my ten thousand dollars in different banks and insurance companies. They all failed! I lost all! all but my luck-penny, my silver sixpence. What I have now, I've earned, and I've saved all I earned. I have always meant it should go to Mr. Clarence' son when I am dead and gone, and I pray he prove no spend-thrift of my hard-gotten gains. All I have got now I've come by honestly. I never was guilty of but the one crime, and I was sore—sore tempted. It is my intention, before I die, to employ an attorney to draw my will; but it's a great cost, and for fear of accidents, I have written this paper, and hereunto I put my name and seal.

"JOHN SAVIL.

"August, 5th, 181–."

All the evidence in the case was now before the court. The defendant's counsel rose to sum up. He contended that the evidence, on the part of his client, deemed sufficient in England, where it was necessary to overcome the universal and strong feeling against alienating property, still remained in full force. He insisted that it was overthrowing the basis of human confidence, to withdraw their faith from men of the age and unimpeached integrity of his client and his witnesses, and transfer it to an ignorant unprincipled foreigner, who had no name and no stake in society. There were thousands of such men in the city, they could be picked up any where, from the swarms about the cathedral, to the dens of Catharine-lane; men who for a few dollars or *shillings*, would swear whatever pleased their purchasers. Was the property and reputation of our best citizens to be put in jeopardy by such testimony? 'One of the plaintiff's counsel,' (and he glanced his eye with honest scorn at Rider,) 'was a man familiar with the use of such instruments; he had been long suspected of practices which should exile him from the society of honest men; which should banish him from this honorable tribunal, and that by their own official sentence.' The counsel was interrupted, and reminded that such vituperation was irrelevant and not admissable.

He contended that it was in order, and a necessary defence against a secret and criminal proceeding, which could only be exposed by unmasking the true character of the chief agent, who had sheltered himself from suspicion behind the unspotted shield of his able and upright associate. Testimony brought forward under the auspices of this gentleman would receive a false value. Advantage had been taken of his client's conscious integrity, and

his just confidence in the sufficiency of the testimony he had adduced to support his cause. Conolly was absent from the city at the time his client
prepared the documents to be sent to England, and
deeming his testimony superfluous, he had taken no
pains to obtain it. For the same reason, and because he had not before adduced it, he had omitted to
bring him forward on the present occasion. His
client had been betrayed by his confidence in the
truth of his cause. He had not anticipated that
the instrument he thought worthless, could be whetted to his destruction; he would not believe it
could be so; it would recoil from the armour of
honesty, the ' panoply divine,' in which his client
was encased. There had been a dark conspiracy
to defraud and ruin, but ' even-handed justice ' would
return the ingredients of the poisoned chalice, to
the lips that had dictated, and had borne false witness. He declared that the evidence for his client,
which he luminously and forcibly recapitulated,
could not be overthrown by a thousand such witnesses as Conolly. He begged that the jury
would not permit their minds to be warped by
the train of singular circumstances that had led
his client to the discovery of his parent. He admitted they had been correctly stated by the oppo-
sing counsel; but what then? was not the remark
as true as it was trite, that the romance of real life
exceeded the most ingenious contrivances of fiction?
Who should prescribe, who should limit the mysterious modes by which Providence brought to
light the secret iniquities of men? He intreated
that gentlemen would allow due weight to that cir-

cumstance which ought to govern their decision—
the character of his client. The opposite counsel,
coerced by his own sense of justice, had paid it
involuntary tribute, when he conceded all testimony
on that point to be superfluous. The same just
homage had been rendered to the witness, Doctor
Eustace, a man of whom he might say what had
once been as truly said of the political integrity of
an honorable citizen: ' The king of England was
not rich enough to buy him.' He then adverted to
the testimony of the child, and asked if it were cre-
dible that the father should be the corrupter of his
son—the destroyer of his innocence?

All these and other arguments were urged
at length, and so ably, that when the counsel
finished, the current seemed to have set in Mr.
Carroll's favor. Animated whispers of encouragement were heard from his friends, and Rider,
who had hitherto been forward and officious, was
quite silent and crest-fallen, and slunk away as far
as possible from observation.

The counsel for the plaintiff now rose to make
his closing argument. He began by expressing
his deep and unaffected regret that he must be the
instrument of justice in exposing to dishonor and
scorn, the character of two gentlemen who had been
held in esteem by the community. It had become
his painful duty to array circumstances in such a
light that it could no longer be doubted that the defendant's integrity had been too deeply infected with
human infirmity to resist the solicitations of temptation, temptation double-faced, alluring him with
offers of fortune, and of rank.

It might seem strange—it was most strange that man should barter virtue for money. But had not this base instrument slain its thousands and its tens of thousands? He would refer those who questioned whether it were of all agents most powerful in vanquishing human virtue, to the daily occurrences of their commercial city, to the records of their courts, to their own observation, to the page of history, to its darkest, most affecting page—the story of thirty pieces of silver.

He would not magnify the crime it was his duty to unveil. He wished that all the indulgence might be extended to the defendant which human frailty claimed; for the sins of our common nature should be viewed in sorrow rather than in anger.

He should endeavor to show how the unhappy man had been led astray; how temptation had at first suggested but a slight departure from the straight path; but *that* once left, how her victim had been darkened, entangled, and lost.

He adverted to Frank Carroll's first accidental meeting with the deceased. He dwelt on his father not only having permitted, but encouraged the child's intercourse with the repulsive stranger.

Subsequently when he was seized with a frightful disease, and apparently near death, the defendant, instead of suffering him to receive relief through the appropriate and adequate channels of public charity—or, even like a Howard or a man of Ross, maintaining him in a private lodging suited to his apparently humble condition—had removed him to his own house, placed him, not in some attic room, or homely apartment suited to a mendicant, bnt in the best apartment of his house, with a nurse, an expensive male nurse, especially provided for him, and the luxury of medical attendance twice and thrice a day. It must be remembered that the defendant was a man, not of wasteful, nor even of free expenditure, but of very limited means, and living carefully within his means. It had not been pretended that the defendant had been led on by the mysterious instinct of nature—no, the circumstances remained unexplained, unadverted to by the defendant's sagacious counsel. Where then was the key to this extraordinary, this romantic charity? Was it not possible that the defendant was previously acquainted with the real condition of his pensionary? His person was well known in a sister-city—his immense wealth and peculiarities had been a topic of common conversation there. The supposition that the defendant was in possession of this knowledge, and kept it secret, furnished a complete, and the only solution to the riddle. He saw a lone old man, on the verge of life, divorced from his species, without apparent heirs. Why should he not take innocent measures to attract his notice, and secure his favor?

It certainly was not an unnatural nor extravagant hope, that the old man's will, made under the impression of recent kindness, should render an equivalent for that kindness. Thus far the defendant's fraud was not of a deep dye, and probably would not offend against the standard of most men's virtue.

" The instruments of darkness
Win us with honest trifles to betray us
In deepest consequence."

It is a presumptuous self-confidence that hopes to set. limits to an aberration from the strict rule of integrity. Had a voice of prophecy disclosed the dark future to the still innocent man, would he not have shrunk with horror from the revelation? But temptation, fit opportunity, convenient time, assailed him, and he fell!

He now begged the particular attention of the jury to a most important circumstance in the testimony, the private interview which occurred between the defendant and the deceased, three days before his death.

The late Mr. Clarence, as the defendant's counsel had admitted, then disclosed to him the particulars of his life. The effort of recalling past events, and living over far-gone griefs, brought on a recurrence of his disease.

He had revealed, among other events of a clouded life, one which naturally struck the imagination of the defendant.

The old man, seven and twenty years before, had lost a child at sea. The defendant, about the same time, had been abandoned at the gate of our city alms-house!

He did not allude to the circumstance as a reproach to the defendant. He did not unnecessarily present it before the public; but he would ask what feeling was more natural, more universal, than a desire of honorable parentage? He could almost forgive the defendant for grasping an opportunity to wash this stain from his family escutcheon. His family escutcheon! alas, it was a blank! He dated his existence from the moment when, a desert-

ed, shivering, half-starved, half-clad child, he was
received under the shelter of public charity!

Is it strange that the project being once conceived
by evil inspiration, of ingrafting himself on the stock
of an honorable family, his invention should have been
quickened to fertility in producing and maturing the
means? The old miser's singular and solitary
death was remembered. The documents in question
might be forged; who should disprove its authen-
ticity? It might be pretended that it was received
through the hands of the deceased Mr. Clarence!

Still it was an unattested and insufficient document; and other testimony must be provided—
where was it to be obtained? Where!—Did the enemy of our souls ever fail to present fit agents to execute a plotted mischief?

He would only remind the jury of the protracted and secret interview between the defendant
and the physician, immediately after Mr. Clarence'
death.

He could not raise the protecting curtain of secresy;
he could not paint the first shrinking of the confede-
rate—he could not calculate the amount of the bribe
—it had been enough for the price of integrity, but
not enough to stifle the voice of conscience, as they
had all witnessed in the consequences of her violated law, the blundering and confusion of the
testimony given by a man, on all ordinary occasions,
clear-headed and self-possessed. Much had been said
by the opposite counsel on the superior claims of this
medical gentleman to their confidence, over the
humble witness of his client. Did he hear this argument brought forward in a country of boasted

equal rights? A new privileged class! a new aristocracy was this! that was to monopolize esteem
and confidence, and to disqualify and disfranchise
the poor and humble. Thank God, truth and virtue
grow most sturdily in the lowly bosom of humility!
The opposite counsel had adopted a plausible explanation of what he no doubt felt to be a very suspicious circumstance—the neglect of the defendant
to take the testimony of Conolly. He would sug-
gest the obvious explanation; it had probably already
occurred to them. The defendant had not anticipated a legal investigation in this country. He had
calculated wisely the amount of proof necessary for
the agents in England. It was certainly prudent to
have as few instruments as possible in a conspiracy
of this dark nature. Conolly, as was apparent, was
of that frank, sociable, communicative disposition,
which characterizes his amiable nation. If it had
been possible to corrupt him, he might, in some con-
vivial moment, disclose a secret which neither involved his fortune nor reputation. Fortune, poor
fellow! he had none; and reputation, alas! it had
been seen at what a rate the reputation of a poor
Irishman was valued.

He begged the jury would not be misled by the
relative standing of the witnesses, but in their verdict would imitate that holy tribunal, that was 'no
respecter of persons.'

He had now come to the last point of the evidence. He would willingly pass it over; he would
for humanity's sake efface it from their memories.
But his duty to his client forbade this exercise of
mercy. He need not tell them he alluded to the

testimony of the child. Surely the unhappy father must have stifled the voice of nature—must have ' stopp'd up the access and passage to remorse,' before he practised on this innocent boy—before he effaced or blotted the handwriting of the Creator, still fresh on his beautiful work. But he had not effaced it. All had witnessed the struggles of Heaven and truth in that little heart against falsehood, fear, and authority. All had seen him yield at last with tears and sobbings to the stern parental command.

He begged the jury would mark by what apparently feeble instruments Heaven had thwarted a well-contrived plot; and finally, he resigned the cause to them, confident, that guided by the light which Providence had thrown across their path, their verdict would establish his client's right.

We have given an imperfect abstract of a powerful argument, but inadequate as it is, it may show how ably men may reason on false premises; how honestly good men may pervert public opinion; and how hard it is to adjust the balance of human judgment.

The Judge then proceeded to charge the jury. He told them that the question before them was one of fact, to be decided by them alone ; that they must perceive that the testimony of the Irishman was utterly irreconcileable with the truth of the defendant's witnesses. It was for them to estimate the credibility of his apparently honest testimony. A great array of circumstances, favorable to the plaintiff's claim, had been presented before them. It was for them to decide what weight should be allowed to them. On the other hand, they must determine how much consideration should be accorded to the hitherto unassailed reputation of the defendant and his witnesses. Their good faith established, the defendant's right to the property was incontestible. Thus he dismissed them with the unadjusted balance in their hands; and the court was adjourned to the following morning.

CHAPTER VIII.

"Dead! art thou dead? alack! my child is dead;
And with my child, my joys are buried!"

ROMEO AND JULIET

MR. CLARENCE returned to his home at a late hour in the afternoon, in a state of mind in which there was nothing to be envied but a consciousness of rectitude. For six months his righteous claim had been suspended, and by the interposition of Winstead Clarence, that man, who, of all the world ought not to have profited by the fortune of his injured relative; and now, when Mr. Clarence had flattered himself that all uncertainty was about to end, his reputation had become involved with his fortune, and both were in jeopardy. He had never coveted riches; neither his day nor his night dreams had been visited with the sordid vision of wealth. He had had the good sense and firmness never to attempt to conceal, or forget, or cause to be forgotten, the degraded condition of his childhood; and he now thought there was a species of injustice, a peculiar hardship in his suffering the reproach and consequences of these vulgar passions, and disquietudes. It was true, that since he had known himself to be the heir of wealth, the exemptions and privileges of fortune had obtained a new value in his eyes. His usual occupations and pleasures had lost their interest in the anticipation of elegant leisure, refined pursuits, and the application of adequate means to high objects.

There was a feeling too, not uncommon when any thing extraordinary and peculiar occurs in our own experience; a feeling of the interposition of Heaven in our behalf; a communication with Providence; an intimate revelation of his will, and his concurrence in our strongest and secret wishes. Mr. Clarence' ruling sentiment was his parental affection; his children appeared to him, and really were, highly gifted. His boy had been the instrument, as far as human agency was concerned, of the singular turn in the tide of his fortunes, and he had regarded him as distinguished by the signal favor of heaven, and destined to gratify his honorable ambition. These had been his high and happy visions; but he had been harassed by suspense and delay, and he was now beset with unexpected dangers, and tormented with unforeseen anxieties.

After the adjournment of the court, he had passed some hours with his lawyers in balancing the chances for and against him, and had pretty well ascertained their opinion of the desperateness of his cause. As he entered his house he met his little girl, Gertrude, in the entry. She bounded towards him, exclaiming, " Good news! good news! dear father!"

" What news? what have you heard, Gertrude?"

" I have received the first prize in my class," and glowing with the emotion she expected to excite, she drew from beneath her apron a prize-book, bright in new morocco and gilding.

"Pshaw!" exclaimed her father, "I thought
you"—had heard some news from the jury, he
was going to add ; but he suppressed the last half
of the sentence, half-amused and half-vexed at his
own weakness. He then, almost unconsciously,
kissed the little girl, and turning from her, paced
the room with an air of abstraction and anxiety.

"You don't seem at all delighted, father," said
the disappointed child, "I am sure I don't know
the reason why ; you used to seem so pleased when
I only got the medal."

Her father made no reply, and a few moments
after Frank came limping into the room. Mr.
Clarence turned short on him, "A pretty piece of
blundering work you made of it in court, Mr.
Frank, how came you to disgrace yourself and me
in that manner ?"

"Oh, father, I was so horribly frightened, and
besides, sir, you know I felt sick."

"Sick ! what ailed you ?"

"Father, have you forgotten that I run a nail
into my foot yesterday?—I have not been well
since."

"My dear boy, I beg your pardon ; but I have
had concerns of so much more moment on my hands.
If your foot still pains you, go and ask your mother to poultice it."

"Mother has gone to Brooklyn. She said she
should get a nervous fever, if she staid at home
waiting for the decision of the cause."

"Well, go to Tempy ; she will do it as well."

"Tempy has gone to Greenwich, to speak to her
brother about coming to live with us, for mother

says we must have a man-servant immediately after we get the cause."

"Have a little patience, Frank, I am going to Doctor Eustace's, and I will ask him to step over and look at your wound." Mr. Clarence snatched up his hat and went to Doctor Eustace's; but in his deep interest in discussing the occurrences of the day with his friend, he forgot the apparently trifling malady of his boy.

"Gertrude," said Frank, as his father shut the door, "don't you wish our grandfather had not left father any money?"

"No, indeed, I don't wish any such thing. But why do you ask me, Frank? I am sure it is all the same, since he has not got it."

"No it is not all the same, by a great deal, Gertrude. Don't you see how different father has been ever since: he does not play to us and talk to us as he used to; he never helps me with my lessons; he always seems to be thinking, and every body is talking to him about the cause; and mother, too, she seems more different than father."

"How do you mean, Frank?"

"Why, she always used to be at home, and had something pleasant for us when we came from school, and so forth; but now she is always talking about how we are going to live, and what she is going to buy when we get the cause."

"Oh, but Frank, we shall have such pleasant times then; mother says so. She says we shall be richer than cousin Anne! and I shall have a piano; and we shall keep a carriage of our own; and we shall have every thing we wish—and that will be like having Aladdin's lamp at once, you know."

"Oh, dear me! all I should wish if I had Aladdin's lamp, would be for somebody to cure my foot. Can't you be my good Genius, Gertrude?" said the poor boy, with a forced smile.

"Yes, Frank. Just stretch your leg out on the sofa, and lay your head in my lap, and I will read to you a beautiful Arabian tale out of my prize-book. You will forget the pain in a few minutes."

The sweet oblivious draught administered by his sister's soothing voice, operated like a charm. Frank's attention was rivetted, and though he now and then startled Gertrude with a groan, he would exclaim in the next breath, "Go on—go on!" She continued to read till he fell asleep. Neither his father nor mother returned till a late hour in the evening.

Early next morning it was known to all persons interested in the cause, that the jury were still in solemn conclave, and it was rumored that they were nearly unanimous in favor of the plaintiff. Those who understood the coercive power of watching and fasting over unanimity of opinion, predicted that the verdict would be forthcoming at the opening of the court.

It is an admitted fact, that notwithstanding the precautions that are taken to maintain the secresy of a jury's deliberations; notwithstanding the officer who attends them, and who is their sentinel, locks them in their apartment, and is sworn neither to hold nor permit communication with them; the state of their opinions does marvellously get abroad. What is the satisfactory solution of this mystery to those

who believe that the nobler sex scorn the interchange
of curiosity and communication?

At the opening of the court, the court-room was
crowded as if a judicial sentence were about to be
passed upon a capital offender, but by a different
and higher class of persons. Some were attracted
by the desire to see how Mr. Clarence would receive
the annunciation of the ruin of his hopes ; how he and
his friend Dr. Eustace would endure the consequent
dishonor. These were disappointed, for neither of
these gentlemen were any where to be seen; Gerald Roscoe too was absent—he who the day before had so boldly scorned every opinion unfavor-
able to Mr. Clarence. There could be no *coup de
theatre* without the presence of these parties. The
general conclusion was, that they were too well apprised of the probable result to meet it in the public
eye.

The proper officer announced that the jury were
ready to present their verdict. They were accordingly conducted to their box, and the foreman arose
to pronounce their verdict for the plaintiff, when he
was interrupted by a noise and altercation at the
door, and Gerald Roscoe entered, and pressed im-
patiently forward. He was followed in the lane he
made by an old woman, who seemed utterly regard-
less of the dignity of the presence she was in, looked
neither to the right nor left, and elbowed her way as
if she had been in a market-house. The young
man cast one anxious glance back to see she followed, and then sprang forward and whispered to Mr.
Clarence' counsel. This gentleman was electrified
by the communication; but he was anxious not to

betray his sensations, and he rose, and with great coolness begged the suspension of the verdict, and the indulgence of the court for a moment. His young friend, Mr. Gerald Roscoe, he said, had found a witness whose testimony might have an important bearing on the case.

Rider interrupted him. He was astonished at such an application. The gentleman must be aware that it was utterly inadmissible; he seemed to have forgotten all legal rules, and all his judicial experience. Had he taken counsel of the unfledged youth who was certainly a most extraordinary volunteer in the defendant's cause? The young man's impertinent obtrusion of his sympathies on the preceding day had deserved reproof; he trusted his honor the Judge would not pass by this gross violation of the decorum of that tribunal.

Roscoe's boyish, slightly-knit frame seemed to dilate into the stature of manhood, as he cast an indignant glance at Rider, whose eye fell before him, and then turning to the court, he said, "I pray the Judge to inflict on me any penalty I may have incurred even in that man's opinion," pointing to Rider, "by my unrepressed sympathy with integrity; but I entreat that my fault may not prejudice Mr. Clarence' cause."

"It shall not," said Rider's associate counsel, willing to humor what he considered the impotent zeal of the youth. "I pray your honor that the new witness may be heard. In the present state of our cause, we have nothing to fear from the machinations of this young counsellor—our beardless brother will scarcely untie our gordian knot."

The judge interposed. " This is somewhat irregular, but as the counsel on both sides consent, let
the witness be sworn." She was so.

" Be good enough to tell us your name, Mistress,"
said Mr. Clarence' counsel.

" Olida Quackenboss."

" You keep a lodging-house in William-street,
Mrs. Quackenboss ?"

" You may call it what you like ; it's my own
house, and I take in a decent body or two now and
then, as sarves my own convenience."

" Did a man, calling himself Smith, die at your
house last April ?"

" No, he died there the thirtieth day of March ;"
then, in an under voice, and counting on her fingers,
' Thirty days hath September,' and so on—" No,
no but, it was the thirty-first of March."

" That is immaterial, good woman."

" What for did you ask me then ?"

" Because I wanted to ask you further, if you
knew any thing of a certain purse, which this man,
calling himself Smith, died possessed of?"

" Yes, do I ; and the lad there," pointing, or rather jerking her elbow, towards Gerald Roscoe,
" laid down ten dollars to answer for it, if any of
you wronged me out of it ; and that would not be as
good as the purse, for it's got Smit's luck-penny in it."

" How came you by it, Mrs. Quackenboss ?"

" Honestly, man."

" No doubt; but did Smith give it to you ?"

The old woman grinned a horrible smile. " Are
you a born-fool, man, to think Smit, a sensible
body, would give away money like your thriftless

spend-all trash, that's flashing up and down Broadway? Why look here, man;" and she thrust her
arm to the almost fathomless abyss of her pocket,
and brought up an old sometime snuff-box, which
she opened, took from it the purse, undrew the
string, and piece by piece dropped into her hand,
the half jo, the Spanish dollar, the English pennies,
and the lucky sixpence, specified in Smith's document. "All this was in it, good money as ever rung
on a counter."

"Then it was paid to you as due from Smith,
was it?"

"Not that neither; Smit paid his own dues; all
but a week's hire of the place, that run up against
him, poor man, while he lay sick and arning nothing. But leave me be; I'll just tell you how it
was. You see, the man that they call the public
administrator came to take Smit's strong box, and
he said the money was all to go into the public chist;
and right glad was I it was to be locked up, and not
go to any heirs, to be blown away with a blast like
the leaves that's been all summer a growing. And
so when this man that they call the administrator
came, I helped him fetch the box from the garret,
and he looked round poor Smit's room upon his
clothes that were hanging about as if they were but so
many cobwebs dangling there, and he said to me,
'You may keep these duds—they'll serve you for
dusting cloths.' I asked him, 'Do you mean I shall
keep them, and all that's in them?' and he said
'Yes;' and to make sure, I called in a witness, and
he said 'Yes' again. And then I shut and locked
the door after us; for I knew of the purse, that

Smit once showed me in his life-time, and I went straight back and got it, and it has not seen the light since till the lad came this morning; and now no man, nor lawyer either, dare to take from me what's honestly mine own. And now ye may take one look at it; it's just as good as when his granny knit it for him, with them words in it—next to a gospel verse are they—' *a penny saved is a penny gained;*' and if ye'd all hare to it, especially yon gay-looking younkers, ye'd have mighty less need of your courts, and your judges, and your lawyers, and your jails. Now you have my word and my counsel, ye may let me go."

"Stop one moment, Mrs. Quackenboss. Who apprised the public administrator that Smith had left the money?"

"He told me one Mr. Carroll had sent him there."

The truth of the miser's document was now attested, and the evidence, of course, conclusive in Mr. Clarence' favor. All, who had watched the progress of the trial, remembered that he might have rested a claim to the miser's money, on the declaration of his manuscript; and his delicacy and disinterestedness in avoiding to do so swelled the tide that was setting in his favor. Murmurs of honest joy, at the triumph of innocence, ran through the court-room. The counsel for the plaintiff rose; '. he had nothing, he said, to allege in answer to the last witness. He was himself convinced,' he magnanimously added, ' of the validity of the defendant's claim to the name and fortune of the late Edmund Clarence, Esquire.'

" Ye're right, your honor, ye're right," cried a voice that made breathless every other in the court-room, " and didn't I tell ye, Lawyer Rider, didn't I tell ye that I heard Clarence that's dead tell him that's living, that he was his own father's son ; didn't I tell ye so, Lawyer Rider?—spake man."

But Rider did not speak. He had no portion of the warm-heartedness of the poor misguided Irishman. He could not throw himself on the wave of generous sympathy, and forget it might engulf him.

Both the offenders were ordered into custody, and both subsequently punished. Rider with the heaviest, Conolly the most lenient infliction the law permitted.

Nothing now remained but for the jury to make out their formal verdict. As soon as this was done, Gerald Roscoe, to whose thought and ingenuity the happy issue of the cause was owing, rushed from the court-room to be the bearer of the happy tidings to Mr. Clarence. He ran breathless to Barclay-street. His glad impatience could not brook the usual formalities. The street door was open. He entered—he flung open the parlor-door; no one was there. He heard footsteps in the room above ; he sprang up stairs, threw wide open the door, and the joyful words seemed of themselves to leap from his lips, " It's yours—it's yours, Mr. Clarence !"

Not a sound replied—not an eye was lifted. Silence, and despair, and death, were there ; and the words fell as if they had been uttered at the mouth of the tomb. Where were now all the hopes, and fears, and calculations, and projects, that a few hours before agitated those beating hearts?

Where was that restless, biting anxiety, that awaited the decision of the cause as if it involved life and happiness? Gone—forgotten; or if it for a moment darted through the memory, it was as the lightning flashes through the tempest, to disclose and make more vivid all its desolation!

What was wealth? what all the honor the world could render to that father on whose breast his only beloved son was breathing out his last sigh? What to the mother who was gazing on the glazed, motionless, death-stricken eye of her boy? What to the poor little girl whose burning cheek was laid to the marble face of her brother, whose arms were clasped around him as if their grasp would have detained the spirit within the bound of that precious body?

The flushed cheek of the messenger faded. His arms that a moment before had been extended with joy, fell unstrung beside him; and he remained awe-struck and mute till the physician who stood bending over the foot of the bed, watching the sufferer for whom his art was impotent, moved round to his side, and bending over him, uttered those soul-piercing words, "*he is gone!*"

Gerald Roscoe closed the door, and with slow footsteps, and a beating heart, returned to the bustling court-room.

CHAPTER IX.

"The graceful foliage storms may reave,
The noble stem they cannot grieve."   Scott

OUR readers must allow us to take a liberty with
time, the tyrant that takes such liberties with us all,
and passing over the three years that followed the
events of the last chapter, introduce them into the
library of Gerald Roscoe's mother, now a widow.
The apartment was in a dismantled condition. A
centre-table was covered with files of papers. The
book-cases were emptied of their precious contents.
The walls stained with marks of pictures just taken
down. The centre-lamp removed from its hang-
ings, vases from their stands, and busts from their
pedestals, and the floor encumbered with packages,
labelled with various names, and marked ' sold.'

Mrs. Roscoe was sitting on a sofa beside her son,
and leaning her head on his shoulder. Their faces
in this accidental position, had the very beauty and
expression that a painter might have selected to
illustrate the son and mother—the widowed mother.
The meek brow on which the fair hair, unharmed
by time, was parted, and just appeared in plain
rich folds from beneath the mourning-cap ; the
tender, vigilant, *mother's* eye ; the complexion, soft,
and fair, and colorless, as a young infant's ; and the
slender form, which, though it had lost all beauty
but grace and delicacy, retained those eminently ;

wereall contrasted as they should be with the firmly
knit frame and manly stature of her son; with the dark
complexion, flushed with the glow of health; a profusion of wavy jet black hair; the full lustrous eye
of genius; an expression of masculine vigor and
untamed hope, softened by the play of the kind
affections of one of the most feeling hearts, and
happiest temperaments in the world. One could
not look at him without thinking that he would
like to take the journey of life with him; would
select him for a *compagnon du voyage*, sure that he
would resolutely surmount the steeps, smooth the
roughnesses, and double the pleasures of the way.
And who to look at the mother would not have
been content to have travelled the path of life with
her, ' heaven born and heaven bound,' as she was,
unencumbered with the burden of life, and unsullied
with any thing earthly? She bore the traces of
grief, deep and recent, but endured with such filial
trust that it had not disturbed the holy tranquillity
of her soul. There was such feminine delicacy in
her appearance, her voice was so sweet and low-
toned, her manners so gentle, that she seemed made
to be loved, cherished, caressed, and defended from
the storms of life. But she was overtaken by them,
the severest, and she endured them with a courage
and fortitude, not derived from the uncertain springs
of earth but from that fountain that infuses its own
celestial quality into the virtue it sustains.

" This has been a precious hour of rest, my dear
Gerald," said his mother, " but we must not prolong it. We have still some matters to arrange
before we leave the house."

"No, I believe all is finished. I have just given your last inventory and directions to the auctioneer."

"Then nothing remains but to dismiss Agrippa. I had determined to have no *feelings*, but I am not quite equal to this task. You must do it for me, Gerald."

"I have already arranged that business. Agrippa would not be dismissed. He says he is spoiled for new masters and mistresses; and to tell you the truth, my gentle mother, Agrippa is half right, your servants are not fit for the usage of common families.

"I certainly would retain Agrippa, Gerald, if we had any right to such a luxury as the indulgence of our feelings. But my annuity will hardly stretch to the maintenance of a servant, and you, my dear boy, have yet to learn how hard it is to earn your own subsistence."

"That's true, mother; but it will be only a little harder to earn Agrippa's too; and I shall work with a lighter heart, if I toil for something beside my own rations. Thank heaven! in our plentiful country there is many an extra cover at nature's board, and those who earn a place there, have a right to dispense them. Agrippa, poor fellow, would follow our fortunes even though 'he died for lack of a dinner.' When I asked him where he meant to go when we left the house, he drew up with the greatest dignity, and said, 'With *the family*, to be sure. Who could ever think of madam and Mr. Gerald living without a servant?'"

"Well, Gerald, if the fancy that his services conter granduer or benefit on us, makes him happier, we will not destroy the illusion. Your exertions to support the old man will give me more pleasure than a thousand servants. My mind has, of late, been so occupied with inventories, that I have thought of making a list of my compensations for the loss of fortune. I should place first the power of adversity to elicit the energies of a young man of eighteen."

" Pass over the *mother's* compensations, if you please, and specify some other particulars. For instance, is adversity the touchstone of friendship ?"

" No, I think not—that is the common notion ; but it seems to me that the misanthropic complaints of human nature, with which most persons embitter their adversity, result from accidental connnctions and ill-assorted unions. In prosperity intimacies are formed, not so much from sympathy of taste and feeling, as from similarity of condition. We associate with those who live in a certain style, and when this bond is dissolved, why should not the friendship be ?"

" Friendship ! mother ?"

" True, Gerald, it is an absurd misnomer. · We fancy the shadow is a substance, and when the light enters complain that it vanishes. Those who are not intoxicated by fortune, nor duped by vanity, do not need adversity to prove their friends. I have been disappointed in one instance only, and there the fault is my own. I humbly confess I was blinded by his flattery. I ought always to have known there was nothing in Stephen Morley to de- serve our friendship."

" Stephen Morley ! the poor scoundrel, he does
not deserve a thought from you, my dear mother."

" But we must bestow a few thoughts upon him
just now, Gerald.   Run your eye over that power
of attorney," she added, giving him a paper, " and
if you find it correct, send it to Denham."   The
paper authorized Denham, Mrs. Roscoe's lawyer,
to convert a certain property into money, and
therewith to pay a debt due to Stephen Morley
from the late Edward Roscoe, Esquire.

" This is superfluous," said Gerald, " Morley's
debt is already provided for in the assignment."

" True, but Morley is dissatisfied and impatient."

" Good Heaven! does the fellow dare to say so?"

" Read his note, Gerald, and you will think with
me that a release from even the shadow of an obligation to Mr. Morley is worth a sacrifice."   Gerald read the following note :

" My dear Madam—A severe pressure of pub-
" lic business (private concerns I should have put
" aside) has prevented my expressing in person, the
" deep sympathy I feel in your late bereavement.
" The loss of a husband, and *such* a husband is
" indeed a calamity ; but we must all bow to the
" dispensations of an all-wise Providence.

" It is painful to intrude on you, my dear madam,
" at *such* a moment a business concern, and no-
" thing but an *imperative* sense of duty to my fa--
" mily, would compel me to do it.   I understand
" you have assumed the settlement of my late friend's
" affairs—a task, suffer me to say, my dearest madam,
" en parenthése, ill-suited to one of your delicate
" sensibilities.

" I hesitate to allude to my late friend's debt to
" me—a debt, I am bound in justice to myself to
" say, contracted under *peculiar* circumstances; still
" I should not refer to them as a reason for an
" earlier settlement of my claim than is provided
" for by your assignments, (which Denham has ex-
" hibited to me,) was I not constrained by that *stern*
" necessity that knows *no* law, to intreat you to
" make arrangements for an *immediate* payment.

" Believe me, my dear madam, with the sincerest
" condolence and respect,

" Your very humble, and
" devoted Servant
" STEPHEN MORLEY."

Gerald threw down the note; " the sycophantic,
selfish rascal!" he exclaimed, "yes, pay him, my dear
mother—if it were the pound of flesh, I would pay
him—' *peculiar circumstances,*' peculiar enough,
Heaven knows! The only requital he ever made for
loans from my father that saved him, time after time,
from a jail—' peculiar,' peculiar indeed, that after
our house has been a home to him he should be the
only one of all the creditors dissatisfied. Pay him!
Yes, mother, pay him instantly."

A servant opened the door "Mr. Morley, madam!
He asks if he can see you alone."

"Show Mr. Morley up—leave me, Gerald."

Gerald paused at the door: "Let me see him,
mother," he said earnestly; " he does not deserve"
—his sentence was broken off by Morley's entrance.
Gerald looked as if he longed to give him the intimation the Frenchman received who said of the

gentleman who kicked him down stairs, 'he intimated he did not like his company.' Morley seized his hand, gave it a pressure, and said in a voice accurately depressed to the key of condolence, " My dear Gerald!" and then elongating his visage to its utmost stretch of wofulness he advanced towards Mrs. Roscoe. She baffled all his preparations by meeting him with a composure that made him feel his total insignificance in her eyes. The bidden tear that welled to his eye was congealed there, and the thrice conned speech died away on his lips. " You have business with me, Mr. Morley," she said in a manner that excluded every other ground of intercourse.

" Yes, my dear madam, I have a small matter of business; but it *is* particularly painful to intrude it at this moment. I am really quite overwhelmed with seeing preparations for an auction in *this* house. God bless me, my dear Julia, was it not possible to avoid this consummation of your misfortunes? And now, when the details of business must be so extremely trying to you?"

" On the contrary, Mr. Morley, they are of service to me."

" Ah! I fear you are overtaxing yourself—an unnatural excitement, depend on it. I fear too—suffer me to be frank—my deep interest in you must be my apology—I fear you have been ill-advised. In your peculiar circumstances, nothing would have been easier than a favorable compromise with the majority of your creditors—certain debts, of course, to be excepted."

" Fortunately, Mr. Morley, there was no neces-

ity for exceptions; I have the means to pay them
all."

"Undoubtedly, madam; but by the surrender of
your private fortune—to that my friend's creditors
had no claim; of course I except those debts in
which my friend's *honor* was involved."

"You must pardon me, Mr. Morley; as a woman, I am ignorant of the nice distinctions of men
of business. Gerald has not yet learned an artificial code of morals; and we both thought all honest
debts honorable."

"Undoubtedly, madam, in one sense; you have
high notions on these subjects; the misfortune is,
they do not accord with the actual state of things;
such sacrifices are not required by the sense of the
public."

"Perhaps not, Mr. Morley, but we were governed by our own moral sense."

"Fanciful, my dear madam; and suffer me to say
that whatever right you may have to indulge your
romantic self-sacrifice, you seem to me to have
overlooked your duty to Gerald."

"A mother," replied Mrs. Roscoe, with a faint
smile, "is not in much danger of overlooking such
duties to an only son. Had our misfortunes occurred at an earlier period of Gerald's life, the surrender of my fortune would have been more difficult.
But Gerald has already had, and availed himself
worthily, of every advantage of education that our
country affords. His talents, zeal, and industry—I
speak somewhat proudly, Mr. Morley—are his present means, and adequate to his wants. His agency

11*

for Mr. Clarence, and another honorable employment he has been so fortunate as to obtain, will furnish him a respectable support without encroaching on his professional studies.''

'' Very fortunate, very respectable, undoubtedly, my dear madam ; but then my friend Gerald is so very promising—such an uncommonly elegant young man—he would have come into life under such advantages. Why, there are the Vincents, Mrs. Roscoe. Who are more sought and visited than the Vincents? Mrs. V. was left in circumstances precisely analogous to yours. She had, I may say, if not an able, a fortunate adviser at least. We called the creditors together, and exhibited rather a desperate state of affairs. She was, you know, at that time a remarkably pretty woman, and looked uncommonly interesting in her widow's weeds; her children were assembled around her in their deep mourning—it was quite a scene. I assure you the creditors were touched ; they signed a most favorable compromise—compounded for ten per cent. I think. Mrs. Vincent lived in great retirement while her daughters were being educated—spared no expense—and now they have come out in the very first style, I assure you. Nobody has a more extensively fashionable acquaintance—nobody entertains in better style, than my friend Mrs. Vincent.''

'' I believe I must remind you that you have business with me, Mr. Morley.''

Morley bit his nails ; but after a moment he recovered his self-possession, and reverted from the na-

tural tone into which he had fallen, to that of sentimental sympathy. "Yes, my dear madam, I have
business; but really my own concerns were quite
put out of my head, by seeing this house, in which I
have passed so many pleasant hours, in preparation for
an auction! I hardly know how to proceed; I could
not fully explain myself in my note. It is too delicate an affair to commit to paper—I was particularly
solicitous not to excite your feelings." Mrs. Roscoe
listened with that quiet attention, that said, as plainly
as words could speak it, *You* cannot excite my feelings, Mr. Morley. She was however mistaken.
Morley proceeded: "I perceive, by the exhibit of
your affairs, that you have placed me on the same
footing with the other creditors of my late friend;
I know it is your intention they shall all be fully
paid, principal and interest—but permit me to say
this is a fallacious hope—a case that rarely occurs;
there are invariably great losses in the settlement of
estates—if the creditors get fifty per cent., they esteem
themselves fortunate. I am compelled to say, though
reluctantly, that there is something a little peculiar
in this debt to me, which renders its immediate and
entire payment very important—important, I mean,
to the memory of my late friend."

"Will you have the goodness, Mr. Morley, to
explain to me the peculiar circumstances attending
this debt?"

"Excuse me, my dear madam; it would be too
painful a task; take my assurance that my friend's
honor is implicated. I beg," he added, lowering
his voice, "that you will not communicate to Gerald what I am going to say. He is hot-headed, and

might be rash. An exposure of the circumstances attending the loan would be most unfortunate; I could not avert the consequences to my friend's reputation. The dishonor, I am sorry to say it, would be great, and the disadvantage to your son, inestimable. It is therefore on his account, far more than my own, that I urge immediate payment."

"Let me understand you distinctly, Mr. Morley; do you mean that there were circumstances attending the borrowing of that money dishonorable to my husband?"

"I grieve to say there were, madam."

"And those circumstances must transpire if the money is not immediately refunded?"

"This is the unhappy state of the case."

"Will you run your eye over that power of attorney, Mr. Morley?" Morley did so, and felt a mingled sensation of joy, at finding himself so secure of immediate possession of the total amount of his debt, and of vexation that he had taken so much superfluous trouble; however, the pleasure preponderated and sparkled in his eyes, as he said, "This is perfectly satisfactory, my dear madam, entirely so; it wants nothing but your signature."

"And my signature, sir, it never will receive." Morley's face fell. He looked as if he felt much as a fox might be supposed to feel, who sees the trap-door fall upon him, just as he is in the act of grasping his prey. "Mr. Morley," continued Mrs. Roscoe, "that instrument will convince you how solicitous I was to escape from a pecuniary obligation to you—galling as it is, I will continue to endure it,

to show you that neither your broad assertions, nor
malignant insinuations, can excite one fear for the
honor of my husband's memory. I shall *not* communicate what you have said to my son, for he
might not be able to restrain his indignation against
a man who has slandered his father, to his mother's
ear. Our business is now, sir, at an end." Mrs.
Roscoe rang the bell. Morley fumbled with his
hat and uttered some broken sentences, half remon-
strating, and half apologizing. The servant appeared. " Agrippa, open the street-door for Mr.
Morley." Mr. Morley was compelled to follow
Agrippa, with the mortifying consciousness of
having been penetrated, baffled, and put down, by a
woman.

It may appear incomprehensible to our readers,
that Stephen Morley should ever have been honored
with the friendship of the Roscoes, but they must
remember we have shown him without his mask.
—" The art of pleasing," says Chesterfield, " is
the art of rising in the world," and one of the
grossest but surest arts of pleasing is the art of
flattery. Morley flattered women for their love ;
men for their favor, and the people for their suffrages.
From the first he received all grace, from the second,
consideration, and from the last, office and political
distinction. When the Roscoes were affluent and
distinguished, Morley was as obsequious to them as
an oriental slave to his master. But when a sudden
turn in the tide of fortune changed the aspect of
their affairs, and cloud after cloud gathered over
them, Mr. Stephen Morley, who resembled the fe-

line race in their antipathy to storms, as well as in some other respects, shook the damps from his coat, and slunk away from the side of his friends.

The Roscoes, occupied with deep sorrows and difficult duties, had almost forgotten him, when he consummated his meanness by the conduct we have related,

CHAPTER X.

By my troth, we that have good wits have much to answer tor
AS YOU LIKE IT.

THE following letter was addressed by Mrs. Layton, whom we take the liberty thus unceremoniously
to present to our readers, to Gerald Roscoe, Esq.

" *Upton's-purchase, June,* 18—.

" Tell me, my dear friend, if you love the coun-
" try, (to borrow your legal phrase,) *per se?* Here
" I am surrounded by magnificent scenery, in the
" midst of ' bowery summer,' in the month of flowers,
" and singing-birds, the leafy month of June, and
" yet I am sighing for New York. It is Madame
" de Staël, I think, who says that ' love and religion
" only can enable us to enjoy nature.' The first,
" alas! alas! is (for *is* read *ought to be,*) passé to
" me; and the last I have exclusively associated with
" the sick-chamber and other forms of gloom and
" misery.

" I honestly confess, I do love the town; I prefer
" a walk on a clean flagging to daggling my
" flounces and wetting my feet in these green fields.
" I had rather be waked in the morning, (if waked
" I must be) by the chimney-sweeps' cry, than by
" the chattering of martins. I prefer the expressive
" hum of my own species to the hum of insects, and
" I had rather see a few japonicas, geraniums, and

"jasmines, peeping from a parlor-window, than all
"these acres of wheat, corn, and potatoes.

"Oh, for the luxury of my own sofa, with the
"morning-paper or the 'last new novel' from Good-
"rich: with the blinds closed, and the sweet security
"of a 'not at home' order to faithful servants.
"Country people have such a passion for *prospects*,
"as if there were no picture in life but a *paysage*;
"and for light too, they are all Persians—worship-
"pers of the sun.　My friends here do not even
"know the elements of the arts of life.　They have
"not yet learned that nothing but infancy or such
"a complexion as Emilie's can endure the revela-
"tions of broad sunshine.　It would be difficult, my
"dear Roscoe, to give you an idea of the varieties
"of misery to which I am exposed.　My friends
"pride themselves on their hospitality—on their de-
"votion to their guests.　They know nothing of
"the art of 'letting alone.'　I must ride, or walk,
"or sail.　We must have this friend to dine, or
"that 'charming girl to *pass the day*.'　My old
"school-mate, Harriet Upton, whom in an evil hour
"I came thus far to see, was in her girlhood quite
"an inoffensive little negative.　She is now a posi-
"tive wife—a positive house-wife—a positive mo-
"ther—and Mrs. Balwhidder, the busiest of bees,
"nay, all the bees of Mount Hymettus are not half
"so busy as Harriet Upton.　She has the best din-
"ners, pies, cake, sweetmeats, in the country—her
"house is in the most exact order, and no servants—
"or next to none—a house full of children too, and
"no nursery!　She is an incessant talker, and no
"topic but husband and children and house-affairs.

" She is an *economist* too, and like most female sages
" in that line, that I have had the misfortune to en-
" counter, she loses all recollection of the end in her
" eternal bustle about the means. Every thing
" she wears is a *bargain*. All her furniture has
" been bought at auctions. She tells me with infi-
" nite naïveté (*me* of all subjects for such a boast)
" that she always makes her visits to town in the
" spring, when families are breaking up, and mer-
" chants are breaking down—when to every tenth
" house is appended that prettiest of ensigns, in
" her eyes, a *red* flag, and half the shop-windows
" are eloquent with that talismanic sentence, ' selling
" off at cost.' Oh Roscoe! would that you could
" see her look, half incredulous and half contemptu-
" ous, when I tell her that my maid, Justine, does
" all my shopping, and confess my ignorance of the
" price of every article of my dress.

" But even Dame Upton, a mass of insipidities as
" she is, is as much more tolerable than her hus-
" band, as a busy, scratching, fluttering, clucking
" motherly hen, than a solemn turkey-cock. He,
" I fancy, from the pomp and circumstance with
" which he enounces his common-places is Sir Ora-
" cle among his neighbors. He is a man of great
" affairs, president of an agricultural society, colo-
" nel of a regiment, justice of the peace, director of
" a bank—in short, he fills all departments, milita-
" ry, civil, and financial, and may be best summed
" med up in our friend D.'s pithy sentence—' he is
" all-sufficient, self-sufficient, and insufficient.'

" I am vexed at myself for having been the dupe
" of a school-day friendship. You, Roscoe, are

" partly in fault for having kept alive my youthful
" sentimentalities.　What a different story would
" Emilie tell you, were she to write!　Every thing
" is *couleur de rose* to her; but that is the hue of se-
" venteen—and besides, from having been brought
" up in a tame way with her aunt, common plea-
" sures are novelties to her.　From the moment we
" left New York, she had a succession of ecstacies.
" The palisades were 'grand;' the highlands
" ' Alps;' and the Caatskills 'Chimborazo,' and
" ' Himlaya.'　She could have lived and died at
" West Point, and found a paradise at any of those
" pretty places on the Hudson.　Albany, that little
" Dutch furnace, was classic ground to her, and she
" dragged me round at day-light to search among
" the stately modern buildings for the old Dutch
" rookeries that the alchymy of Irving's pen has, in
" her imagination, transmuted to antique gems.
" Even in traversing the pine and sandy wilderness
" from Albany to Schenectady, she exclaimed, 'how
" beautiful!' and when I, half vexed, asked ' what
" is beautiful?' she pointed to the few spireas and
" sweetbriars by the road-side.　Alas for her poor
" mother! the kaleidescope of her imagination was
" broken long ago, and trifles will never again
" assume beautiful forms and hues to her vision.
" There are pleasures, however, for which I have
" still an exquisite relish—a letter from you, my
" dear Gerald, would be a ' diamond fountain' in
" this desert.

" By the way, what do you know of the Cla-
" rences of Clarenceville?　They called on us a
" few days since; the father, daughter, and a young

" man by the name of Seton, an artist, who resides
" in the family and teaches the young lady paint-
" ing. She, if one may judge from the poor fellow's
" blue eye and sunken cheek, has already drawn
" lines on his heart, that it will take a more cunning
" art than his to efface. He seems to regard her as a
" poet does his muse, or a hero his inspiring genius,
" as something to be worshipped and obeyed, but
" not approached. She appears a comely little body,
" amiable, and rather clever—at least she looked
" so : she scarcely spoke while she was here ; once
" I fancied she blushed—and at what, do you think?
" Your name, Gerald. The father was very curious
" about you. He is a ' melancholy Jacques' of a
" man, but he is a dyspeptic, which accounts for all
" moral maladies. They are evidently the lions of
" this part of the world. Harriet Upton has a con-
" stitutional deference for whatever is *distingué* in
" any way ; and she was in evident trepidation lest
" Mr. Clarence, who, she took care to tell me, was
" ' very particular,' should not accord his suffrage
" to her friend. I was piqued, and determined to
" show her there was more in woman's power than
" was dreamt of in her philosophy. I succeeded so
" well that she kindly assured me she had never
" seen Mr. Clarence ' take so to a stranger,' and
" ' husband said so too.' ' Husband says,' in Harriet
" Upton's mouth, is equivalent to ' scripture says'
" from an orthodox divine.

" Mr. Clarence betrayed some surprise at my
" particular knowledge of you, and your affairs ; for
" to confess the truth, I was a little ostentatious of
" the flattering fact of our intimacy. I cannot ac-

" count for his curiosity about you, but on the—*fe-*
" *minine* supposition, you will call it—that he has
" designs, or rather hopes, in relation to you; and
" on some accounts the thing would do remarkably
" well. But then there is your genuine antipathy
" to rich alliances to be overcome; and, Gerald, you
" are such a devotee to beauty, that this young lady
" would shock your beau-ideal; and besides, to a
" young man who is a romantic visionary in affairs
" of the heart, there is something chilling and re-
" volting in the sort of exemplary, mathematical cha-
" racter that I take Miss Clarence to be; and finally
" —and thank Heaven for it—you are not a marry-
" ing man, Gerald.

" I wonder that any man—that is, any man of
" society—should trammel himself with matrimony,
" till it becomes a refuge from old-bachelorhood.
" An old bachelor is certainly the poorest creature
" in existence. An old maid has a conventual asy-
" lum in the obscurity of domestic life; and besides,
" it is *possible* that her singleness is involuntary, and
" then you feel more of pity than contempt for her;
" but an old bachelor, whether he be a fidgety, cy-
" nical churl, or a good-natured tool who runs of
" errands for the mamas, dances with the youngest
" girls in company, (a sure sign of dotage,) and
" feeds the children with sugar-plums; an old ba-
" chelor is a link dropped from the universal chain,
" not missed, and soon forgotten.

" But to the Clarences once more. Miss Clarence
" and Emilie have taken a mutual liking, and Emilie
" has accepted an invitation, received to-day, and ex-
" pressed in the kindest manner, to pass a week at Cla-

" renceville. The invitation to the Uptons and me is
" limited to a dinner. If Miss Clarence were a wo-
" man of the world, she would not care to bring her-
" self into such close comparison with such exqui-
" site beauty as Emilie's. Is it not strange that
" Emilie, Hebe as she is, should have so little influ-
" ence over the imagination. She is a great deal
" more like Layton than like her poor mother. By
" the way, will you tell Layton he must remit us
" some money, and also that I shall conform to *his*
" wishes in respect to going to Trenton, and shall of
" course expect the necessary funds. Be kind enough
" to say I should have written to him if I had had
" time.

 " Oh, that my friend would write—not a book—
" heaven forefend! but a letter. Do gratify my
" curiosity about the Clarences. I mean in rela-
" tion to any particular interest they may have in
" you. I know generally the history of Mr. C.'s
" discovery of his father, and his law-suit.

 " Adieu, dear Gerald. Believe me with as much
" sentiment as a wife and matron may indulge,

" Yours,

" GRACE LAYTON."

Gerald Roscoe to Mrs. Layton.

" *New York, June,* 18—.

 " My dear Madam—It is I believe canonical to
" answer first the conclusion of a lady's letter. My
" reply to your queries about the Clarences will ac-
" count for Mr. C.'s interest in me, without involv-
" ing any reason so flattering as that you have sug-

12*

" gested. My uncle, Gerald Roscoe, was one of
" that unlucky brotherhood that have fallen under
" your lash, and so far from being a ' dropped link,
" not missed, and soon forgotten,' he had that
" warmth and susceptibility of heart, that activity
" and benevolence of disposition, that strengthen
" and brighten the chain that binds man to man,
" and earth to heaven. Blessed be his memory!
" I never see an old bachelor that my heart does
" not warm to him for his sake. But to my story.
" My uncle—a Howard in his charities—(you
" touched a nerve, my dear Mrs. Layton, when
" you satarised old bachelors)—my uncle, on a
" visit to our city alms-house, espied a little boy,
" who, to use his own phrase, had a *certain some-*
" *thing* about him that took his heart. This certain
" something, by the way, he saw in whoever needed
" his kindness. The boy too, at the first glance
" was attracted to my uncle. Children are the
" keenest physiognomists—never at fault in their *first*
" *loves.* It suddenly occurred to my uncle, that an
" errand-boy was indispensable to him. The child
" was removed to my grandfather's, and soon made
" such rapid advances in his patron's affections that
" he sent him to the best schools in the city, and
" promoted him to the parlor, where, universal
" sufferance being the rule of my grandfather's
" house, he was soon as firmly established as if he
" had equal rights with the children of the family.
" This child was then, as you probably know,
" called Charles Carroll. He was just graduated
" with the first honors of Columbia College, when,
" within a few days of each other, my grandfather

" and uncle died, and the house of Roscoe & Son
" proved to be insolvent. Young Carroll, of course,
" was cast on his own energies. He would have
" preferred the profession of law, but he had fallen
" desperately in love with a Miss Lynford, who
" lived in dependence in her uncle's family. He
" could not brook the humiliations which, I suspect,
" he felt more keenly than the subject of them,
" and he married, and was compelled, by the actual
" necessities of existence, to renounce distant ad-
" vantages for the humble but certain gains of a
" clerkship. These particulars I had from my mo-
" ther. You may not have heard that at the moment
" of his accession of property he suffered a calamity
" in the death of an only son, which deprived
" him of all relish, almost of all consciousness, of
" his prosperity. He would gladly have filled
" the boy's yawning grave with the wealth which
" seemed to fall into his hands at that moment, to
" mock him with its impotence. The boy was a
" rare gem. I knew him and loved him, and hap-
" pened to witness his death ; and being then at the
" impressible season of life, it sunk deeply into
" my heart. It was a sudden, and for a long time,
" a total eclipse to the poor father. The shock
" was aggravated by a bitter self-reproach, for
" having, in his engrossing anxiety for the result of
" his pending lawsuit, neglected the child's malady
" while it was yet curable.

" He was plunged into an abyss of melancholy.
" His health was ruined, and his mind a prey to
" hypochondriac despondency. He languished for
" a year without one effort to retrieve his spirits.

" His physician prescribed entire change of scene,
" as the only remedy, and a voyage to Europe was
" decided on.   His daughter was sent to Madame
" Rivardi's in Philadelphia, where, by the way, if
" she had been of a, polishable texture, she would
" now be something very different from the unembel-
" lished little person you describe. Mrs. Clarence went
" abroad with her husband.   My mother, who is a
" sagacious observer of her own sex, says she was a
" weak and worldly-minded woman, quite unfit to
" manage, and certainly to rectify, so delicate an
" instrument as her husband's mind.   They had
" been in Europe about eighteen months, when Mr.
" Clarence received the news of my father's death,
" the last, and bitterest of our family misfortunes.
" This event roused Mr. Clarence' generous sym-
" pathies.   It gave him a motive for return and ex-
" ertion.   He came home to proffer assistance in
" every form to my mother.   He found that she
" had heroically surmounted difficulties with which
" few spirits would have struggled; that she had
" declined a compromise with my father's creditors,
" and had succeeded in paying off all his debts;
" and that we were living independently, but with
" a severe frugality almost unparalleled in our boun-
" tiful country.   I mention these particulars in jus-
" tice to Mr. Clarence, and to do honor to my
" mother.   My mother! I never write or speak
" her name without a thrill through my heart.   A
" thousand times have I blessed the adversity that
" brought forth her virtue in such sweet and beau-
" tiful manifestations.   It was there, like the per-
" fume in the flower, latent under the meridian sun,
" but exhaled by the beating tempest.

" I should not care my wife should honor my me-
·" mory by mausoleums, cherished grief, and moping
" melancholy, and their ostentatious ensigns. Deep
" and even *unchanging* weeds, do not excite my
" imagination; but the tender, cheerful fortitude
" with which my mother endured pecuniary reverses;
" the unblenching resolution with which she met
" all the perplexing details of business, never falter-
" ing till my father's interrupted purposes were
" effected, and till his memory was blessed, even by
" his creditors; this is the honor that would make
" my ghost trip lightly through elysium—shame
" on my heathenism!—that would enhance the hap-
" piness of heaven.

" But to return to Mr. Clarence. He insisted
" that he owed a debt to my father's family, and that
" my mother ought not to withhold from him the
" right as he had now the opportunity to can-
" cel it.

" My mother, with the scrupulousness which, if
" it is an infirmity, is the infirmity of a noble mind,
" recoiled from a pecuniary obligation. Mr. Cla-
" rence, however, was not to be baffled. Inspired
" with confidence in me, as he said, by the ability
" with which I had assisted my mother in the man-
" agement of our private disastrous affairs, he made
" me his man of business, and paid me a salary that
" relieved us at once from our most pressing neces-
" sities. I soon after entered on my profession, and
" from that time have received a series of kindnesses,
" which, in the temper of his noble nature, he has
" bestowed as my dues, rather than as his favours.
" It is now five years since I have seen him. His

" daughter I have never seen since her childhood ;
" though far less striking than her brother, she
" was then interesting. I am mortified, on her
" father's account, that she should have turned out
" such an ordinary concern. But it is a common
" case ; the fruit rarely verifies the promise of the
" bud. However, I fancy her father has his conso-
" lations. I infer from his letters that she is ex-
" emplary in her filial duties. They have resided at
" Clarenceville ever since her mother's death, when
" Miss C. was withdrawn from school. It is cer-
" tainly a merit in a girl of her brilliant expecta-
" tions to remain contentedly buried alive in the
" country—a merit to point a moral, not adorn a
" tale. Is it natural depravity, my dear Mrs. Lay-
" ton, or artificial perversity, that makes us during
" the romantic period of life so insensible to useful
" home-bred virtues? 'A comely little body—
" amiable and rather clever !' Heavens! such a
" picture would give Cupid an ague-fit. The words
" raise the long forgotten dead in my memory and
" carry me back to good Parson Peabody's, in
" Connecticut, where I was sent to learn Latin and
" Greek, and where, even then, my wicked heart
" revolted from ' a comely little body—amiable and
" rather clever,' a Miss Eunice Peabody—a pat-
" tern damsel. I see her now knitting the parson's
" long blue yarn-stockings, and at the same time
" dutifully reading Rollin, Smollett, (his history !)
" and Russell's Modern Europe—knitting, and read-
" ing by the mark. Many a time in my boyish
" mischief I have slipped back her mark, and seen
" her faithfully and unspectingly retrace the pages,

" though once, when 1 had ventured to repeat the
" experiment on the same portion of the book, she
" very sagely remarked to the admiring parson 'that
" there was considerable repetition in Rollin..' How-
" ever, I beg Miss Clarence' pardon, and really
" take shame to myself for any disrespect to
" one so nearly and dearly allied to my excellent
" friend, her father. The truth is, I have been a
" good deal vexed by having her seriously proposed
" to me as a most worthy matrimonial enterprise,
" by several of my friends, who flatter me by say-
" ing, it would be an acceptable alliance to the
" father, and that I want nothing but fortune to
" make a figure in life. Now that is just what I
" do not want. I have my own ambition, but,
" thank God, it does not run in that vulgar channel.
" I honor my profession, among other reasons, be-
" cause it does not hold forth the lure of wealth.
" I would press on in the noble career before me,
" my eye fixed on such men as Emmet and Wells,
" and if I attain eminence it shall be as they have
" attained it, by the noblest means—the achieve-
" ments of the mind; and the eminence shall be
" too, like that 'holy hill of the Lord, to which
" none shall ascend but those that wash their hands
" in innocency.' If you have the common prejudices
" against my profession, you may think this holy
" hill as inaccessible to lawyers, as the promised
" land was to the poor sinning Israelites. But
" allow me, by way of an apt illustration of my own
" ideas, to repeat to you a compliment I received
" from Agrippa, an old negro-servant of my fa-

" ther. He came into my office and looking
" round with great complacency, said, 'Well, Mas-
" ter Gerald, you've raly got to be a squire.'

" 'Yes, Grip; but I hope you do not think that
" lawyers cannot be good men.'

" 'No, that I don't sir; clean hands must do a
" great deal of dirty work in this world.'

" I shall never undertake a doubtful cause—a ne-
" cessity which I believe the best ethics include
" among our legal duties—without consoling myself
" with Agrippa's apothegm. But enough, and too
" much, of egotism. One word as to your womanly
" fancy that Miss Clarence blushed at the mention of
" my name; I never knew a woman that had not a gift
" for seeing blushes and tears. Poor Miss Clarence!
" Never was there a more gratuitous fancy than
" this.

" And now, my dear madam, for a more agreea-
" ble topic. When do you return to the city? I
" am becoming desperate. My dear mother has
" been at Schooley's mountain for the last four
" weeks; and since your parting ' God bless you,'
" I have not exchanged one word with ' Heaven's
" last, best work.' My condition reminds me of a
" play, written by a friend of mine, which was re-
" turned to him by the manager, with this comment,
" 'It will not do, sir. Why there is not a woman in
" it; and if your men were heroes or angels, they
" must be damned without women.' Now I am far
" enough from being hero or angel; but there is no
" paradise to me without women—without you, my
" dear madam——and—my mother. I put her in,

"not so much for duty's, as for truth's sake. Com-
"mend me to Miss Emilie; it is no wonder she
"should love the country—all that is sweet, beau-
"tiful, and inspiring in nature, is allied to her.

" My temper was put to the test the other day on
"her account; or more on yours, than hers. Tom
"Reynolds joined me on the Battery. ' So,' said
"he, ' your friend Mrs. Layton has made a grand
"match for her peerless daughter!'

" ' How? to what do you allude?'

" ' Bless me! you have not heard that Emilie
"Layton is engaged to the rich Spaniard, Pe-
"drillo?'

" ' Pshaw! that is too absurd. Pedrillo is a fo-
"reigner, unknown, and twice Miss Layton's age.'

" ' Mere bagatelles, my dear sir. He is rich; and
"put what you please in the other scale, and it kicks
"the beam, that is, if fathers and mothers are to
"strike the balance.'

" ' Upon my word, you do them great ho-
"nor; but in this case I fancy Miss Layton's own
"inclinations will be consulted.'

" ' *Tant mieux*. Pedrillo is a devilish genteel
"fellow, handsome enough, and has a very insinu-
"ating address. What more can a girl ask for?'

" I was not, as you may suppose, my dear ma-
"dam, fool enough to throw away any sentiment on
"a man destitute of the first principles on which
"sentiment is founded. So we parted; but I was
"indignant that rumor should for a moment class
"you with persons who are degraded far below the
"level of those pagan parents who abandon their

" children to the elements, or sacrifice them to their
" divinities. Of all the mortifying spectacles of ci-
" vilized life, I know none so revolting as a parent
" —a *mother*—who is governed by mercenary mo-
" tives in controlling the connubial destiny of a
" daughter! But why this to you, who are inde-
" pendent, to a fault, (I should say, if the *queen* could
" do wrong,) of all pecuniary considerations?

" But my letter is so long, that my moral has
" little chance of being read; so here is an end
" of it. Return, I beseech you, my dear Mrs. Lay-
" ton; nothing has any tendency to fill the vacancy
" you make in the life of your devoted friend and
" servant,

" GERALD ROSCOE."

CHAPTER XI.

"Rural recreations abroad, and books at home, are the innocent
pleasures of a man who is early wise, and gives fortune no more
hold of him than of necessity he must."   DRYDEN.

THE sentiment of Dryden, which we have prefix-
ed to this chapter, accorded with Mr. Clarence'
views, and will in part explain his preference of a
rural life. But he had other reasons—reasons that
neither began nor terminated with himself. The
formation of Gertrude's character was the first object
of his life, and he wished, while it was flexible, to secure
for it the happiest external influences. He believed
that direct instruction, the most careful inculcation
of wise precepts, and the constant vigilance of a single individual, (even though that individual be a
parent,) are insignificant, compared with the indi-
rect influences that cannot be controlled, or with
what has been so happily called the 'education of
circumstances.' He wished to inspire his child with
moderation and humility. She was surrounded by
the indulgencies of a luxurious town-establishment,
and exposed to the flatteries of the frivolous and
foolish. He wished to give her a knowledge and
right estimate of the just uses and responsibilities of
the fortune of which she was to be the dispenser.
His lessons would be counteracted in a society where
wealth was made the basis of aristocracy and fashion.
He wished to infuse a taste for rational and intellec-

tual pursuits. How was this to be achieved amidst the 'dear five hundred friends' she had inherited from her mother—the flippant idlers of fashionable life'?

Mr. Clarence was too much of a philosopher to condemn *en masse* the class of fashionable society. He knew there were individual exceptions to its general character, but he regarded them as the golden sands borne on the current, not giving it a new direction. He esteemed the devotees to morning visits and evening parties as the mere foam on the fountain of life—as having no part in its serious uses or purposes. He felt a benevolent compassion for them; they seemed to him like the uninstructed deaf and dumb, beings unconscious of the rich faculties slumbering within them; faculties, that if awakened and active, and directed to the ends for which they were designed by their beneficent Creator, would change the aspect of society.

Mr. Clarence was not diappointed in many of the benefits he expected from his daughter passing the noviciate of her life in the country. She learned to love nature from an acquaintance and familiarity with its sublimest forms, and most touching aspects. Those glorious revelations of their Author refined her taste, and elevated her imagination and her affections to an habitual communion with Him.

In a simple state of society, she felt the power of her wealth only in its wise and benevolent uses. She learned to view people and things as they are, without the false glare of artificial society. Her domestic energies were called forth by the necessities of a country-establishment, which, with all the facilities of

wealth, does, it must be confessed, sometimes require from the lady of the *ménage* the skill of an actual operator.

In this education of circumstances, there was one
which had a paramount influence on the character
of Gertrude Clarence—her intercourse with her
father. Gibbon has said, that the affection subsist-
ing between a brother and sister is the only Platonic
love. Has not that sentiment that binds a father to
his daughter, the same generosity and tenderness
arising from the distinction of sexes, and with that
something higher and holier?

A parent stands, as it were, on the verge of two
worlds, and blends the fears and hopes of both. He
feels those anxieties and dreads that arise from an
experience of the uncertainties of this life, and that
inexpressible tenderness, and those illimitable desires,
that extend to the eternal hereafter.

Mr. Clarence had perhaps an undue anxiety in
regard to the possible evils of the present life. His
mind never quite recovered from the melancholy
infused into it by the relation of his father's history.
The shocking death of his son nearly destroyed
for the time his mental faculties, and perma-
nently impaired his health. He timidly shrunk
from every form of evil that might assail his child,
not considering that she had the unabated ardor, and
the elastic spirit that are necessary to sustain the burden of life. Gertrude's character, originally of a
firm texture, was strengthened by her father's timi-
dity. Her resolution and cheerfulness were always
equal to his demands, and these were sometimes unreasonable. His solicitude sometimes degenerated

to weakness, and his sensibility to petulance. To these Gertrude opposed a resoluteness, and equanimity, that to a careless and superficial observer might seem coldness; but such know not how carefully the fire that is used only for holy purposes is concealed and guarded.

But our fair readers may be curious to know whether Gertrude's rustication was to be perpetual? whether the matrimonial opportunities of a rich heiress, were to be circumscribed to the few chances of a country-lottery? and whether she had arrived at the age of nineteen without any pretenders to her exclusive favor? Certainly not. The spirit of enterprise, in every form, is too alert in our country to permit the hand of an heiress to remain unsolicited, and Gertrude Clarence was addressed by suitors of every quality and degree. Clergymen, doctors, lawyers, and *forwarding merchants*, addressed, we should perhaps say approached her, for they soon found something in the atmosphere of Clarenceville that chilled and nipped their young hopes—they soon felt, all but the most obtuse, that Gertrude Clarence was no game for the mere fortune-hunter.

But, ask my fair young readers, did she pass the most susceptible years of her life without any of those emotions and visions that disturb all our imaginations? She had her dreams, her beau-ideal. Her memory had retained the image of a certain youth who had appeared to her in all the graces of dawning manhood when she was a very young and unobserved child. In her memory he had been associated with her brother, so fondly loved,

so long and deeply lamented. In her hopes—
no, her thoughts did not take so definite a form—
in her visions, there was one personification of all
that to her imagination was noble, graceful, and
captivating. Her father unwittingly cherished this
preposession.

His debt to the Roscoe family, and his love to its
departed members, inspired, naturally, a very strong
interest in Gerald, now its sole representative. Gerald's personal merit confirmed this interest. Mr.
Clarence delighted to talk of him to Gertrude, to
dwell on and magnify his rare qualities. He maintained a constant correspondence with Mr. Clarence,
and his graceful and spirited letters seemed to im-
part to her acquaintance with his character, the
vividness of personal intercourse.

It was natural that Mr. Clarence, in looking forward to the probable contingency of Gertrude's marriage, should in his own mind fix on Gerald Roscoe,
as the only person to whom he would willingly resign her ; but it certainly was not prudent to infuse
a predilection into her mind, and to nourish that predilection without calculating all the chances against
its gratification, and that fatal but unthought of
chance, that her sentiment might not be reciprocated.

But we are in danger of anticipating, and we
proceed to give a day at Clarenceville which will
enable our readers to judge of our heroine's character, from its developement in action, a mode as
much more satisfactory than mere description, as a
book than its table of contents.

Mr. Clarence' house was no 'shingle palace,' but
a well built, spacious, and commodious modern edi-

fice, standing on a gentle slope on the northeast shore of one of the beautiful lakes in the western part of the state of New York. The position of the house was judiciously selected to economize sunshine, and soft breezes, the luxuries of a climate where winter reigns for six months. Literally, the monarch of all he surveyed, Mr. Clarence' right of property had enabled him to save from the relentless axe of the settler, a fine extent of forest trees that sheltered him from the biting north winds, and rising in strait and lofty columns, a ' lonely depth of unpierced woods' offered a tempting retreat to the romantic and the contemplative ; or to those more apt to seek its ' lonely depths,' the sportsman and deer-hunter. Between the house and the lake, not a tree had been suffered to remain to intercept the view of the clear sparkling sheet of water, the soul of the scene.

The lawn was circular, and surrounded with shrubs and flowers, which Gertrude loved better than any thing, not of human kind.

Sweet-briars, corcoruses, passion-flowers, and honey-suckles, wreathed the pillars of the piazza ; and the garden which was a little on the right of the house, and filled with fruit-trees, and arranged in terraces, covered with grapes, tempered the bolder features of the scene with an air of civilization, refinement, and even luxury. The opposite shore of the lake, was mountainous, wild, and rugged, and enriched with many an Indian tradition. The lake was not a barren sheet of water, but dotted with islands, some without a tree or shrub, green, fresh, and smooth, looking as if they might have been the cast-off mantles of the sylvan deities; others were embowered with trees, and overgrown with native grape-vines, that had leaped from branch to branch, and hung their leafy draperies on every bough.

Less romantic, but not less agreeable objects terminated the perspective; a thriving village, with its churches, academy, and court-house, and all the insignia of an advancing, busy population.

The day we have mentioned was that appointed for Mrs. Layton and the Uptons to dine at Clarenceville. Any interruption of his customary occupations was apt, before breakfast, to disturb Mr. Clarence' serenity. The demon of dyspepsia was then lord of the ascendant. When he entered the breakfast parlor, Gertrude and Mr. Seton only were there. "Where is the breakfast, Gertrude?" he asked. "I hope you do not mean to wait for Miss Emilie. Young ladies should really learn that good manners require them to rise at the family hours."

"Emilie was up with the birds, papa, and has gone to walk."

"To walk! my dear child, how could you permit her to expose herself to the morning air?"

"I was asleep."

"Asleep! Nothing is more fatal to health than sleeping in the morning. I have mentioned to you the anecdote of Lord Mansfield, Gertrude?"

"O yes, papa." And Gertrude could scarcely repress a smile, when she recollected how many times it had been mentioned to her.

"I presume, Gertrude, it is not necessary to wait breakfast for Miss Layton."

"Not at all, sir; I have ordered it already."

Mr. Clarence walked to the window, and unhappily espied his favorite riding-horse. "What a stupid scoundrel John is!" he exclaimed, "to leave Ranger in the sun."

Seton started from his seat: "It was not John, sir; I have been riding, and I took it for granted that John would see the horse."

"I beg your pardon, Mr. Seton; but really, sir, it is not agreeable—it is not the thing to use a horse in this way." Poor Seton went with all possible haste to repair his fault, while Mr. Clarence continued, "Such imbecility is really too bad; twenty good shades within as many yards. He 'took it for granted John would see the horse;' this 'taking it for granted' is just the difference between those that get along in the world, and those that slump through. Do you know why Sarah does not bring the breakfast, Gertrude?"

"I hear her coming, sir."

"What are you looking at, Gertrude? Oh, I see—Ranger has got away from Louis; I expected it. Sarah, send John instantly here." Mr. Clarence threw up the sash, and would have expressed his impatient displeasure to Seton, but Gertrude laid her hand on his arm:

"My dear father! Louis is not well this morning."

Mr. Clarence put down the window, walked once or twice across the room, and asked for the Edinburgh-Review. Gertrude looked on the tables, on the book-shelves, on the piano, on every thing that could support a book; but the London Quarterly,

the North American, the Literary Gazette, New
Monthly, Ladies' Magazine, the Analectic, Eclec-
tic, every thing but the Edinburgh, was forthcoming—*that* had vanished.

"There is no use in looking, Gertrude; it's gone
of course; it's of no consequence; the breakfast is
here." They sat down; but here a new series of
trials commenced. The coffee was burned too much,
and Mr. Clarence made his daily remark, that he
believed all the difficulty might be remedied, if people would say *roast* coffee, instead of *burnt* coffee.
Then the dyspeptic bread had been forgotten, and
the family bread was underbaked; the fish was cold,
and the eggs were stale. Sarah was inquired of,
'why fresh eggs had not been gotten from John
Smith's.'

"Mr. Smith don't calculate to part with any
more till after Independence."

"I dare say; it is all independence to our farming
gentry! Has Mrs. Carter brought the fowls for
dinner, Sarah?"

"No, sir; she has concluded not to."

"What is the meaning of that?"

"Why, sir, she says poor Billy reared them, and
she don't love to spare them."

"Nonsense! tell John to go down and tell her I
must have them."

"I have another errand for John to do at the
same time," whispered Miss Clarence to the girl;
"tell him to wait till after breakfast."

While these domestic inquiries had been making,
Miss Clarence had prepared some remarkably fine
black tea, just received from New York—the gar-

dener had sent in a basket of strawberries, the first
product of the season—and the cook had found a
mislaid loaf of the favorite bread ; and when Miss
Emilie Layton returned from her walk, all radiant
and glowing with beauty, health, and spirits, Mr.
Clarence was in the best humor possible. "Up
rose the sun, and up rose Emily!" he exclaimed.
"Pardon me, my dear little girl, I do not often
quote, even prose ; but you look so like the spirit of
the jocund morning"—he drew her chair close to himself, kissed her white dimpled hand—"the privilege
of an old man, Miss Emilie—don't look cast-down,
Louis ; every dog must have his day."

"What delightful spirits you are in, Mr. Clarence!" said the young lady.

"Spirits! ah my dear Miss Emilie, bless your
stars that you did not see me half an hour sooner.
I have been tormenting poor Gertrude and Louis ;
but I can't help it—I believe spirits, sensibility, every thing, as a friend of mine says, depend on the
state of the stomach. Don't eat that egg—take
some of these strawberries, Miss Layton ; they are
delicious *haut bois.*"

"I prefer the egg, sir ; I am very hungry."

"Stop, my dear girl ! don't you know you should
always open an egg at the obtuse end, and if it is
perfectly full to the shell, it is fresh ; I have tried the
experiment all summer, and I have not found half a
dozen good ones."

"And I have broken all mine in the middle, and
never found a poor one," said Miss Layton, dashing
hers out, and proceeding to eat it with the keen relish
of a youthful and stimulated appetite.

·¹ I like that—I like that, Miss Emilie; that makes all the difference in life, the difference between such a poor fidgetty creature as I am, and such a happy spirit as yours. Go on, my dear child, and break your eggs in the middle for ever; but excuse me, I have an errand that must be done immediately," and he rose to leave the room.

"Are you going to the widow Carter's?" asked Gertrude, with a very significant smile.

"Yes," and though Mr. Clarence bit his lip, he smiled in return.

"It is unnecessary. John was directed not to do the errand till after breakfast."

"There it is—see there, Miss Emilie—My good Gertrude has saved me from playing Blue Beard on a poor widow's chickens this morning. The brood of a Heaven-forsaken boy of hers who has been drowned in the lake this summer—the only good thing the graceless little dog ever did, was to rear these chickens. It would have been a worse case than that of the widow's cow, immortalized by Fenelon—all the poultry in Christendom would not have made up the loss to her, and she would have sent them, poor soul! she would have surrendered her life, if either Gertrude or I had required it."

Mr. Clarence had resumed his seat, and taken up a newspaper, when a servant entered with letters from the post-office; they were distributed according to their different directions. Miss Layton looked conscious and disturbed, and retreated to her apartment. Mr. Clarence broke the seal of his, saying it was a short business-letter, and that he had left his spectacles in the library; he asked

Gertrude to read it to him.   She accordingly leaned
over his shoulder, and read as follows : " I have
" thought over and over again what I told you the
" day we parted.   I am right—It is all fudge—there
" is no lion in the way.   I tell you again, make hay
" while the sun shines—strike while the iron is hot
" —clench the nail"—Louis started from his seat,
but Miss Clarence without observing him, read on,
" straws show which way the wind blows.   If I have
" eyes, it sets from the right quarter—delays are
" dangerous.   A certain person's life hangs by a
" thread, and when he's gone, she's off to the city,
" and snapped up by the dandies—three hundred
" thousand ——"

" Stop, for God's sake !" cried Seton, and snatch-
ing the letter, flushed and trembling, he instantly disappeared.   Mr. Clarence closed the door after him,
and turning to Gertrude, asked her what could be
the meaning of this.   Gertrude was in tears ; for a
moment she could not reply, but taking up a letter
Seton had dropped, and, glancing at it and looking
at the signature, " It is so," she said ; " the letters
are both from that vulgar brother of Seton—they
were misdirected—this was meant for you."

The letter designed for Mr. Clarence' eye, was as
follows :   " Respected Sir—I take the liberty, by
" return of mail, to tender my sincere thanks to you
" and Miss Clarence, for your politeness to me
" during my late visit to my esteemed brother.   It
" was very gratifying to me to find your health so
" much improved, and my brother so pleasantly
" situated in your valued family.   I think I may
" say Lewis deserves his good fortune—he has al-

"ways been a remarkably correct young man,
"Louis has. It was a disappointment to my father,
"after giving him a liberal education, that he
"should take such a turn for painting; but Allston,
"our great painter, says he has a remarkable talent
"that way, so that there is a good prospect, if he
"should go to foreign countries, that he may, at some
"future day, become as celebrated as Sir Benjamin
"West; but I for one should be perfectly content to
"have him settle down in the country, and only
"handle the brush for his amusement. My wife
"would be very glad to accept Miss Gertrude's
"invitation, as she is remarkably fond of Louis, as
"indeed we all are. The rose for Miss Gertrude,
"and the calliflower for yourself, I shall do myself
"the pleasure to send by the first opportunity. Till
"then believe me, sir, with much respect and esteem,
"and gratitude, to you and to Miss Gertrude,

" Your very obedient,

" humble servant,

" WILLIAM SETON."

"It is too bad," said Mr. Clarence, "to be expected to be the dupe of such a vulgar, grovelling
wretch. Is it possible, Gertrude, that Louis has
any thing in common with this base fellow?"

"Nothing, my dear father, nothing."

"Has he in any way indicated an intention of
addressing you?"

"Never."

Mr. Clarence paused for a moment, and then
added, "Pardon me, my dear child, for catechising
you a little further: have you any reason to think
that Louis loves you?"

"I believe he does."

Gertrude's tears dropped fast on the letter which she still held in her hand, folding and refolding it. Mr. Clarence walked up and down the room, till suddenly stopping, he said; "Seton is not all I could have wished for you, my dear Gertrude—his delicate health—the nervous, susceptible constitution of his mind, are, according to my view of things, great evils—but he is pure, and disinterested, and talented. I reverence a sentiment of genuine affection. It is cruel to disappoint or trifle with it. I see your emotion, Gertrude, your wishes shall govern mine."

Miss Clarence subdued her agitation—"You misunderstand my emotion, sir," she said; "I was grieved that Mr. Seton should have been so outraged, insulted, that I should myself have dragged forth feelings that he has never betrayed but involuntarily—my dear father, my only wish is to live and die with you."

"Do you mean deliberately to abjure matrimony, Gertrude?" asked her father, reassured, and animated by discovering the real state of his daughter's heart.

"No; that would be ridiculous; but I am sure, very sure, I shall never marry."

"Oh! that is all. That resolution and feeling will last, Gertrude, till you see some one worthy to vanquish it; but that it exists now is proof enough that you are yet fancy free. But what is to be done for poor Seton? one thing is certain, he must leave us."

"Do not say so. We certainly can convince him

how deeply we feel the injustice his brother has done
him—he is sick—at present incapable of the labor
of his profession—he has no refuge but the house of
his sordid brother.   From you, my dear father, I
would not hide a shade of feeling—I do love Louis
Seton—with sisterly affection"—(Mr. Clarence
smiled)—" you are incredulous—I could voluntarily
confess to Louis all I feel for him—can that be
love?"

"No; but how soon may it become so?"

Never—I am confident of that—I have involuntarily robbed Louis of his happiness—I know
the exquisite sensitiveness of his mind—If he
were to leave us now he might never recover the
shock and mortification of his brother's disclosure.
If he remains, I think we may by degrees restore
his self-respect, his self-confidence, and his serenity.
At least let us try."

"Do as you please, my noble-minded girl.   I
am satisfied to trust every thing to you, superior as
you are to the heartless coquetries and pruderies of
your sex; but remember we are handling edged
tools."

"But not playing with them," replied Gertrude
with a faint smile; and then kissing her father, and
thanking him for his compliance, she left him and
went to a difficult task.   She met a servant in the
entry; "Have you seen Mr. Seton?" she asked.

"Yes ma'am; and Miss Clarence," he added,
drawing closer to her, and lowering his voice,
"there's something the matter with Mr. Seton—he
just called me to pack his clothes, and he was all in

a flutter, and just walked about the room without doing the least thing for himself."

"Mr. Seton is ill, John, and insists on leaving us ; but we must prevent him. You would all be willing to nurse him, would you not, John ?"

"Indeed, that would we, Miss Clarance—a nice, quiet young man is Mr. Louis."

"Then I will try to persuade him to stay. Tell him, John, I wish to speak with him in the library." Miss Clarence having thus adroitly averted the gossiping suspicions of the inferior departments of the family, repaired to the library. Seton soon followed her. He had an expression of self-command and offended pride, bordering on haughtiness, and so foreign to his customary, gentle, and sentimental demeanor, that Gertrude forgot her prepared speech and said, "You are not offended, Louis ?"

"Offended, Miss Clarence!—I am misunderstood—defamed—disgraced!"

"Louis, you are unjust to yourself, and unjust to us ; do you think that my father or I would give a second thought to that silly letter ?"

Seton was soothed. He fixed his eye on Gertrude, and she proceeded. "It is essential to our happiness that we should understand one another perfectly. Have we not in two years too firmly established our mutual confidence and friendship to have them shaken by the accidents of this morning ?" She paused for a moment, and proceeded with more emotion. "Louis, you know I lost my only brother. It is long ago that he died, and I was very young at the time, but I perfectly remember the tenderness I felt for him—remember! I still feel it.

The chasm made by his death has never been filled. You know my father is all that a father can be to me, but for perfect sympathy there must be similar age, pursuits, and hopes." While Gertrude dwelt in generals, she could talk with the coolness of a philosopher; but as she again approached particulars, her voice became tremulous.

"I can, I *do* feel for you, Louis, the sentiments of a sister—a sister's solicitude for your honor and happiness. I would select you from all the world to supply poor Frank's place to me. You will not permit false delicacy, fastidious scruples, to deprive me of the brother of my election? Forget the past." Seton made no reply. "You do not mean to reject me, Louis?" she added, playfully extending her hand to him. He turned away from her.

"Oh Gertrude! Gertrude! why should I deceive you? why rather should I suffer you to delude yourself? You might as well hope to distil gentle dews from consuming fire, as to convert the sentiment I feel for you into the tranquil, peaceful, fearless, satisfied love of a brother. Mine was no common love—it subsisted without hope or expectation—a self-sustaining passion—the light of my existence—the essence of my life—a pure flame in the inmost, secret sanctuary of my heart—that sanctuary has been violated. I betrayed, and another has dishonored it. '*Forget the past!*' forget that my thoughts of you have been linked with sordid expectations and base projects. God knows I never, in one presumptuous moment aspired to you, but not because you were rich. In my eyes, your fortune is your meanest attribute—my poverty makes no part of my humility.

"You must not interrupt me, Gertrude. I know your generosity—I know all you would say; but hear me out, now, while I have courage to speak of myself. I have been injured, and the worm trodden on, you know, will turn."

"I must interrupt you, Louis; I cannot bear to hear you speak of yourself in these unworthy, degrading terms."

"You misunderstand me. I do not mean to degrade but rather to justify myself, by making you acquainted with the short, sad history of my mind. I know I am weak and pusillanimous. Nature and circumstances have been allied against me. I was born with a constitutional, nervous susceptibility that none of my family understood or regarded. I was a timid, sensitive boy. My brothers were bold and bustling. They were steel-clad in health and hardihood, while I shrunk, as if my nerves were bare, from every breath. This, in their estimation, was inferiority, and so it became in mine. I was humbled and depressed; my life was an aching void. I rose in the morning, as poor Cowper says he did, 'like an infernal frog out of Acheron, covered with the ooze and mud of melancholy,' and my days flowed like a half-stagnant and turbid stream, that gives back no image of the bright heaven above it, and takes no hue from the pleasant objects past which it obscurely crawls. My spirit was crushed; I felt myself to be a useless weed in creation, and when I first discovered that I possessed one talent—one redeeming talent—my heart beat with the ecstasy that an idiot may feel when his mind is released from its physical thraldom, and throbs with the first pulse of intellectual life. That talent introduced me to you, Gertrude, gave me estimation in your eyes, was the medium of our daily intercourse, and I cherished and cultivated it as if it were, as it in truth was, the principle of life to me. The exercise of this talent, and the secret indulgence of my love for you, were happiness enough. I expected nothing more : I did not look into the future—I forgot the past. I was satisfied with the full, pervading sense of present bliss. But you are wearied, Miss Clarence, and I am intrusive."

"No, no, Mr. Seton," replied Gertrude, raising her head, and removing from her face the handkerchief that had hidden from Seton the deep emotion with which she listened to him. "No, Louis," she continued in the kindest and firmest tone, "but such disclosures are useless—they may be worse than useless."

"Gertrude, I have no terms to keep with consequences, and I pray you to hear me out. My tranquillity vanished like a dream, when, last week, I betrayed my passion to you. Your calmness and gentle forbearance soothed me, but it was not, it is not in your power to restore the self-confidence I felt while my passion was unknown. A fever is preying on my life; my spirits are disordered. This cruel letter of my brother will shorten the term of my insupportable existence—for this I thank him. Nothing now remains but to pray you to render me justice with your father; and to beg you, Gertrude, to bear me kindly in your memory."

He took her hand and pressed it to his burning lips.

Gertrude was agitated with the conflicting suggestions of her own mind. She had sought the interview with a definite and decided purpose. That purpose was now nearly subdued by seeing the strength of a sentiment which she had hoped to modify or change. She shrunk with instinctive delicacy from the manifestation of a passion that had no corresponding sentiment in her own heart. Her first and strongest impulse was to escape from the sight of misery which she could not relieve. But ' were not these selfish suggestions ?'—' Could she not mitigate it ?'—' At least,' she thought, as the current of generous purpose flowed back through her heart, ' at least I will try what persevering efforts may do,' and bodying her thoughts in words, "Louis," she said, "I will not part with you ; you must stay with us. If I have power over you, it shall be exercised for some better purpose than to nourish a sentiment which I can never return. It may be because I am inferior to you—certainly not superior—that was the suggestion of your excessive humility, arising from circumstances to which you have already alluded. You have erred, by your own confession, you have all your life erred in distrusting and undervaluing your own powers. You have now only to put forth your strength to subdue all of your feelings that should be subdued."

" Do you believe this, Gertrude ?"

" Believe it! I am sure of it. The frankness of our explanation has dissolved all mystery. Hobgoblins vanish in the light. Your feelings have been aggravated by concealment. They are too intense for any earthly object. Louis, let me use a sister's liberty and give you sisterly counsel; let me remind you of one of the safest passages of a book that you have read and admired perhaps too much for your own happiness. 'Se rendre digne de l'immortalité est le seul but de l'existence— bonheur—souffrance-tout est moyen pour ce but.'"

Seton caught one moment of inspiration, from the sweet tone of assurance in which Gertrude spoke. 'There is a medicament for my wounded spirit,' he thought; but the light was faint and transient, like the passing gleam reflected by a dark and distant object. "Ah, Gertrude," he said, "you are happy, and have the energy and hope of the happy; but for me there are no bright realities in life; it is stripped of its illusions. Oh, most miserable is he who survives the illusions of life! I am yet in my youth, Gertrude, and I look forward with the dim, disconsolate eye of age. Life is a dreary desert to me, beset with frightful forms, and inevitable perils. I am sick, and steeped in melancholy; why should I drag my body of death along your bright path?"

"You shall not, Louis; we will drive out the foul fiend, and court the spirit of health and cheerfulness. You know I have had all my life to contend with the demons of disease in my father. Practice has given me some skill in detecting and expelling them. I will be your leech; and you shall promise to be docile and obedient. I shall lock up your easel for the present. My father has proposed a jaunt to Trenton. We will go there. Beautiful scenery should 'minister to the mind diseased' of a painter. Shall I tell papa that I have your consent to go with us ?"

"Do what you will with me. You will be blessed in your ministry, if I am not."

This conference, which had been long enough, was now broken off by the entrance of Becky, an old and privileged domestic. "I should think, Mr. Seton," she said, "you might have consideration enough to put off your lessons to-day, when there is but every thing for Miss Gertrude to see to." Seton tacitly acquiesced in the reprimand, and left the apartment.

Gertrude was alarmed and oppressed with the depth of poor Seton's sorrow ; and though, to him, she had assumed a tone of firmness and serenity, his despondency had infected her, and as he left the room, she sunk back in her chair, her mind abstracted from every thing around her, and filled with gloomy and just presentiments.

"Miss Gertrude," said Becky.

Gertrude made no reply, she did not even hear Becky, shrill and impatient as her tone was. Her vacant eye accidently rested on a fine game-piece Seton had recently finished, which was standing before her on the library-table. Becky gave her own interpretation to her mistress' gaze.

"It's well enough done to be sure, but," she added with professional scorn, "it's a shame and a silliness to take the *creaters*' lives in midsummer, just to draw their pictures, when they'd make such a relishing

dish in the fall. But come, Miss Gertrude, I should
be glad you would tell me what we are to do?

"Do, do about what, Becky?"

"Did not Amandy tell you?"

"Tell me what?"

"Why Miss Gertrude; I never saw you so with
your thoughts at the end of the world, when sure we
had never more need of them; but you will have to
make up your mind to it, for the dinner has fallen
through—the whole—entirely."

This was indeed an alarming annunciation to the
mistress of an establishment, who expected invited
company to dinner, and who, like Gertrude, considered a strict surveillance of her domestic concerns
as among the first of woman's temporal duties. She
therefore recalled her thoughts from their wander-
ings, and roused all her powers, to avert the
shower of grievances which she saw lowering on
Becky's clouded brow.

We advise all those who have not experienced the
complicated embarrassments of giving a dinner-par-
ty in a country-town, unprovided with a market
and other facilities, to skip the ensuing conversation,
for they will have no sympathy with the trials that
beset rural hospitality—trials that, like woes, cluster
and sometimes so thick and heavily, that their poor
victim wishes, but wishes in vain for the bottle
which the good little man in the fairy legend gave to
Mick, that did its duty so handsomely, and spread the
poor fellow's table so daintily. But alas, among all
our *settlers*, we have none of these kind-hearted
little people—they are the true patriots and never
emigrate, and unassisted human female ingenuity is

put to its utmost stretch. Fortunately Miss Clarence was not often, and certainly not on the present occasion, of a temper to be daunted by the minor miseries of human life, and she now demanded of her domestic, with an air of philosophy which Becky deemed quite inappropriate, what was the matter?

"Matter, Miss Gertrude! matter enough to turn a body's hair gray; and to cap all, Judge Upton has just sent down word that he shall bring a grand English gentleman with him."

"Oh, is that all, Becky? Then I have nothing to do but to order John to lay an additional plate."

"An additional plate, indeed! I think, ma'am, you had better order something to put on it."

"I ordered the dinner yesterday," said Miss Clarence, with faint voice and faint heart; for she well knew that the result of ordering a dinner, bore a not very faint resemblance to that of 'calling spirits from the vasty deep.'

"Yes, ma'am, I know you ordered it; but I told Amandy to let you know that the butcher did not come down from the village this morning, and we've neither lamb nor veal in the house."

"But we have Neale's fine mutton?"

"Not a pound of it. He came up yesterday to say his fat sheep had all strayed away."

"Why did not you tell me?"

"You were riding out, ma'am, and I sent John to Hilson for a roaster."

"Oh, spare me, Becky; a roaster, you know, is papa's aversion, and mine too."

"I know that, Miss Gertrude, but then I thought

to myself, it's no time to be notional when there's
company invited, and not a pound of *fresh* to be
had for love or money ; but as ill luck would have
it, Hilson had engaged the whole nine for the Independence dinner, a delightsome sight they'll be, all
standing on their feet with each an ear of corn in
his mouth. But thinking of them," added Becky,—
mentally reproaching herself for this gush of professional enthusiasm,—" Thinking of them wont
fill our dishes ; and so, Miss Gertrude, I want you
to send word to the Widow Carter, you must have
her fowls, whether or no. To be sure they'll be
rather tough, killed at this time of day,"

" Yes, Becky, since we know why she refuses
them, they would be too tough eating for any of us.
No, I had rather give our friends a dinner of strawberries and cream."

" Cream ! the thunder turned all that last evening."

" The elements against us too !"

" Elements ! ice creams, you mean. No, ma'am,
they were mixed last night ; but Malviny says she
can't stay to freeze them. She must go down to
the village to Mrs. Smith's funeral. She says the
general expects it."

" It is a hard case, Becky ; but we must make
the best of it. You must not let this Englishman
spy out the nakedness of our land. Your fingers
and brains never failed me yet, Becky. Now let
us think what we have to count upon."

" There's as good a ham as ever came from
Virginia."

" Yes, or Westphalia either, and as beautiful

lettuces as ever grew.   Ham and salad is a dinner
for a prince, Becky ; and then you can make up a
dish from the veal of yesterday with currie—bouillie
a tongue—prepare a dish of maccaroni—see that
the vermicelli soup is of your very best, Becky—
papa says nobody makes it better—and the trout,
you forgot the trout, here comes old Frank up the
avenue with them now—bless the old soul, he never
disappoints us—boil, stew, fry the trout ; every
body likes fresh trout.   As to the ice-creams, tell
Malvina she shall go down to the village to every
funeral for a year to come, if she will give up the
general's lady.   The dinner will turn out well yet,
Becky.   As you often say, ' it's always darkest just
before day.' "

" And you beat all, Miss Gertrude, for making
day-light come," replied Becky, pleased with her
mistress' compliment, and relieved by her ready
ingenuity.   " There's few ladies use what little
sense they have got to any purpose.   If there were
more of them had your head-work, the house-busi-
ness would not get so tangled, and that's what John
and I often say."   Thus mutually satisfied, mistress
and servant parted.

Miss Clarence' thoughts reverted to Seton ; and
she repaired to her own apartment, happy in the
consciousness of a firm resolve to make every
effort to secure his tranquillity.   Alas, that human
judgment should be so blind and weak, that its best
wisdom often leads to the most fearful consequences !

When Gertrude entered her own apartment, she
found Emilie Layton sitting at a writing-desk, busily
employed in answering her letters.   Her face was

drenched in tears, but so unruffled that it seemed as
if no accident could disturb its sweet harmo-
nies. "You put me in mind, Emilie," said Gertrude, kissing her cheek, "you put me in mind of
a shower when the sun is shining."

Emilie dashed off her tears. "I will not be
miserable any longer ; would you, Gertrude ?"

"No, I never would be miserable if I could help
it, Emilie."

"It is too disagreeable," replied Emilie, with
perfect naïveté, "it makes one feel too bad ; but
I really have enough to make me miserable. If I
dared, I would show you all these letters ; but,
dear Gertrude, you can advise me without knowing
what the real state of the case is, only that papa and
mama want me to do something that I hate to do—
that I would rather die than do. Now would you
do it if you were I ?"

Gertrude did not need second sight to conjecture
what the nature of this parental requisition might be.
"It is difficult to answer your question, Emilie ; but
there are things that it is not right to do, even in
compliance with parental authority. This may be
one of them."

"Oh, it is, I am sure. You have divined it
most certainly, Gertrude ; but I have not told you
a word, you know. Mama charges me not in her
letter. I am so glad you think as I do ; but I am
afraid mama will persuade me. She suffers so
much when any thing crosses her. If she could
only be persuaded to think as I do about it. I
have written a letter to a certain person who has
great influence over her. You may read it, Ger-

15*

trude. You cannot understand it, though he will.
Read it aloud, for I want to hear how it sounds.''

Gertrude read aloud, " To my mother's best and
dearest friend."—"Your father, of course?" she
said, looking up a little perplexed at Emilie.

Miss Layton blushed, and there was an expression of acute pain passed over her face, as she said
with quivering lips, "Oh no, Gertrude, I wish it
were so ; but perhaps you think I have addressed it
improperly—if you do, just run the pen through
that line." Gertrude did so, and read on, "As
" mama has told me, Mr. Roscoe, that you already
" know all about a certain affair, I trust I am not
" doing wrong in begging you to intercede with
" my dear mother in my behalf. Do convince her
" that it is not my duty to sacrifice my happiness to
" my father's wishes. It is very hard to make
" one's self miserable for life, and is it not an odd way
" to make one's parents happy ? Papa says there is
" no use in being romantic. I am sure I am not
" so. I would as lief marry a rich man as a poor one,
" if I loved him. Any person, however romantic,
" might love Miss Clarence, in spite of her fortune.
" Therefore it is *not*, as my father says, an absurd,
" girlish notion about ' love in a cottage,' that gives
" me such an antipathy to ———. Do intercede
" for me, if I have not made an improper request,
" and if I have, forget it, and remember only your
" friend, E. L." Gertrude laid down the letter
without comment. " It is a very poor letter" I
know, said Emilie, " and poorly written, for I blotted the words with my tears as fast as I wrote
them."

Gertrude smiled at her simplicity. "No, Emilie, it is a very good letter, for it is true ; and truth from such a heart as yours is always good. But would it not be best to burn the letter ? It seems to me you may trust to your own representations to your mother. No intercessor can be so powerful as her tenderness for you."

"Oh, Gertrude, you do not know mama. She can talk me out of my five senses, and she says nobody in the world has such influence over her as Mr .Roscoe." On second thoughts, Gertrude believed that Emilie might need a sturdier support than her own yielding temper, and she acquiesced in the letter being sent ; and Emilie despatched it, and drove from her heart every feeling of sorrow almost as easily as she removed its traces from her heart's bright and beautiful mirror.

CHAPTER XII.

"I will tell thee a similitude, Esdras. As when thou asketh the
earth, it shall say unto thee that it giveth much mould whereof
earthen vessels are made, but little dust that gold cometh of; even
so is the course of this present world."   ESDRAS.

MADAME ROLAND has left it on record—let any
woman who fancies she may soar above the natural
sphere of her sex, remember who it is that makes
this boast—that she never neglected the details of
housewifery, and she adds, that though at one period
of her life she had been at the head of a laborious and
frugal establishment, and at another, of an expensive
and complicated one, she had never found it necessary to devote more than two hours of the twenty-
four to household cares. While we have this illus-
trious woman before us, as evidence in the case, we
would venture to intimate, in opposition to the vulgar and perhaps too lightly received opinion, that
talents are as efficient in housewifery as in every
other department of life ; and that, cæteris paribus,
she who has most mind will best administer her domestic affairs, whether her condition obliges her,
like the pattern Jewish matron, to 'rise early and
work diligently with her own hands,' or merely to
appoint the labors of others.

If our opinion be not heresy, we would commend
it to the consideration of scholars, and men of
genius, and all that privileged class, (privileged in
every thing else,) who have been supposed to be

condemned by their own elevation to choose an humble, grubbing companion for the journey of life, at best not superior to Johnson's beau-ideal of a female travelling companion.

But to return to our heroine. Her happy genius had rode out the storm threatened in the morning, by her trusty Becky, and she saw the dinner hour draw nigh with a tranquillity that can only be inspired by the delightful certainty that, to use the technical phrase, *all is going on well.* She was in the parlor with Miss Layton, and awaiting her guests, when Judge Upton, who, true as a lover to his mistress, never broke ' the thousandth part of a minute in the affair' of a dinner, arrived. After the most precise salutations to each and all, he expressed his great satisfaction in being punctual. ' He had done, what indeed he seldom did, risked a failure in this point. He must own, that with a certain divine, he held punctuality to be the next virtue to godliness; but it had been impossible for him to dispense with attending the funeral of general Smith's lady. The general expected it; such a respectable person's feelings should not be aggravated on so afflicting an occasion. He must own he had been uncommonly gratified; the general behaved so well; he bore his loss like a general.'

Miss Clarence suppressed, as nearly as she might, a smile at the conjugal heroism of a ' training-day' general, and asked Mrs. Upton why Mrs. Layton was not with her.

Mrs. Upton's volubility, which had emitted in low rumblings such tokens of her presence, as are heard from a bottle of beer before the ejection of the cork gives full vent to the thin potation, now overflowed.

"Oh my dear," said she, "Mrs. Layton chose to come on horseback with Mr. Edmund Stuart, our English visiter. Don't be frightened, Emilie, dear, husband's horses are remarkably gentle; indeed he never keeps any others, for he thinks dangerous horses very unsafe. Oh, Mr. Clarence, by the way, do you know we must change our terms. Mr. Stuart says that it is quite vulgar in England to say, we *ride*, when we go in a carriage. We must call a ride a *drive*—only think! He says we cannot conceive how disagreeable Americanisms are to English ears."

"My dear madam," replied Mr. Clarence, who was rather sensitive on the subject of Anglo-criticism, "do let us remember that in America we speak to American ears, and if any terms peculiar to us have as much intrinsic propriety as the English, let us have the independence to retain them."

"Oh! certainly, certainly," said the good lady, who had no thought of adventuring in the thorny path of philological discussion, "husband says he don't see why *ride* is not as proper as drive, especially for those who don't drive. But girls, I must tell you before Mr. Stuart comes, that he is remarkably genteel even for an Englishman. He is the son of Sir William Stuart, and, of course, you know, will be a lord himself." Our republican matron was not learned in the laws that regulate the descent of titles; but, in blessed unconsciousness of her ignorance, she proceeded: "I was determined he should see Clarenceville, for, as husband says, it is all important he should form favorable opinions of our country,"

" Why important ?" asked Mr. Clarence, in one
of those cold and posing tones that would have
checked a less determined garrulity than Mrs. Upton's. But her impetus was too strong to be resisted,
and on she blundered. " Oh, I don't know exactly, but it is, you know. He is to pass six
months in the United States, and he is determined
to see every thing. He has already been from
Charleston to Boston. Only think, as husband
says, what a perfect knowledge he will have of the
country."

" Does he propose," asked Mr. Clarence, " to
enlighten the public with his observations ?"

" Write a book of travels, you mean, sir ? Oh,
I have no doubt of it, and that made me in such a
fever to have him see the girls. Girls, you must be
on the *qui vive* The dinner party will be described
at full length. Your dinners, Gertrude, are always
in such suberb style. Husband told Mr. Stuart he
did not believe they were surpassed in England."
Gertrude blushed when she thought of the disas-
ters of the larder, and the miscellaneous dinner preceded by such a silly flourish of trumpets. " Oh,
don't be alarmed, Gertrude, dear," continued the
good lady, " I am sure it will be just the thing,
and then you know a beauty and a fortune,"
glancing her little glassy eye, with ineffable gratu-
lation from Emilie, to Gertrude, " a beauty and a
fortune will give the party such eclat ! Oh, I
should have given up, if any thing had happened
to prevent our coming. The children gave me
such a fright this morning ! Thomas Jefferson fell
down stairs ; but he is a peculiar child about falling,

always comes on his feet, like a cat. Benjamin
Franklin is very different. He has never had but
one fall in his life, so husband calls it ' Ben's fall,'
like ' Adam's fall,' you know ; very good, is not it ?"
That solemn, responsible person, 'husband,' whose
sententious sayings were expanded like a drop of
water into a volume of steam, by that wonderful
engine, his wife's tongue, was solemnly parading the
piazza, his watch in his hand, and his eye fixed on
the avenue, while with lengthening visage he groaned
in spirit under that misery for which few country
gentlemen have one drop of patience in their souls
—a deferred dinner.

" Oh, there they come !" he was the first to announce, and after the slight bustle of dismounting,
&c., and a whisper from Mrs. Upton of ' do your
prettiest, girls,' Mrs. Layton entered the drawing-
room, her arm in Mr. Stuart's, who with his hat
under' his other arm, his stiff neckcloth, and
starched demeanor, looked the son of an English
baronet at least. His stately perpendicularity was
the more striking, contrasted with the grace and
elasticity of Mrs. Layton's movements. This lady
deserves more than a transient glance.

Mrs. Layton was somewhere on that most disagreeable stage of the journey of life, between thirty
and forty—most disagreeable to a woman who has
once enjoyed the dominion of personal beauty ; for
at that period she is most conscious of its diminu-
tion. If ever woman might, Mrs. Layton could
have dispensed with beauty, for she had, when she
pleased to command them, graceful manners, spirited conversation, and those little feminine engaging

ways, that though they can scarcely be defined or described, are irresistibly attractive. But never were the arts that prolong beauty more sedulously studied than by this lady. She owed much to the forbearance of nature, who seemed to shrink from spoiling what she had so exquisitely made. Her eyes retained the clearness and sparkling brilliancy of her freshest youth. Her own profuse, dark hair was artfully arranged to shelter and display her fine intellectual brow, and the rose on her cheek, if too mutable for nature, claimed indulgence for the exquisite art of its imitation. She was yet within the customary term of deep mourning for a sister, and as she was not of a temper to crusade against any of the forms of society, her crape and bombasin were in accordance with its sternest requisitions; but their sombre and heavy effect was skilfully relieved by brilliant and becoming ornaments. Like the Grecian beauty who sacrificed her tresses at her sister's tomb, she took care that the pious offering should not diminish the effect of her charms. Mrs. Layton resembled a Parisian artificial flower, so perfect in its form, coloring, and arrangement, that it seems as if nothing could be more beautiful, unless perchance the eye falls on a natural rose, and beholds His superior and divine art whose 'pencil' paints it, and 'whose breath perfumes.' Such a contrast was Emilie Layton to her mother. There was an unstudied, child-like grace in every attitude and movement, the dew of youth was on her bright lip, and her round cheek was tinged with every passing feeling.

Mrs. Layton presented her English acquaintance

to Miss Clarence and her father, and returned their
salutations with an air of graceful self-possession that
showed she was far too experienced to feel a sensation from entering a country drawing-room. Her
brow contracted for an instant as she kissed her
daughter, and whispered, "I see you are going to
be my own dear girl, Emilie." Emilie turned
away, and her mother's scrutiny was averted by the
outbreaking of Mrs. Upton's ever ready loquacity.
"Would you think, Mr. Clarence," she asked,
"that Grace Layton and I were girls together. I
don't deny I have a trifling advantage of you,
Grace, dear; but, as husband says, when I die, you
will shake in your shoes."

"Do, Miss Clarence," interposed Mrs. Layton,
"convince our friend Mrs. Uupton, that such familiarity with time is quite rustic and barbarous
Time is as obsolete in civilized life as his grim personification in the primer. We never talk of
time in good society, Mrs. Upton."

"Not talk of time!" retorted her good-natured
contemporary, "that's odd for a married woman.
Old maids are always particular about their ages,
but it's no object for us; besides, as husband says,
children are a kind of mile-stones that measure the
distance you have travelled. That was quite
clever of husband—was not it? Husband," she
continued, stretching her neck out of the window,
and addressing her better half, "when was it you
made that smart comparison, of children to mile-
stones?"

"Children to mile-stones! what are you talking about, my dear?"

"Oh, I remember, it was not you—it was"—but on drawing in her head she perceived no one was listening to her. Mrs. Layton, unable as she confessed, any longer to endure the odious flapping of time's wings, had adroitly turned the conversation. "What are those pictures you are studying, Mr. Stuart?" she asked.

The gentleman colored deeply, and replied, "Some *American* representations of naval engagements, madam."

"And if the British lion were the painter he would have reversed the victory?" said the lady archly.

Miss Clarence felt that the rites of hospitality demanded the interposition of her shield: "That picture," she said, "does not harmonzie well with our rural scenery, but my father values it on account of the artist, who is his particular friend."

"An *ingenious* young person, no doubt," replied the traveller, with an equivocal emphasis on the word ingenious, and a supercilious curl of his lip.

"Oh, remarkably ingenious," exclaimed Mrs. Upton, "by the way, Gertrude, dear, where is Louis Seton to-day?"

"Confined to his room by indisposition," replied Miss Clarence, without hesitation, or blushing.

"Hem—hem—hem"—thrice repeated the vulgar little lady, who like other vulgar people thought the intimation of something particular between any marriageable parties always agreeable to a young lady. Miss Clarence looked deaf, and Mrs. Upton was baffled; but she good-humoredly continued "I do wish, Mr. Stuart, you could have seen the young gentleman who painted that picture. Husband thinks him an uncommon genius, almost equal to that celebrated American who is such a famous painter—I forget his name—I do believe husband is right, and I am losing my memory; but at any rate I remember the interesting anecdote about him —I forget exactly who told it to me, but I believe it was husband—however, that is of no consequence— yet it is so provoking to forget—if I could only remember when I heard it." ·

"Oh, never mind when," exclaimed Mrs. Layton, " tell the story, Mrs. Upton. We shall never for- get *when* we heard it."

" Well, he was born—oh, where was he born? you remember, Gertrude, dear ?"

" If you mean West, I believe he was born in Pennsylvania."

Oh, yes, it was West; now I remember all about it—it was husband told me—his parents were wretchedly poor ; wer'nt they, Gertrude, dear ?"

" Too poor, I believe, to educate him."

" Oh, yes ; that is just what husband told me— and being too poor, and being born, as it were, a painter, he invented colors—or brushes—which was it, Gertrude, dear ?"

" Neither, I believe," replied Gertrude, suppress- ing a smile, and glad of an opportunity to shelter Mrs. Upton's ignorance, and save her friends from her farther garrulity, she proceeded to relate the well known story of West having made his first brush from the hairs of a cat's tail, and of his having, instructed by the Indians, compounded his first colors from the vegetable productions of the wilds around him. Mr. Stuart took out his tablets apparently to note down the particulars Miss Clarence had related. " I beg your pardon," he said, " have the goodness again, Miss Clarence, to tell me the name of the painter of whom you spoke."

" West."

" West! ah, the same with our celebrated artist."

" Is there an English artist of that name ?" asked Mrs. Layton, with seeming good faith.

"Indeed is there, madam, an exceeding clever person too, Sir Benjamin West ; his name is known throughout Europe, though it may not have reached America yet, owing probably to the ignorance of the fine arts here. My eldest brother received with the estate two of his finest productions. One of the happy effects of our law of entail, is that it fosters genius by preserving in families the chef d'œuvres of the arts. It is much to be regretted," he continued turning to Mr. Clarence, " that your legislators have deemed this law of primogeniture incompatible with your republican institutions. It is an unfortunate mistake, which will for ever retard your advance in the sciences, arts, and manners."*

" Do manners go with the estate ? How can that be ?" asked Mrs. Upton in all simplicity. Whatever replies to this question might have been suggested by the presence of the *unportioned* younger son, they were suppressed by the common instincts of good breeding, and dinner fortunately being an-

---

* There may appear to be a striking coincidence between the opinions of our traveller and those announced in Captain Basil Hall's travels; but no allusion was intended to those volumes. This chapter was written a year before their appearance.

nounced, the party repaired to the dining-room, where we shall leave them to the levelling process of satisfying appetites whetted to their keenest edge by an hour's delay of a country dinner. Perhaps, in confirmation of the assertion already made of Miss Clarence' housewifery, it should be stated, that there was not a dish on table of which Mrs. Upton did not taste, and ask a receipt.

The dinner being over, Mrs. Layton, evidently anxious for some private conversation with her daughter, proposed a stroll in the wood.

She arranged the party according to her own wishes. " Mr. Clarence," she said, " you are, I believe, condemned to some business discussions with the judge. Mrs. Upton, Miss Clarence, I am sure, will give you a quiet seat in the library, and her receipt book. Miss Clarence, you will do Mr. Stuart the honor to point out to him the beauties of an American forest ; and Emilie shall be my Ariadne. I wish," she added in a voice spoken alone to Miss Layton's ear, " that like her you were dreaming of love."

" Pshaw ! mother," replied Emilie. . There was nothing in her words, but there was something in her manner and looks that abated her mother's hopes. She had, however, too much at stake to leave any art untried to achieve her object; and when, after an hour's walk, Miss Clarence again met the mother and daughter, Emilie's cheek was flushed, and her eyes red with weeping. Her practised mother veiled her own feelings, and inquired of Mr. Stuart, with as much carelessness as if she had thought of nothing else since they parted, " how he liked an American forest ?"

" With such a companion," he replied, courteously bowing to Miss Clarence, " quite agreeable, but in itself monotonous."

" A quality, I presume," answered Mrs. Layton, " peculiar to *American* forests. But, my dear girls, where are you going ?—spare me a little longer from the din of Mrs. Upton's tongue. I had as lief be doomed to turn the crank of a hand-organ. My dear Miss Clarence, you must not be all Emilie's friend. Sit down on this rustic bench with me, and let Emilie show Mr. Stuart the pretty points of view about the place. He has come forty miles to see the lake, or the fair lady of the lake," she whispered, as the gentleman withdrew with Miss Layton. " I see everywhere about your place, Miss Clarence," continued Mrs. Layton, plucking a honeysuckle from a luxuriant vine that embowered the seat where she had placed herself, " indications of the refinement of your taste. Flowers have always seemed to me the natural allies and organs of a delicate and sensitive spirit. I admire the oriental custom of eliciting from them a sort of hieroglyphic language, to express the inspirations of love—love, ' the perfume and suppliance of a moment,' so beautifully shadowed forth in their sweet and fleeting life. I see you do not agree with me."

" Not entirely. Flowers have always seemed to me to be the vehicle of another language : to express their Creator's love, and, if I may say so, his gracious and minute attention to our pleasures. Their beauty, their variety, their fragrance, are

gratuities, for no other purpose, as far as we can
see, but to gratify our senses, and through those
avenues to reach the mind, that by their ministry
may communicate with the Giver. To me the
sight of a flower is like the voice of a friend. You
smile, but I have great authority on my side. Why
was it that the French heroine and martyr could
exclaim, ‘ J’oublie l’injustice des hommes, leurs sottises, et mes maux avec des livres et des fleurs,’ but
because they conveyed to her the expression of a
love that made all mortal evils appear in their
actual insignificance.’’

“ Bless me, my dear Miss Clarence! how seclusion
in a romantic country does lead one to refine and spin
out pretty little cobweb systems of one’s own.   Now
my inference would have been that Madame Roland’s
books and flowers helped her to forget cabals and
guillotines, and perhaps I should have come as near
the truth as you. You are a very Swedenbor-
gian in your exposition of nature. However, you
have no mawkish, parade sentiment, and your hidden and spiritual meanings certainly exalt flowers
above mere ministers to the senses. But how did
we fall into this flourishing talk ? I detained you
here to make a confession to you.’’

“ A confession to me !’’

“ Yes; you know I told you you must be my
friend as well as Emilie’s.’’ ‘ Ah,’ thought Gertrude, ‘ she is going to confide to me poor Emilie’s
affair. I will have the boldness to give her my real
opinion.’ Mrs. Layton proceeded, “ I must be
frank with you, Miss Clarence—frankness is my
nature. I have wronged you.’’

" Wronged *me*, Mrs. Layton ?"

" Yes, my dear Miss Clarence, in the tenderest point in which a woman can be injured ; but do not be alarmed, the injury is not irreparable. You recollect the day you called on me at Mrs. Upton's with that woe-begone, love-stricken devotee of yours ?"

" Mr. Seton ?"

" Yes, Mr. Seton. Now spare me that senti- mental, rebuking look. I will not be irreverent to the youth, though I know better than to give credit to the gossip of Goody Upton, and her cummers about you. His love-passages, poor fellow, will never lead to your hymeneal altar. But to my confession. You must know that on the aforesaid day I had a fit of the blues, and I saw every thing, even you, through a murky cloud. To speak lite- rally, (ergo disagreeably,) I did not perceive one of your charms."

" Oh, is that all, Mrs. Layton ?—woman as I am, I can pardon that."

" All ! no, if it were, I would not have mentioned it, for one *woman's* opinion of another is a mere ba- gatelle. Idleness, you know, is the parent of all . sin. I had nothing to do, and moved and incited thereto by the demon of ennui, I sat down and de- scribed you to one of my correspondents as you had appeared to my distempered vision."

" And is *that* all ?"

" Yes, that is all; but that you may know the whole head and front of my offending I must show you my cerrespondent's reply."

" Do so—that may make a merit of my pardon."

Mrs. Layton took a letter from her reticule, but
before she opened it she said, "I must premise in
my own justification, not to conciliate you, that
when I met you to-day you seemed perfectly trans-
formed from the little demure lady you appeared at
first. I feel now as if I had known you a year and
could interpret every look of your expressive face.
Something had happened this morning—I am sure
of it—to give a certain elevation to your feelings. I
' would not flatter Neptune for his trident, nor Jove
for his power to thunder.' I could not flatter *you*, Miss
Clarence, and it is no flattery to say your beauty is
of that character which Montesquieu pronounces the
most effective. It results from certain changes and
flashes of expression—it produces the emotion of
surprise. When you speak and show those brilliant
teeth of yours, your face is worth all the rose and
lily beauties in Christendom. You remind me of
Gibbon's description of Zenobia—do you remember it?"

"No; I seldom remember a description of personal beauty."

"I never forget it. You have not been enough
in the world to learn that beauty is the *sine qua non*
to a woman—a young woman—unless, indeed, she
has fortune."

"We are graduated by a flattering scale, truly!"

"Yes, my dear girl, but you may as well know
it; there is no use in going hoodwinked into society! But now for our document." Mrs. Layton
unfolded Gerald Roscoe's letter, which our readers
have already perused, and read aloud from the passage beginning, 'Is it natural depravity,' and end-

ing with the anecdote of Miss Eunice Peabody.
When she had finished reading, 'a comely little body, amiable and rather clever,' " is a quotation from
my letter," she said, " and was my libellous description of you, Miss Clarence."

" Libellous! Mrs Layton. I declare to you
after your frightful note of preparation it sounds
to me quite complimentary ; but who is the gentleman to whom I have this picturesque introduction ?"

" Ah! there's the rub. He is undoubtedly the
most attractive young man in New York—the prince
of clever fellows ; and, honored am I in the fact—
my selected, and favorite, and most intimate friend."

' Oh!' thought Gertrude, ' Emilie said Roscoe
was her mother's most intimate friend,' and the pang
that shot through her heart at this recollection was
evident in her face, for Mrs. Layton paused a moment before she added—" Gerald Roscoe." At
this confirmation of her mental conjectnre, Gertrude
involuntarily covered her face with her hands, and
then, disconcerted to the last degree at having betrayed her sensations, she said, half articulately,
something of her being taken by surprise at the
mention of Gerald Roscoe's name, that he was her
father's friend, but she concluded with hoping Mrs.
Layton would not think she cared at all about it.
But Mrs. Layton was quite too keen and sagacious
an observer to be imposed on for a moment by such
awkward hypocrisy as Gertrude's. She saw she
did care a great deal about it, and giving a feminine
interpretation to her emotion, and anxious to efface
every unpleasant impression from her mind, she said
in her sweetest manner, " I enjoy in anticipation

Roscoe's surprise when he shall see you. It will be quite a *coup de théatre.* On the whole, Gertrude— I must call you Gertrude—*dear* Gertrude—I think I may claim to have done you a favor. I have prepared Roscoe's mind for an agreeable surprise, and for the still more agreeable feeling that his taste is far superior to mine—that to him belongs the merit of a discoverer, and as he is after all but a man, he will enjoy this, and I shall enjoy particularly your triumph over his first impressions."

' Ah,' thought Gertrude, ' those impressions will never be removed, I shall be paralyzed, a very Eunice Peabody, if ever I meet him.' But she smiled at Mrs. Layton's castle-building, and though she assured that lady that nothing was more improbable than that she should ever encounter Gerald Roscoe, as he never left town, and she never went there, yet she did find something very agreeable in Mrs. Layton's perspective ; and being human and youthful, she was not insensible to the flatteries addressed to her by the most fascinating woman she had ever seen.

Mrs. Layton's expressions of admiration were not all flattery. There was something in Gertrude that really excited her imagination. She saw she was of a very different order from the ordinary run of well-bred, well-informed, decorous, pleasing young ladies—a class particularly repulsive and tiresome to Mrs. Layton. She foresaw that Miss Clarence, far removed as she was from being a beauty would, set off by the *éclat* of fortune, become a *distingué* whenever she appeared in society, and she took such measures to ingratiate herself as she had found most generally successful. She had shown Roscoe's letter to manifest and enhance the value of her changed opinion. She spared no pains to efface the impression the letter evidently left on Gertrude's mind. She taxed all her arts of pleasing—talked of herself, alluded to her faults, so eloquently, that the manner was a beautiful drapery that covered up and concealed the matter. She spoke with generous confidence of the adverse circumstances of her matrimonial destiny, and Gertrude, in her simplicity, not doubting that she was the sole depository of this revelation, felt a secret self-gratulation in the qualities that had elicited so singular a trust, and the tenderest sympathy with the sufferer of unprovoked wrongs. Then Mrs. Layton again reverted to Roscoe, the person of all others of whom Gertrude was most curious to hear. She had a kind of dot and line art in sketching characters, and with a few masterly touches presented a vivid image. She spoke of society; and its vanities, excitements and follies, like bubbles catching the sun's rays, kindled in the light of her imagination.

Gertrude listened and felt that her secluded life was a paralyzed, barren existence. Her attention was rivetted and delighted till they were both aroused by the footsteps of a servant, who came to say that Judge Upton's carriage was at the door. Half way to the piazza they were met by Mrs. Upton. " Gertrude, dear," she said, " I hope you *will* excuse our going rather early. You know I am an anxious mother, and the Judge is so important at home—but we have had a charming day! I am sure Mr. Stuart has been delighted. I asked him if he had ever seen any thing superior to Clarence-

vjlle as a whole, and I assure you he did not say
yes. Indeed, sub rosa, (you understand, between
you and I,) I do think you have made a conquest."

"Do not, I entreat you, Mrs. Upton, ask the
gentleman whether I have or not."

"Oh no, my dear soul; *do* you think I would
do any thing so out of the way ? I understand a
thing or two; but I do long to know which will
carry the day, you or Emilie—fortune versus—
as husband says—versus beauty. One thing I am
certain of, we shall all be in the book."

"Not all," said Mrs. Layton, and added in a
whisper to Gertrude, "who but Shakspeare could
have delineated Slender ?"

Gertrude was surprised and disappointed at finding Emilie on the piazza, prepared to return with
her mother; but there was no opportunity for ex-
postulation. Judge Upton stood at the open carriage door, as impatient as if a council of war were
awaiting his arrival at home, and the ladies were
compelled to abridge their adieus.

When Mr. Clarence had made his last bow to
his departing guests, he seated himself on the
piazza. "There goes our English visiter, Gertrude," said he, "enriched no doubt with precious
morceaus for his diary. Judge Upton will repre-
sent the class of American country-gentlemen, and
his miscellaneous help-meet will sit for an American
lady. I heard him ask Mrs. Upton, who has, it
must be confessed, an anomalous mode of assorting
her viands," (Mr. Clarence spoke with the disgust
of a dyspeptic rather than a Chesterfieldian,)
"whether it were common for the Americans to eat

salad with fish? Notwithstanding her everlasting good nature, she was a little touched at his surveillance, and for once replied without her prefix 'husband says,' that she supposed we had a *right* to eat such things together as pleased us best."

"It is unfortunate," said Gertrude, "that travellers should fall into such hands."

"No, no, Gertrude; it makes no difference with such travellers. They come predetermined to find fault—to measure every thing they see by the English standard they carry in their minds, and which they conceive to be as perfect as those eternal patterns after which some ancient philosophers supposed the Creator to have fashioned the universe. I had a good deal of conversation with this young man, and I think he is about as well qualified to describe our country, and judge of its real condition, as the fish are to pass their opinion on the capacities and habitudes of the birds. I do not mean that ours is the superior condition, but that we are of different elements. It does annoy me, I confess, excessively, that such fellows should influence the minds of men. I do not care so mnch about the impression they make in their own country, as the effect they have in ours, in keeping alive jealousies, distrusts, and malignant resentments, and stirring up in young minds a keen sense of injustice, and a feeling of dislike bordering on hatred to England— England, our noble mother country. I would have our children taught to regard her with filial veneration—to remember that their fathers participated in her high historic deeds—that they trod the same ground and breathed the same air with Shakspeare, and Milton, and Locke, and Bacon. I would have them esteem England as first in science, in literature, in the arts, in inventions, in philanthropy, in whatever elevates and refines humanity. I would have them love and cherish her name, and remember that she is still the mother and sovereign of their minds."

"But my dear, dear father, you are giving England the supremacy and preference over our own country."

" Our country ! she speaks for herself, my child; if there were not a voice lifted throughout all this wide spread land of peace and plenty, yet how 'loud would be the praise !' I do not wish to hear her flattered by foreigners, or boasted or lauded by our own people. Nor do I fear, on her account, any thing that can be said by these petty tourists, who, like noisome insects, defile the fabric they cannot comprehend."

CHAPTER XIII.

" Is there in human form that bears a heart—
    A wretch! a villain! lost to love and truth!
'That can with studied, sly, ensnaring art,
    Betray sweet Jenny's unsuspecting youth ?"   BURNS

Gerald Roscoe to Mrs. Layton.

" ON looking over your letter a second time, my
" dear Mrs. Layton, I find there is enough of it
" unanswered to give me a pretence for addressing
" you again; and as I know no more agreeable
" employment of one of my many leisure hours
" than communicating with you, I will contrast
" your picture of the miseries of rustic hospitality
" and rustic habits, with the trials of a poor devil,
" condemned to the vulgarity and necessity of drag-
" ging through the summer months in town.   We
" all look at our present, petty vexations, through
" the magnifying end of the glass, and then turning
" our instrument, give to the condition of others, the
" softness and enchantment of distance.

" But to my picture.   Behold me then, after
" having waited through the day in my *clientless*
" office, retired to my humble lodging, No. —
" Walker-street, in a garret apartment, (by courtesy
" styled the attic,) as hot, even after the sun is
" down, as a well-heated oven when the fire is with-
" drawn, or as hot as you might imagine ' accom-
" modations for a single gentleman' in tophet.   The

17*

" room is fifteen feet square, or rather the floor,
" as the ceiling descends at an angle of forty-five
" degrees, so that whenever I pass the centre of my
" apartment I am compelled to a perpetual salam,
" or to having my head *organized* in a manner that
" would confound the metaphysical materialism of
" a German.

" My dear mother, nobly as she has conformed
" herself to our fallen fortunes, has not yet been able
" to dispense with certain personal refinements for
" herself, or for her unworthy son.   I believe in my
" soul, she has never wafted a sigh from our land-
" lady's sordid little parlor to the almost forgotten
" splendors of our drawing-room; but there is
" something intolerably offensive to her habits and
" tastes in the arrangements of a plebeian bed-room.
" Accordingly she has fitted up my apartment with
" what she considers necessaries ; but that first ne-
" cessity—that chiefest of all luxuries—space, she
" cannot command ; nor can all her ingenuity over-
" come the principle of resistance in matter, so that
" my ' indispensable' furniture limits my locomotive
" faculties to six feet by four.   The knocks I get
" in any one day against my bureaus, writing-
" table, book-case, &c., would convert a Berkleian
" philosopher.

" I have but one window, an offset from the roof,
" to which my dormant ceiling forms a covert way.
" My horizon is bounded by tiled roofs and square
" chimneys.   No ·graceful outlines of foliage ; no
" broad lake to sparkle and dimple on the verge of
" the starry canopy ; no 'heaven-kissing hill ;' but

" chimneys and roofs, and roofs and chimneys, for
" one who counts it high pleasure to behold

> ' The lofty woods—the forest wide and long,
>   Adorn'd with leaves and branches fresh and green,
> In whose cool bowers the birds, with many a song,
>   Do welcome with their quire the summer's queen;
> The meadows fair, where Flora's gifts among
>   Are intermix'd with verdant grass between;
> The silver scaled fish that softly swim
>   Within the sweet brook's crystal, watry stream.'

" These are the sorrows of my exile from nature
" in this her glorious ascendant. I say nothing,
" my dear Mrs. L., of being chained to the city,
" when the sweet spirits that gave it life are fled.
" In short, I will say nothing more of my miseries
" and privations. I will even confess that my little
" cell has its pleasures; humble though they be, still
" they are pleasures. I do not mean the dreams
" and visions that sport about the brain of a young
" man who has his own fortunes to carve in the
" world, and who of course indemnifies himself for
" the absolute negation of his present condition by
" the brilliant apparition of the future. It is well
" for us that our modesty is not gauged by our an-
" ticipations ! My humble attic pleasure consists in
" looking down, like Don Cleofas, on my neigh-
" bors—in guessing at their spirit and history from
" their outward world. You, my dear madam,
" who live in the courtly luxury of ——— street, if
" your eye ever glanced through your curtained
" window at the yards of your neighbors, would
" only see the servile labors of their domestics.
" You can therefore have no imagination of the

"revelations of life to my eye. A curious contrast
"there is between the front and rear of these esta-
"blishments of our humble citizens—the formal
"aspect of the ambitious front parlor, and the *laisser*
"*aller* style of the back apartments. Suffer me,
"in this dearth of parties, operas, and whatever
"makes an accredited drawing-room topic, to in-
"troduce you to one of my neighbors and his '*petit*
"*paradis*,' for so Abeille calls and considers his
"yard, a territory of about thirty feet by fourteen.
"Poor Abeille!—poor—what can make a French-
"man poor? They ride through life on the 'virtu-
"oso's saddle, which will be sure to amble when
"the world is at the hardest trot.' They have
"heaven's charter for happiness.

"Abeille was a seigneur of St. Domingo, and
"possessed one of the richest estates of that Hes-
"perian island. Did you never observe that a
"Frenchman's temperament is the reverse of the
"ungracious state that 'never is, but always to be
"blessed.' Let his present condition be abject as it
"will, he *has been* blest. Abeille revels now in the
"retrospective glories of his seigniory, from which
"the poor fellow was happy to escape, during the
"troubles, with his life, his family, and a few jew-
"els, with the avails of which he has since purchased
"this little property, and a scene of perfect *French*
"happiness it is. Abeille has two lodgers, an old
"bachelor, bitten with the mania of learning French,
"and a clerk qualifying himself for a supercargo.
"He teaches young ladies to paint flowers. His
"pretty daughters, Felicité and Angélique, embroi-
"der muslin and weave lace, and by these means,

" and the infinite ingenuity of a French *ménage*
" they contrive to live in independence, and so far
" from any vain misery about their past magnifi-
" cence, it seems merely to cast a vivid hue—a sort
" of sunset glory over their present mediocrity.

" Abeille's little parterre gives him far more
" pleasure, he confesses, than he ever received
" from his West-India plantation. This parterre is
" the triumph of taste over expense. He has
" covered with a trellis a vile one story back-build-
" ing, that protrudes its hideous form the whole length
" of the yard, and conducted over it a grape-vine, that
" yields fruit as delicious and plentiful as if it grew
" in sunny France. The high board-fence, over
" which once flaunted a vulgar creeper, is now em-
" bossed with a multi-flora. In the angle of the
" yard next the house, and concealing with exquisite
" art an ugly indentation of the wall, is a moss-rose,
" Abeille's *chef d'œuvre*. This he has fed, watered,
" pruned, and in every way cherished, till it has
" surmounted the fence; and to-day I saw him
" gazing at a cluster of buds on the very summit, as
" a victor would have looked on his laurel-crown. At
" the extremity of the yard is a series of shelves ar-
" ranged like the benches of an ampitheatre, (mark
" the economy of space and sunshine !) filled with
" pots containing the finest flowers of all seasons.
" The back windows are festooned, not screened—
" a Frenchman never blinds his windows—with
" honeysuckles, coquetting their way to two bird
" cages, where, embowered and perfumed, are
" perched canaries and mocking-birds, who enjoy

" here every sweet in nature but liberty, and the
" little servile rogues sing as if they had forgotten
" that; and to finish all, the few unoccupied feet of
" the '*petit paradis*,' just leaving space for Abeille
" to meander. among the flowers, are set with me-
" dallions of carnations, tulips, hyacinths, and mig-
" nonette. I must not omit the tame crow, Abeille's
" esquire, who follows him like his shadow, and
" madame's pets and darlings, an enormous parrot,
" the most accomplished of his tribe—a Mathews
" among parrots—and the largest and ugliest shock
" that ever lay in a Frenchwoman's lap. There sits
" madame, at this moment, coquetting with the par-
" rot, scolding Belle, and taking snuff, her only
" occupations in life. ' Pauvre femme,' Abeille
" says, ' elle ne sait pas travailler—toutes les femmes
" de St. Domingue sont ainsi paresseuses, mais,
" elle est si bonne, si œconome, et si fidelle !'
" ' Pauvre femme' indeed ! Abeille looks at her
" through the vista of long past time, or he would
" not account the latter quality such a virtue. But
" if madame does not, her pretty daughters do
" know how to work. Felicité wrought herself into
" the heart of a youth, who in spite of her poverty,
" and in spite of the Yankee prejudice of all his kin-
" dred against a *French* girl, married her, and toiled
" hard to support her, when last week, like the gifts
" of a fairy tale, came a rich legacy to Felicité from
" Port-au-Prince, the bequest of a ci-devant slave.
" Never were people happier. I see them now
" prettily grouped at their chamber-window, Felicité
" leaning on her husband's shoulder, and playing

" bopeep with her child, the child in the arms of her
" old maiden aunt 'Eli, who has forgotten to put on
" her false curls, even forgotten her matin mass
" ever since this bantling came into the world. So
" easy is it, my dear Mrs. Layton, for the affections
" of your sex to revert to their natural and happiest
" channel.

" But the prettiest flower of my neighbor's gar-
" den, the genius loci of his *petit paradis*, is An-
" gélique. She is much younger than her sister.
" From my observations from winter to summer for
" the last three years, I take it she is about the
" poetic age of seventeen.

" With all the facilities of my observatory, and
" the advantage of occasional explanatory notes
" from Abeille, I am extremely puzzled by Angé-
" lique. During the past winter, I used every eve-
" ning to see her, the very soul of gaiety, at the
" little *réunions* at her father's. Her sylph-like
" figure was always flitting over the floor. She danced
" with her father's old French friends, and frolicked
" with the children, the veriest romp and trickster
" among them. She would sew the skirts of pére
" Baillé's coat to old 'Eli's gown; drop icicles un-
" der the boys' collars, and play off on all, young
" and old, her feats of fearless frolic. As the spring
" opened, I heard her sweet voice outsinging the
" birds, her light heart seemed instinctively to echo
" their joyous notes; and many a time have I
" thrown down my book, and involuntarily respond-
" ed to her merry peals of laughter. Soon after
" this there was a sudden transition from the gay
" temper of the girl to the elaborate arts of the

"young lady. She dressed ambitiously, always
" with exquisite taste, as if she had studied her fa-
" ther's flowers for the harmony of colors, but with
" a restless vanity and expense that seemed the out-
" breaking of her West-India nature. A few weeks
" since she had the fever of sentiment upon her—
" would sit whole evenings by her window alone,
" and sang more plaintive ditties than I supposed
" there were in the French language. Now, she
" sings nothing, gay or sad, but sits all day over
" her lace without raising her eyes. Her face is so
" pale and pensive that I fancy, even at this dis-
" tance, I see the tears dropping on her work.

" Her father called me to the fence to-day to give
" me a carnation. I remarked to him, that made-
" moiselle was too constantly at her work. ' Yes,'
" he said, ' but she will work and she is so
" triste, Monsieur Roscoe. Sacristie ! we are all
" triste, when Angélique will not smile.' ' Ah !
" monsieur, mon cœur pleure.' I felt a sort of
" shivering as if a storm were gathering over this
" sunny spot. Heaven grant that this little hum-
" ble *paradis* may not be infested by evil spirits.
" Do not, my dear Mrs. Layton, give the reins to
" your feminine fancy. My interest in Angélique
" is all ' en philosophe,' or if you please, ' en phi-
" lanthropiste ;' a little softer and deeper it may be,
" than 'Eli or even Felicité, or any less beautiful
" than Angélique could excite."

" I left my letter last evening and strolled down
" to the Battery. It should have been a moon-
" light night but the clouds had interposed, and the

" few loiterers that remained there chose the broad
" walk at the water's-side. I saw an acquaint-
" ance whom I was in no humor to join, and I
" retired tò a more secluded walk, where I encoun-
" tered a pair who had evidently gone there to avoid
" observers, for on seeing me approach they turned
" abruptly and departed. Soon after, in going
" up Broadway, I met the same couple. They
" were just separating; the lady came towards
" me; she was shawled and veiled, but as I was
" passing her, her veil caught in the railing of an
" area and her face was exposed. It was, as I had
" conjectured, Angélique. I walked on without
" seeming to notice her, and I perceived that her
" attendant had turned and was hastily retracing his
" steps after her. I cast a scrutinizing glance at
" him, and though his hat was drawn close over his
" eyes, and he held his handkerchief to his face, I
" believed then, and still believe, he was *Pedrillo*.
" He has a certain gait and air that cannot be mis-
" taken, and though he had not on the famous
" Spanish identifying cloak that you used to say
" was managed more gracefully than any other in
" Broadway, yet I am sure I am right in my conjec-
" ture. If I am, ' curse on his perjured arts!' "

" My dear Mrs. Layton :—My letter had swollen
" to such an unreasonable bulk that I threw it aside
" as not worth the postage. But some facts having
" come to my ear which have made me give unwill-
" ing credence to the possibility that you may be in-
" duced to favor Pedrillo's suit to Emilie, I have
" determined to communicate certain particulars to

" you, that I think will influence your opinion of
" this gentleman.

  " The evening after the encounter with Pedrillo
" I have already mentioned, I was returning late to
" my lodgings—there should have been a waning
" moon to light the city, but the heavens were over-
" cast, one of the possible vicisitudes of weather,
" which, (if we may judge from the economy of lamp-
" oil,) is not anticipated by our corporation.   The
" night was dark and drizzling.   It was past one
" o'clock.   I was musing on the profound stillness—
" what stillness is so eloquent as that of a populous
" city ?—and in part confused by the darkness, I
" turned down White instead of Walker street.   I
" did not perceive my mistake till I had made some
" progress, and then my attention was attracted by
" a carriage drawn up close to the flagging ; the
" steps were down, the door open, and the coach-
" man on his box.   There was no light from
" the adjoining houses ; no sound, no indication
" of any kind that a creature was awake there.
" I thought the poor devil of a coachman over-
" wearied had fallen asleep on his box, and I stop-
" ped with the intention of waking him, when I
" heard three low notes whistled by some person
" a few doors in advance of me, and directly half
" the blind of a parlor window was opened, and by
" the faint light that penetrated the misty atmos-
" phere, I perceived a man's figure before the win-
" dow of *Abéille's* house.   Imperfect and varying
" as the light was, I saw the person was addressing
" imploring and impatient . gestures to some one
" within.   My first impulse was that natural to a

" mind of common manliness and delicacy, to avoid
" any interference with the secret purposes of an-
" other, and I crossed the street, designing to pass
" immediately down on the other side. But as the
" purpose of this untimely visit flashed upon my
" mind, I felt that there was something cowardly in
" my retreat. It might be possible, even at this
" late moment to save the infirm Angélique (for
" I had truly divined the actors in the scene) from
" the power of the villain Pedrillo. I was forti-
" fied in my hope when 1 saw Angélique, in the
" act of putting her hat on her head, throw it
" from her, and cautiously raise the window-sash.
" She spoke to Pedrillo, but in so low a voice that
" I only caught a few words. Something she said
" of her mother being sick. That she faltered in
" her purpose of quitting the paternal roof was plain
" from Pedrillo's vehement gestures, and from the
" agony of indecision with which she paced the
" room, wringing her hands, and balancing, no
" doubt, the pleadings of honor and filial duty,
" against the passionate persuasions of her lover.

" I too thought of poor Abéille—the fond old
" father—of his ' petit paradis,' and his cheerful and
" grateful enjoyment of the wreck of his splendid
" fortune, and of this his loveliest flower trampled in
" the dust. Images of the ruin and desolation that
" awaited the amiable Frenchman nerved my reso-
" lution, and the possibility that I might avert the
" instant danger, made my heart throb as if my own
" dearest treasure were in jeopardy. What, thought
" I, ought I to do? What can I do, to counteract
" one who has so far succeeded in his purposes?

" I may alarm the neighbors by my outcries, and
" rouse Abéille, but the wretch will escape with his
" prey, before he can be intercepted : or, at best,
" Angélique will be disgraced by the exposure of
" her intentions. Thus puzzled, I ceased to measure
" obstacles, dismissed all calculations, and just fol-
" lowed the impulse and guidance of my feelings.
" I advanced with cautious foot-steps towards
" Abeille's door-step. Pedrillo was already on it,
" and as yet unaware of my proximity.

" The light moved from the parlor, and flashed
" through the fan-light above the street-door. An-
" gélique had then decided her fate. There was
" another pause in her movement. I was now
" so near to Pedrillo that I heard him breathe
" through his shut teeth, ' Ye furies ! why does
" not she open the door ?' and as if answering
" to his words, Angélique gave audible tokens
" of her decision. The bolts were slowly with-
" drawn, the door opened, and Pedrillo sprang
" forward to receive his prize, when with one arm
" I hurled him back. I know not how far he fell,
" nor where, I had no time to give him one glance ;
" with my other arm I had grasped Angélique, and
" dragging her within the door, I instantly reclosed
" and rebolted it.

" I never shall forget, and I am sure I can never
" describe, Angélique's first look of terror, astonish-
" ment, and inquiry, and the overwhelming shame
" with which she dropped her head on her bosom,
" when she recognised me. Fortunately she did
" not speak. I listened intently for some indica--

" tion of our baffled knight's intentions, at this un-
" expected turn in his affairs. I heard nothing till
" the sound of the retiring carriage-wheels proved
" that he had retreated. I then graced myself with an
" apology to Angélique. I am not sure that she was
" not, when her first surprise was over, a little vexed
" with my interference, but I was so fortunate as to
" give a better direction to her feelings, and with-
" out preaching about her duties, or dictating them,
" I set before her such a picture of her fond old fa-
" ther, that her tender heart returned to its loyalty
" to him, to duty, and to happiness, and shuddering
" at the precipice from which she had escaped, she
" most solemnly vowed for ever t o renounce, and
" shun Pedrillo.

" That it is better to save than to destroy, no one
" will dispute. I believe it is easier—far easier to per-
" suade the infirm to virtue than to vice. There is an
" unbroken chord in every human heart, that vibrates
" to the voice of truth. There is there an undying
" spark from the altar of God, that may be kindled
" to a flame by the breath of virtue. If we felt this
" truth more deeply, we should not be so reckless of
" the happiness of our fellow-beings, and so negli-
" gent of any means we may possess of cherishing
" and stimulating their virtue.

" I did not embarrass Angélique with my pre-
" sence one moment after I was assured that her
" right resolution was fixed ; but I hesitated whether
" to retire through Abéille's yard to my lodgings,
" or to go into the street, where Pedrillo might pos-
" sibly still be lurking. I wished that, if possible,
" he should think Angélique had been rescued by

18*

"' some one who had a natural right to interpose in
" her behalf. But as I thought there was little
" chance of encountering him, and as I had knocked
" off my hat in entering the house, I withdrew that
" way in the hope of finding it. I did not; and I
" have since suspected that Pedrillo ascertained my
" name from it, for I have met him once since, and
" I thought his face flushed and his brow lowered
" as he passed me.

" Now, my dear Mrs. Layton, have I not by
" giving you a true account of the sober part I
" played in this little drama, proved to you my dis-
" belief in the slander that claims the paramount
" favor of your sex for men *à bonnes fortunes?*
" However, to confess the truth, my motive in the
" communication was quite foreign to myself; but
" I must indulge my egotism by relating my own
" part in the characteristic finishing of the tale.
" Old Abéille came to my room this morning with
" a note from Angélique. She informed me that
" her poor mother had just died; that she had be-
" stowed ' such praise' on her when she gave her
" her last blessing. ' The praise,' she said, ' she
" had not-deserved by her virtue, she would by her
" penitence, and she had fallen on her knees and
" confessed all to her mother ; and her mother had
" then blessed her more fervently than ever, and
" blessed Monsieur Roscoe, both in one breath. And
" if the prayer of the dying was heard,' adds Angé-
" lique, ' no trouble nor sin will ever come nigh to
" Monsieur Roscoe, nor to any thing Monsieur
" loves.' Her note concludes with the information

" that she is going to the convent at Baltimore ' to
" pray to God and make penitence *for a little*
" *while.*' It was evident the old man had a burden
" on his heart that could only be relieved by words ;
" but there are feelings of a nature and force to
" check the fluency even of a Frenchman ; and
" Abéille was mute, save in the eloquence of tears.
" He took out his snuff-box, which serves him on all
" occasions as a link to mend the broken chain of
" his ideas ; but now it would not do. I had not
" yet read Angélique's note, and I naturally referred
" his emotion to the death of his wife, to which I
" adverted in a tone of condolence. " Ah, 'tis not
" that, Monsieur Roscoe,' he said, ' il faut mourir—
" and my wife—pauvre femme !—was good to die.
" Certainement c'est un grand malheur ; but every
" body can speak of his wife's death—but, sacristié !
" when I think of *that*, my tongue will not move,
" though my heart is full of gratitude to you, Mon-
" sieur Roscoe. Ah, you have saved us all, et de
" quelle horreur !' Here Abéille burst into a fresh
" flood of tears, and again had recourse to his snuff-box.
" I could no longer appear ignorant of his meaning.
" ' My good friend,' said I, ' I understand you per-
" fectly ; but this is not a subject to talk about. Let me
" only say to you, that Angélique was even more
" ready to spring from the toils than I was to extri-
" cate her.' ' Ah, Dieu soit béni—veritablement—
" elle est un ange. Ah, Monsieur Roscoe, you
" have said that good word of ma petite pour
" m'encourager. Vous savez,' he continued, for
" now he had recovered all his volubility, ' vous

" savez quelle est belle—la reine de toutes mes
" fleurs—ah! n'est ce pas, Monsieur—and she is
" always so douce et gaie—si gaie—toujours—
" toujours—and now, Monsieur Roscoe, we must
" speak English; *that* always have a very plain mean-
" ing. My claim on my country is partly allowed,
" and I have received fifty thousand francs. Now I do
" not want this money; I am very happy, and my
" poor girl shall have it all—ten thousand dollars—
" and when she has made her penitence you shall
" have her hand, Monsieur Roscoe, and all the
" money in it. Ah, do not speak—vous le méritez.'

" I certainly was not prepared to reply to so un-
" expected an expression of Abéille's gratitude.
" However, I had frankness enough to · say that
" marriage must be an affair of the heart entirely.
" ' You,' I said, ' my friend Abéille, cannot answer
" for Angélique at the end of a twelvemonth, nor
" can I foresee in what disposition I shall then find
" myself.' 'Ah but,' iuterrupted Abéille, ' we will
" shorten Angélique's retirement to a few weeks—
" elle est si jeune,—il ne faut pas penser et prier
" Dieu too long.' I was driven to an evasion; for
" I have too much chivalry interwoven in the very
" web of my nature to reject a ' fair ladye' in plain
" terms, and I said, scarcely controlling a smile at
" the resemblance of my reply to the formula of a docile
" miss, at her first offer ; I said that my mother felt
" on these subjects quite ' *en Américaine*,'—that she
" had her prejudices, and I feared it would break
" her heart if I married any other than one of my
" own countrywomen, and therefore I must not

" admit the thought of aspiring to the hand of
" Mademoiselle Angélique.

" ' Est-il possible,' cried Abéille, ' q'une femme
" raisonnable, peut être capable de telles sottises,
" pauvre garçon!' This was spoken in a tone of
" deep commiseration. ' I pray the bon Dieu will
" reward your filial piety; but where will madame
" find une Américaine comparable à mon Angélique?
" Toujours, toujours you shall be mon fils, if
" you cannot be the mari of my belle Angé-
" lique. Eh bien!—chacun à son goüt—mais,
" une Américaine préférable à mon Angélique!'
" The old man took a double pinch of snuff.
" ' Adieu, Monsieur Roscoe; you will come to
" the cathédrale to hear the miserére chanted for
" poor Madame Abeille.' I assured him I would
" do so, and thereupon we parted.

" My dear Mrs. Layton, allow me the happiness
" of soon hearing from your own lips, or your own
" pen, that Senor Pedrillo's suit has met its merited
" fate.

" And in the meantime, believe me, as ever,

" Your devoted friend and servant,

" GERALD ROSCOE."

Roscoe was right in his conjecture that Pedrillo
had ascertained who had intercepted his success.
When he rose from the prostrate position in the middle of the street where Roscoe had thrown him, he
stumbled over a hat. He perceived that the noise
at Abéille's door had attracted the observation of
one of the guardians of the night, and he thought
proper to retreat. He took the hat with him, and

when he exposed it to the light, he found within it the name that of all others was most likely to give a keen edge to his resentment. He had met Roscoe often at Mrs. Layton's, and had had some corroding suspicions that Emilie's indifference to his addresses proceeded from preference to Roscoe. He torĕ off the name, and threw the hat into the street, saying as he did so, "I have found out the *object*, and I will make the *opportunity* of revenge."

It must be confessed there is a charm to our republican society, in a foreign name and aristocratic pretensions, like the fascinations of a fairy tale to children. Our tastes are yet governed by ancient *prĕstiges*—cast in the old mould. We profess the generous principle that each individual has a right to his own eminence, whether his sires commanded the heights, or drudged obscurely in the humblest vale of life ; but artificial distinctions still influence our imaginations, and the spell has not been dissolved by the repeated detection of the pretensions of impostors with foreign manners, and high-sounding titles who have obtained the entrée of our fashionable circles.

Henriques Pedrillo had far more plausible claims to favor than certain other vagrant foreigners who have played among us too absurd and notorious a part to be yet forgotten. He had in the first place ' nature's aristocracy,' a person and face of uncommon symmetry and elegance, and these advantages he cherished and set off with consummate art, steering a middle course between coxcombry and negligence, the Scylla and Charybdis of the gentleman's toilette. His conversation did not indicate any more

erudition than he might have imbibed at the play-
house, and by a moderate intercourse with cultivated society. He spoke English, French, and
Spanish equally well ; and so well as to leave his
hearer in doubt which was his vernacular; and he
had the insinuating address—the devotion of look
and manner, in his intercourse with ladies, that
marks the exotic in America. In common with
most Spaniards who come among us, he cast his na-
tivity in old Castile, though he confessed he had
been driven to the new world to repair the abated
fortunes of his ancient family. He was not precise
in communicating the particulars of his career; but
the grand circumstance of success, if it did not ex-
tinguish curiosity, at least repressed its expression.
He had been recently known to some of our first
merchants, as the principal in a rich house in the
Havana. This was enough to satisfy the slight
scrupulosity Jasper Layton might have felt in introducing him to his wife and daughter. Mrs. Layton at first courted Pedrillo merely as a brilliant
acquisition to her *coterie.* She confessed she had
no affinities for American character—tame, unex-
citable, and unadorned as she deemed it. She
spoke French and Spanish remarkably well, and
the desire to demonstrate these accomplishments did
not betray a very culpable vanity. She first sedulously cultivated Pedrillo's acquaintance ; ' Eve did
first eat ;' but Mrs. Layton, no more than our first
mother, foresaw the fatal consequences of what appeared a trivial act. Their relations soon became
interesting and complicated. Pedrillo was capti-
vated by Emilie's pre-eminent beauty. Her inno-

cence and sweetness touched all that remained of
unextinguished goodness in his nature. The evil
spirits look back with lingering affection to the
heaven they have forfeited.

Layton, a man of lavish expense, found Pedrillo
a most convenient friend. Pedrillo was profuse,
but not careless. He had the acute habits of a man
of business, and even in his pleasures he nicely balanced the amount he gave against the consideration he expected to receive. When, therefore, he
from time to time, lent Jasper Layton large sums of
money, he gloried in the secret consciousness of the
power he was accumulating. Their intimacy grew
till Layton gave him the last proof of his confidence
and good fellowship, by introducing him to a club
of gentlemen who met privately every night at a
gambling-house, and indulged there to great excess
this keen and destructive passion.

Pedrillo had acquired in scenes of stirring excitement and imminent peril, such command over his
turbulent passions, that to the eye of an observer the
fire that was merely covered, seemed extinguished.
So at least it appeared to Layton, when after a night
of various fortune and feverish excitement, they
emerged from their club-room, just as the city
lamps were dimmed by the approaching day.
"Pedrillo, my dear fellow," said Layton, "you
are a philosopher : you win and lose with equal
nonchalance—I—I confess it—I am giddy with my
enexpected luck."

"*Unexpected ?*" replied Pedrillo.

"Yes, unhoped for ; Pedrillo, I will tell you a

secret. When I entered that room to-night I was utterly ruined."

" A secret!—ha! ha!"

" A secret—yes, *you* might have guessed it, for God knows you were deeply concerned in it—but all scores are wiped out now, hey, Pedrillo? That last bragger cleared off the last five thousand—and my loss to that devilish fellow Martin, that is balanced too; thank Heaven I am my own man again; a timely whirl of the wheel it was. Fortune, blind goddess as thou art, I still will worship thee!"

" Do we visit her temple to-morrow night?"

" Certainly."

" Au revoir, then." They parted; Layton went one way, intoxicated with success, humming glees and catches, now twisting his cane around his fingers, now striking it on the pavement, and even attracting the eye of the drowsy watchmen by his irregular movements. His spirits would have fled if he had penetrated Pedrillo's bosom, and seen the keen, vigilant suspicion he had awakened there.

The next night they met again at the gaming-table. Fortune maintained her perch on Layton's cards; Pedrillo lost large sums. Again they left the house together. Pedrillo appeared even more unmoved than he had on the preceding night. He congratulated Layton with as much seeming unconcern as if the subject in question were a mercantile speculation in which he had no personal concern. Layton was in ecstacies—" You may defy the world, Pedrillo!" he said in a tone of the highest good humor, " and all its turns, tricks, and shufflings. Those poor devils we have left behind us are ready

to cut their own throats, or mine. Zounds! my dear
fellow, you are high-souled and whole-souled—"

" Have you heard from Miss Emilie, to-day ?"
asked Pedrillo, rather abruptly interrupting his
companion's strain of lavish compliment.

" Yes."

" Does she permit me to follow her ?"

Layton's elated tone was changed to one more
conciliatory, as he replied, " Why, to tell you the
truth, Pedrillo, she seems disinclined ; and on the
whole we may as well consider the affair as ended."

" *When* did you come to that conclusion, sir ?"

" When ? what difference does that make, if it be
a wise conclusion ?"

" Do we meet to-morrow night ?"

" As you please ; after my run of luck it does not
become me to propose it."

" We meet then ; and *after* we will speak of Miss
Emilie."

" Eh bien ; but of course Pedrillo, you understand that I shall never consent to put any force on
her inclinations."

" You shall do as you choose"—and he added
mentally, " you shall *choose* it, Jasper Layton, as
surely as a man chooses life rather than death."

The next evening found them at their accustomed
haunt. After Pedrillo and Layton had played one
game, Pedrillo threw up the cards, alleging a pain
and dizziness in his head. Another took his place.
He continued to stride up and down the room, sometimes pausing beside Layton, and always keeping
his eye fixed on him. Layton had a dim consciousness, as some sensitive persons have in their sleep, of

a steady gaze, and once or twice he looked up, startled and inquiring, but instantly his attention reverted to the portentous interests of the game.
From time to time angry and half-smothered exclamations broke from his companions, at his obstinate
luck ; still they continued with fatal desperation to
wager and lose, and when the play was finished,
they had lost, and Layton had won all. Accustomed as they were to sudden and violent fluctuations
of fortune, their continued losses on the present occasion had exhausted their patience, and deprived
them of the power of quelling the expression of
their excited passions. Despair, madness, and
worse than all, suspicion, burst forth in loud impre-
cations, or in half audible murmurs. Layton's
cheek burnt, and his hand trembled, with triumph,
or resentment, or consciousness, but he uttered not
one word ; and when, as they left the apartment, he,
as usual, thrust his arm into Pedrillo's, Pedrillo
withdrew from him, and fixed on him a cold pene-
trating glance that thrilled through his soul. He
involuntarily shivered—they emerged from the long
dark passage, that led from their secret haunt to the
street, into a damp, hot, steaming atmosphere. " A
singular morning for agues !" said Pedrillo, looking
contemptuously at Layton, while he took off his
own hat and fanned himself, as if to stir some living
principle in the suffocating air. Layton turned
his eye timidly to Pedrillo ; their glances met—a
keen intelligence, a malignant triumph, and piti-
less contempt, spoke in Pedrillo's ; the shame, and
fear, and misery of detected villany, in Layton's.
They walked on in silence to the head of the street,

where, instead of parting as usual, Pedrillo drew
nearer to Layton, took his arm, and went on with
him. "A word to the wise," he said, in a low thrill-
ing voice, "a word to the wise, for wise I think
you will be after this folly—the ass should not attempt a cheat in the presence of the fox, Layton.
I suspected your trick the first night—the second my
suspicions were confirmed—to-night I have detected you. Let this pass. You have been rash—
imprudent in your practice, my good friend; you
should have calculated more nicely the chances of
detection. Other suspicions than mine are awakened, but there is an immeasurable distance between
suspicion and certainty, and we may continue to wi-
den that distance; that is, if," and as he finished his
sentence, every word seemed measured and weighed,
and sunk like lead into Layton's heart,—"if in
future we are friends?"

The tone was interrogative, and Layton replied
gaspingly, "certainly, certainly."

"Well, very well; we understand each other, do
we not?"

"Yes, yes, perfectly."

"Then let that pass—'Il ne faut pas être plus
sage qu'il ne faut'—details are disagreeable and you
are sure, quite sure there is a clear mutual compre-
hension?"

Layton felt at every word as if a new manacle were
rivetted on him. Still, safety on any terms, were
better than destruction, and while he writhed under the power, he dared not resist; "Proceed," he
cried, "for God's sake—you know I understand
you."

"Then, Layton," he resumed in a familiar, every-day tone of voice, " my lips are sealed—as to the few thousands you have won from me, retain them, as a consideration in part for the treasure you en-sure me—*ensure* me, mark my words; and, Lay-ton, if in future you get becalmed, do not attempt to raise the wind by such desperate expedients. There are a few situations in life where honesty *is* the best policy, and the gaming table is one of them. But before we part, let us settle our plan of action. Suspicion is awake, go again to-morrow night, and lose your winnings liberally! this will baffle their sagacity, and what is more, appease their resent-ment. Do you like my counsel?"

"I will take it."

"Good night then, or rather good morning, for I think the sun is glimmering through the scalding fog." They parted, and Layton sprang on his own door-step, as a newly captured slave would dart from the presence of his master. "One word," said Pedrillo, turning back, "you write to Miss Emilie to-morrow?"

"Yes, yes, I will communicate my determination to her."

"Oh! 'of course,'" replied Pedrillo, with a 'laughing devil in his eye,' and quoting Layton's last words of the preceding evening, "'of course you will put no force on her inclinations.'" An oath rose to Layton's lips, but he suppressed all ex-pression till secure from observation in his own room, he gave vent to a burst of passion; but re-sentment, remorse, and parental tenderness, were now alike unavailing. He was inextricably involved with Pedrillo, and his own safety could only be secured by the sacrifice of his beautiful child.

Jasper Layton was the only son of a man of talent, virtue, and fortune, and he never quite lost the sense of the responsibility such an inheritance involved; and to the last, the fear of publicly disgracing his honorable name, was a source of the keenest suffering to him. Unfortunately he came into possession, by his father's death, of a large fortune, before he had sufficient strength of principle, or habit, to encounter its temptations. He was not destitute of kind, or even tender affections; but what good thing thrives without culture? and frivolous pursuits and selfish indulgences had rendered his callous. Still, they had not perished, and it was after many heart-writhings, and after a long interview with Pedrillo on the subsequent morning, that he wrote the following letter to his wife—to a wife who, if she had rightly employed her superior powers, might have saved him from the wreck of virtue and happiness.

"Madam—I enclose you a remittance, according "to the *conjugal* request you did me the honor to "transmit through Gerald Roscoe, Esq.; and at the "same time, I take the liberty to forewarn you, that "unless you second—energetically second, my "views and wishes in the ——— affair, I shall lose "the ability, as I have long ago lost the inclination, "to answer the demands arising from your habits of "reckless expense. I expect you to be at Trenton "by the first of next month. Pedrillo will follow "you there; and there, or at Utica (he leaves all

" minor points to her decision) he expects to re-
" ceive Emilie's hand. He loves Emilie—upon
" my soul I believe de does—devotedly.

" God knows I have taken every care of her hap-
" piness in my arrangements with P——. He has
" made a magnificent settlement on her, and pro-
" mises never, but with her consent, to take her to
" Cuba. Do not moralize (it is not your forte)
" about P.'s foibles. I know the world; we must
" take our choice between unmasked frailty, and
" hypocrisy. I, for one, prefer the former. P.'s
" liberality covers a multitude of sins. Women
" *must* be married. Emilie, poor girl, will not it is
" true, marry for love; but *we* married for love!
" and what has come of it? ha! ha! It is well
" enough for boys and girls to dream about, and
" novelists to string their stories on; but you and I
" know it is all cursed dupery. All that can be
" *secured* in matrimonial life is pecuniary indepen-
" dence. To this I have attended with parental
" fidelity.

" You must do your part; your influence over
" E. is unbounded; and if you choose to exercise it.
" you can *incline* her (force is of course out of the
" question) to do that, on which, let me tell you,
" madam, your as well as my happiness—happiness!
" existence depends. We are ruined, *dishonored*,
" if this affair is not brought to a fortunate conclu-
" sion. . I tell you this because it is necessary you
" should know the worst, to second me as you
" should; but make no unessential communications
" to poor E. God preserve that cheek from shame

" that has never been dyed but with the pure blush
" of innocence.

" Do your part, I beseech you, and do it well,
" and effectually; you *can* act like a woman of
" sense. But I am urging where I should com-
" mand. Remember you have other children, and
" will have future wants. Can you look poverty
" and disgrace in the face ? If not, you know the
" alternative.   Yours, &c.

            " JASPER LAYTON."

While the episode in Pedrillo's life related in
Roscoe's letter, and the transactions of the gaming-
house were passing in New York, Gertrude Clarence was enjoying an almost daily interchange of
visits with her new friends, and an acquaintance
that promised nothing but happiness was ripening
into intimacy. Mrs. Layton found herself compelled by the receipt of her husband's letter, suddenly to suspend this intercourse, and she despatched the following note to Gertrude, in which, as will
be seen, she did not hint at the place of her destina-
tion after she left Upton's-purchase. She had her
reasons for this reserve. She feared that Mrs. Upton would propose to accompany her, as a ride to
Trenton from her residence was a convenient and
tempting jaunt of pleasure; and she meant that her
going there should appear to have been the consequence of a subsequent arrangement.

" It is with inexpressible sorrow, my sweetest
" friend, that I am compelled to bid you adieu with-
" out again seeing you. We take our departure

" early in the morning. Poor Em' is quite heart-
" broken about it. We are both under the tyranny
" of destiny. I resign all to the despot, save my
" affections; and of those, you, dearest, have taken
" complete possession. It is not because you are
" a heroine of the nineteenth century; that is, prac-
" tical, rational, dutiful, and all the tedious *et ceteras*
" that I admire you. No, these are qualities that, like
" bread and water, are the gross elements of every
" day life, but they have nothing to do with that
" fine accord of finely touched spirits that common
" minds can no more attain than common senses can
" take in the music of the spheres. There is no
" describing it, but we understand it; do we not?
" Dear Gertrude, you must be my friend, you must
" love me ; you will have much to forgive in me. I
" am a wayward creature. Oh, heavens! how infe-
" rior to you! but there have been crosses in my
" destiny. Had I known you sooner, your bland
" influence would have given a different color to
" my life. You understand me. I disdain the
" Procrustes standard of pattern ladies who admit
" none to the heaven of their favor, but those
" who can walk on a mathematical line, like that
" along which a Mahometan passes to his paradise.
" My best regards to your father. I wish he
" could have looked into my heart and seen how I
" was charmed with his manners to you ; the chival-
" ric tenderness of the lover mingling with the calm
" sentiment of the father. Would that poor Em'
" had —— but on certain subjects unhappy wo-
" man is forbidden to speak. To you, my loveliest
" friend, a husband would be a superfluity—at pre-

" sent. But to poor Em' how necessary. You
" *must* come to us this winter. I shall make a
" formal attack on your father to that effect. I
" shall bring out all the arts of diplomacy ; but I
" shall need no arts. I have good sense on my
" side, and ' good sense' is the oracle of every man
" past forty. Clarenceville is, I allow, in the sum-
" mer, a most delicious residence, the favored haunt,
" the home of the genius of mountain and lake ;
" but in winter, when the grass withers, the leaves
" fall, the running stream runs no longer, and the
" winds are howling through these sublime forests,
" (a nervous sound of a dark day or cloudy night,)
" then come to the luxuries of civilization in town.
" Man was not made to contend alone with nature ;
" and, with honest Touchstone, I confess that the
" country in respect ' it is in the green fields, is
" pleasant ; but (at all seasons) in respect it's far from
" court, it is tedious.' But pardon me, I had for-
" gotten this was a note. One is so beguiled
" into forgetfulness of every thing else when com-
" muning with you, dearest ! Emilie begs me to
" say farewell for her." Here followed half a
dozen lines so carefully effaced, that the keenest
curiosity could not discover a word. The note
proceeded : " These crossed lines prove how invo-
" luntarily my heart flows out to you—how unwil-
" lingly it bears the cold restraint of prudence ; but,
" after a few days, such restrictions will be unne-
" cessary. Till then, believe me, dear Gertrude,
                " Yours, most truly,
                        " GRACE LAYTON."
    " N. B, My mind was so engaged with matters

" of deeper interest that I forgot to mention the
" total wreck of poor Upton's expectations of
" making a family piece in an English book. She
" has exhausted her hospitalities on this son of an
" English baronet, in the hope of seeing herself, and
" the Judge, and all the little Uptons in print, when
" lo ! she has found this morning, in the course of one
" of her housewife explorations, a leaf from the travel-
" ler's note-book. I can stop to give you but a
" few specimens from the memorandum. I am vexed
" at the fellow's impertinence towards you ; but you
" are a *femme raisonnable*, and know that fortune
" must be thus taxed. ' Mem. Upton's-purchase,
" residence of a country justice—convenient vicinity
" to some celebrated lake-scenery—staid here on
" that account. American scenery quite savage—
" Justsce U. an abyss of ignorance—wife, a mighty
" vulgar little person—children, pests—no *servants*
" —two *helps*. Dined at Clarenceville. The C.s
" great people in America—giants in Lilliput !—
" Amer'n table barbarisms—porter and salad with
" meats ! peas with currie !—no poultry—no butch-
" er's meat. Query, do the inferior animals as well
" as man uniformly degenerate, and become scarce
" in America ? Miss C. an only daughter—a pro-
" digious fortune—pretty good air too—do very
" well *caught young*—but can't go again. Devilish
" pretty girl here—mother a knowing one.' You see,
" dear Gertrude, we have all a part in these precious
" notes. Poor little Upton half cried as she read
" them. We are philosophers and may laugh.
" Again, and at each moment more tenderly,

" Yours,   G. L."

" One more nota bene and I have done.   I have
"just received a folio from Gerald Roscoe—Oh !
" what a lover he will be ! how I could have loved
" such a man !   Who is it that says (too truly!) that
" ' la puissance d'aimer est trop grande, elle l'est trop
" dans les ames ardentes!'

Farewell, dearest,

G. L."

Gertrude wondered that Mrs. Layton should be
so reserved about Emilie's affairs, when she manifested such singular confidence, and unbounded tenderness ; for measuring her new friend by her own
purity and truth, she gave full credit to all her expressions.   Contrasted with the simple regard and
unexaggerated language of Gertrude's common acquaintance, they were like the luscious fruits of the
tropics, compared with our cold northern productions.

· But she had now no time to analyze her fascinating friend.   The jaunt to Trenton, to which her
father had at once consented, on Seton's account
had been delayed from day to day, for two weeks,
from the daily occurrence of the rural affairs of
midsummer, that seem to country gentlemen, of the
first importance.   In the mean while, Seton was
becoming worse.   The family physician, announced
the approach of a nervous fever, that could only be
averted by change of air ; and Mr. Clarence put
aside every other concern ; and, on the very day of
Mrs. Layton's departure, he set off with Gertrude
and Seton, and servants competent to the care of
the invalid, in case he failed to derive the benefit

they hoped, from the journey. Mr. Clarence was usually particularly annoyed by the discomforts of travelling ; his philosophy completely subdued by bad roads, bad coffee, bad bread, and worst and chiefest of all plagues, by the piratical ' red rovers' that ' murder sleep ;' but his benevolence now got the better of the habits generated by ill health and indulgence—he thought, and cared only for Seton.

If the unhappy patient's malady had been within the reach of art, it must have been subdued by Gertrude's ministrations; for with that exquisite sensibility, which vibrates to every motion of another's spirit, she watched all the variations of his mind, and imparted or withheld the sunshine of her own, as best suited his humor ; but, in spite of skill and patience, and sisterly vigilance, the nervous fever predicted by the physician made hourly encroachments ; and the necessity of a few hours' delay at one of the noisiest inns of that noisiest of all *growing* towns, thronged busy Utica, exasperated the disease to an alarming degree.

As may be supposed, Mr. Clarence had not come to the most public hotel of a town, abounding in every species and grade of receptacle for travellers, till he had unsuccessfully applied for admittance to the other more private, but now overflowing houses.

The travellers, on alighting, were shown into the common receiving parlor, a large apartment opening into the public hall, and near the general entrance door. Mr. Clarence, after vainly attempting to obtain audience of the official departments of the house, and after a fruitless quest for some private and unoccupied apartment, was compelled to content himself with securing the exclusive possession of a settee, which had the advantage of a position removed as far as the dimensions of the apartment admitted, from either of the general passage doors, through which the full tide of human existence ebbed and flowed. Here, he, Gertrude, and Seton, seated themselves; and here they might for a little time, but for poor Seton, have been well enough amused with the contrast to the seclusion, quiet, and elegance of their home.

The front windows of the apartment looked into the most public, and *par excellence* the busiest street of the town, the avenue to the great northern turnpike. Stage-coaches were waiting, arriving, departing, driving to and fro, as if all the world were a stage-coach, and all the men and women merely travellers.

The 'window privilege' (as our New-England friends would say) at the side of the room, was no way inferior to that in front. This afforded a view of the canal, and of the general debouching place of its packet-boats—all elements are here tributary to the *forwarding* system.

There were servants and porters hustling baggage off and on the boats—stage-coach proprietors persecuting the jaded passengers with rival claims to patronage—agents clothed in official importance—idlers, for even here are idlers, and all 'as their tempers were,' muttering, sneering, scolding, joking, laughing, or silently submitting to their fate. The way-worn, weary travellers, as they poured into the hotel, seemed the victims, instead of the authors, of this hurly-burly.

A female, with a highly decorated pongee riding-dress, gaudy ear-rings, a watch at her side, with half a dozen seals, and a gold safety chain, as big as a cable around her neck—in short, with the aspect of a half gentlewoman, seated herself beside Miss Clarence, and very unceremoniously began a conversation with her.   " Are you going on in the pioneer line, Ma'am ?" " No." " Oh, in the telegraph—so are we, it is much more select; but I tell my husband, that all the stages are too levelling to suit me"—a pause ensued, and soon after the lady beckoned to her husband. " My dear, who is that foreign looking gentleman, that says he is going on in the pioneer-line?"   " The Duke of Monte-Bello!"   The lady looked all aghast at the untimely discovery, that levels might be raised as well as lowered in a stage-coach.

The only apparently perfectly cool member of this bustling community, was a ruddy-faced, tight-built, active, little man, not far declined from his meridian, who was walking in and out, and up and down the room, addressing the individuals of this motley crowd, with the easy air of a citizen of the world.   He approached Mr. Clarence, and by way of an introductory salutation observed, that it was a 'warmish day.'   The mercury stood at ninety, and Mr. Clarence' blood at fever heat.

" Intensely hot," he replied, without turning his head or moving his eye from the ark-like boats, which were gliding under the bridge that crossed the canal.

"A pretty sight that!" continued the good-natured man, " especially, to one, who, like myself, has travelled through this town many and many a day, in fair weather and foul, with the mail on my back."

" You, my friend, you do not look older than myself !"

I think I have some dozen years the advantage of you, sir ; but I have led a stirring kind of a life, and kept my blood warm, and courage up. Yes, sir, just where the grand *canaul* goes, I used to whistle along a foot-path; and here, where the folks are now as thick as blades of grass in June, stood my log-house ; and my wife, and four flax-headed little boys, were all the inhabitants. I love to look back upon those times, though I have now seventy drivers in my employ; but we grow with the country, and get to be gentlemen before we know it ; excuse me, sir, my coaches are getting under way."

A fresh bustle now broke out ; Babel was nothing to it; for no post-coaches stood at its devoted doors. "Hurra for the western passengers!" Gentlemen and ladies for Sacket's harbor—all ready!" "Hurra for Trenton !" "Pioneer line—ready !" "Gentlemen and ladies for the Telegraph!" "The bell is ringing for the Adams boat—going out !" "Horn blowing for the Jackson—coming in."

Where was poor Seton, and his nerves, in this *mêlée.* "It will certainly kill him," thought Gertrude, and calling to a black fellow, who was hurrying hither and thither, as if he were the ruling spirit of the scene ; "my good friend," she said, imploringly, "cannot you get a private room, for that sick gentleman ?"

Blackey grinned from ear to ear; " Missess can't suspect a private room in a public-house."

Happily, his reply, half impudent, and half simple, caught the ear of our friend, the some-time mail-bearer; who ordered the servant, instantly, to find private apartments, and accompanied his command with such demonstrations of his having ' come to be a gentleman,' as none may give, in our country, but those who have *worked* their passage to that elevation ; and none will receive, but those, whose color stamps their subordination.   When blackey had recovered from the impetus, that had hurled him from one extremity of the room to the other, his chastiser ordered him to show the lady to the square-room ; and said, he would himself conduct the gentlemen to the best apartments the house afforded.   Most gratefully did they all follow, blesssing the timely interposition of the bustling little man in authority.

Miss Clarence took possession of her apartment, opened the sashes, closed the blinds, and was just throwing herself upon the bed, when, a horribly scrawled half-sheet of paper, caught her eye.   She picked it up, and taking it for granted, that it was some discarded scrawl, and without once doubting, whether it were proper to read it, and having nothing else to do, she began it ; and once begun, it was read, and re-read.   There was no address, no signature ; it was not folded, or finished.   It ran thus :

" You will be surprised at this addenda to the " folio I have just despatched ; if, indeed, you can " decipher it, written, as it must be, with a bar-room " pen, and diluted ink.   Since I put that in the P.

" Office, I have had positive information—there is
" no longer any doubt remaining. The poor girl is
" passive, and P. is to follow them to Trenton.
" What horrible infatuation! You may think me as
" infatuated to hope to prevent it; bnt I cannot look
" on, and see a creature so young, so innocent, and
" so lovely, on the brink of a precipice, and not
" stretch out my arm to rescue her from destruction.
" I will communicate the terrible suspicions that are
" abroad ; if my efforts are abortive, why, I shall have
" made them, and that will be some consolation. I
" think if I see ——, I can dissipate her delusion ; if,
" indeed, it be delusion ; but if, as I rather think, it is
" a timid submission to tyranny, I shall try to rouse
" her courage to rebellion. This crusade, of course,
" prevents my paying my respects at Clarenceville;
" I understand there are troops of pilgrims to that
" shrine. Let them bow before the golden idol—I
" reserve my worship, for the image to be set np in
" my heart. Report says that Miss C——"

Here the letter had been interrupted, and as Gertrude hoped, unintentionally left, for she could not
believe that a person who could indite a decent
epistle would expose such allusions to public in-
spection. ' Who could have written it ?' She ran
over the whole catalogue of her own, and her father's acquaintance. Not one appeared as the probable writer. She thought of Gerald Roscoe, but
she was familiar with his autograph, and, ' thank
heaven, it was not he,' she ejaculated audibly,
and smiled involuntarily at the sensation of escape
she derived from this assurance. ' Why was it
she had rather it had been any other man living

than Gerald Roscoe?' Before she had given this
self-interogation fair hearing, and while she was
folding the manuscript with the intention of showing it to her father, she heard a tap at the door,
and the voice of the negro-servant, saying, 'Won't
missess please to hand me a written letter, lying on
the table under a handkerchief, and won't missess
please to keep the handkerchief tight over it, *case*
the gentleman's very *pa'tic'lar* not to have me, nor
nobody read it."

She looked around the room, saw a cambric
handkerchief, not far from the place where she had
found the letter, and scrupulously covered it; but
she did not transfer it to the servant till (as every
woman will believe) she had vainly investigated every
corner for a mark. She was gratified with this indi-
rect assurance that the exposure of the letter had
been accidental and limited to herself, and probably
owing to the draft of wind occasioned by her throwing open the window when she entered the apartment.

But what could console the high-minded Gertrude
Clarence for the conviction that continually pressed
on her from every quarter, and in every form, that
the accident of fortune, a distinction that she had
never sought, and never valued, exposed her to
slights and ridicule; to be dreaded and avoided by
one class, courted and flattered by another. She
thought of Seton, and it cannot be questioned that
she felt a glow of satisfaction that she had excited
one pure, disinterested sentiment; and a secret regret that affection was in its nature so independent
and inflexible, that, though she would, she could not

love him who so well deserved her love. Then came the bitterest reflection of all; her fortune had envenomed the shaft that wounded Seton's peace.

What would become of envy and covetousness, and all their train of discontent, evil, and sin, if the external veil were lifted, and the eye could penetrate the secrets of the heart ?

Miss Clarence was roused from a long reverie to which we have merely given the clue, by a notice that Mr. Seton was so much refreshed as to be able to proceed on his journey.

Nothing can be more beautiful, more soothing and refreshing, than the coming on of evening after the fierce heat of one of our midsummer days. It is a compensation for the languor and exhaustion of mid-day—or rather it is the best preparation for the full and exquisite enjoyment of the delicious coolness, the deepening shadows, and the fragrance that exhales from woods, flowers, and and fields. A summer's evening in the country is a paradise regained ; but, alas ! evil spirits could leap the bounds of paradise ; and melancholy interposed her black pall between poor Seton and the outward world. In vain did Gertrude point out the rich hills and valleys of Oneida—the almost boundless view of a country so recently redeemed from savages and savage wildness, and now rich, populous, and cultivated. He scarcely raised his heavy eye-lids ; and his faint and irrelevant replies indicated that his brain was already touched by his disease.

All other interest was now lost in anxiety to reach Trenton; and after as rapid a drive, as roads, at their

best indifferent, would permit, they arrived at the
' rural resort,' the neat inn in the vicinity of the falls.
Fortunately there were no visiters there at the moment of our travellers' arrival, and they had an opportunity of selecting their apartments, and for
Seton, the most retired and commodious one the
house afforded, to which he was borne in the arms
of his attendants.

The consciousness of sacrificing one's private inclinations and comforts for the good of another is
always pleasant to a benevolent mind; and Mr.
Clarence, whom nothing but an errand of kindness
would have tempted from his home to a gathering-
place, was in unexpected good spirits. He already
' felt quite renewed by his journey.' ' Gertrude
looked better than he had seen her for six months.'
' He was sure Louis wanted nothing but a little rest.'
He was delighted with the deep retirement and *ru-
ralities* of the situation, and ' charmed with the
neatness, civility, and quiet of the house.' The
last quality was not of long duration. One or two
stage-coaches arrived, and the consequent and inevitable bustle ensued. The guests were judiciously
disposed in a part of the house as remote as possible from that occupied by Mr. Clarence; and
Gertrude passed the evening in her father's apartment, reading aloud to him, according to her
usual custom. The lecture was of course interrupted by Mr. Clarence' frequent visits to Seton's
room. His mind was still wandering, and his fever
increasing; but after a while, a powerful opiate took
effect, and he sunk into an unquiet, artificial sleep.
His attendant, however, reported that he was doing

well, and Gertrude, after giving her last minute
directions, bade her father 'good night.'

As she shut the door of his apartment, her book
in one hand, and lamp in the other, her foot was
entangled in the cloak of a gentleman who was
standing muffled in the little gallery. In extrica-
ting herself from the awkward embarrassment, her
lamp fell. The gentleman recovered it, and gracefully apologizing for the accident, he relighted the
lamp by the lantern suspended in the gallery. This
was an operose business. The cloak encumbered
him, he threw it aside, and Gertrude could not but
notice, with a curiosity stimulated by the concealment for which the cloak had obviously been
worn—for nothing could be more agreeably tempered than the atmosphere—the fine figure and
classic head thus accidentally and unintentionally
disclosed. Every one knows how slow and almost
impossible the process of ignition appears when
waited for. The gentleman made some common-
place, but, as Gertrude thought, pleasant remark
about it, which was suddenly cut off by a servant,
who came up the stairs and whispered to him. He
returned the lamp to Miss Clarence, bowed, and
hurried away. She turned to inquire the stranger's
name of the servant, but half ashamed of her curiosity, she hesitated, and while she hesitated, he disappeared.

Gertrude then went to her own apartment.
After remaining there a while, she missed her
keys, and recollecting she had left the bag that
contained them in the parlor, she went down stairs
in quest of them. As she approached the parlor-

door which stood a-jar, she heard voices in low and
earnest conversation.   She listened ; one was Mrs.
Layton, her heart beat, and she sprang forward,
and again stopped, for she perceived that her
friend was deeply absorbed in a *tête à tête*, evidently private, with the stranger whom she had
met in the gallery.   They had been quite too much
interested in their own affairs to hear Miss Clarence'
light tread, and there being no light in the passage,
she stood for a moment without the fear of observation.   Mrs. Layton leant against the window, her
handkerchief at her eyes, and her back to the light,
which fell strongly on the stranger's face.   His fine
features were kindled with a glow of earnest feeling,
he spoke in a tone of mingled supplication and remonstrance.   ' Such a man could scarcely speak
in vain,' thought Gertrude, as she turned away, and
stole back to her own apartment.   There she re-
volved in her own mind the probable meaning of
Mrs. Layton's unexpected appearance at Trenton—
the obscure intimations in relation to Emilie in her
farewell note—this private interview with the elegant
stranger—the Utica scrawl ; and she would probably have arrived at the right exposition, if that
had not involved Mrs. Layton in deep reproach.
Of course, that was rejected ; and after going round,
in the same circle, she gave up the subject as
inexplicable, and resigned her mind to the sweet
fancies awakened by a dewy moonlight evening.

Gertrude Clarence, in daylight, and amidst the
real affairs of life, was truly what Mrs. Layton had
called her, a fit heroine for the nineteenth century ;
practical, efficient, direct, and decided—a rational

woman—that beau-ideal of all devotees to the ruling
spirit of the age—utility. But it must be confessed
she had certain infirmities of olden and romantic
times clinging to her; that she loved in moonlight
and retirement, to abandon herself to the visions of
her imagination; that she sought and loved the
beauty and mystery of nature; that she gave her
faith to the poetry of life—the sublime virtue that is
sometimes manifested in actual human existence,—
and that always visits the dreams of the enthusiast,
as the fair forms of their divinities were presented to
the inspired vision of the Grecian sculptors.

CHAPTER XIV.

" Is't possible that on so little acquaintance you should like
her ?—that but seeing you should love her ?"

AS YOU LIKE IT.

WE have violated the consecrated privacy in
which Miss Clarence sheltered her romantic taste,
to prepare our readers for a sally that might other-
wise appear extravagant. It was a night to call
forth all the secret correspondencies between the
spirit and the outward world ; a night when the
soul responds harmonious to the voice of nature ;
when the intellectual life, that like the electric principle, pervades the material world, becomes visible
and audible, is seen in the starry depths of heaven,
and speaks in the ' viewless air.' It was a night—
just such as every body has seen, though perchance
not thus marked—in midsummer, sweet, bright, and
soft. There had been a slight shower, and the
atmosphere was charged with the perfume of all the
wild flowers that abound in the forest in June—the
month of flowers. The clouds had broken away
and dispersed, save here and there a few light
silvery forms, that as they melted away in the moon-
light, seemed the very coinage of the brain, shaped
in fancy's changing mould ; now winged spirits,
now graces wreathing themselves in flowers ; now
fairies at their elfin gambols, and now—nothing.
On such a night it is treason against nature to
steep the senses in sleep ; voluntarily to close the

natural entrances to all this glory; at least, so
thought Gertrude, and obeying a sudden impulse,
she threw on her shawl, and creeping softly down
stairs, she entered the apartment where the only
member of the family who was out of bed, was
drowsily adjusting his ledger. " I am going down
to the falls," she said.

" Miss! you'll see them far plainer by daylight."

Gertrude did not think it worth while to explain
the advantage of the *claire obscure*, and simply
requested a lamp might be left standing in the
entry for her. The man assented without expressing any inconvenient curiosity or surprise. The
head of the financial department of the ' rural resort' was a little ancient gentleman, (gentleman by
courtesy—illimitable republican courtesy!) who
trudged on in his narrow walk of life without looking to the right or left to scan the motives, or even
observe the conduct of his fellow-travellers. That
a lady should desire to see the falls by moonlight,
appeared to him no more strange than that she
should wish to view them by daylight. If he
valued falls, it was as ' water privileges ;' and the
only ' view' he took of picturesque objects was of
their effect on the bright side of the landlord's
ledger. Gertrude, therefore, happily escaped a
remonstrance, and soon found herself in the little
path traversing the deep wood which borders the
precipitous bank of the West Canada creek—a narrow, deeply embedded stream, that after winding,
leaping, and foaming in its unnoticed solitude for
centuries, has, within the last few years, become one
of the staple curiosities of the country.

Miss Clarence had passed a few weeks of the preceding summer at Trenton, and was secure in her
familiarity with the forest-paths. It seemed as if all
nature were hushed in silence to listen to the music
of the dashing waters. Not a breath of air was stirring. The leaves reposed in the still atmosphere.
The moon looked as if she were immoveably set in
the far, cloudless depths of the heavens, and where
her rays stole in through the lofty branches, and
slept on the moss-grown trunks, or dewy herbage,
not the slightest quivering of the leaves broke or
varied the clear defined outline of the bright spaces.
There is something vast and oppressive in such im-
mobility and stillness, and Gertrude felt, in approaching the brawling, noisy, little stream, as if it
were a living soul—a being endowed with feeling
and sympathy, and voice to speak them. She rapidly descended the several flights of steps, that afford but a slippery and inconvenient passage down
a precipitous rock of a hundred feet in height—so
grudgingly does art seem to have lent her aid to her
mistress nature—but here nature may well scoff at
her handmaid's negligence, for here she reigns a
queen of beauty; every heart does her homage;
every heart! the very trees, as they bend from the
walled banks and almost embower the sportive
stream, seem in the act of reverence.

Gertrude pursued the usual walk along the margin of the stream, now passing with security over
the broad, flat rocks, and now cautiously creeping
around the jutting buttresses, whose bases are fretted
by the foaming torrent, and whose sides afford a perilous passage along a shelving ledge, scarcely wide

enough for a heron's foot. Fortunately, Gertrude
had none of the physical sensitiveness that renders
some persons incapable of approaching a rapid
stream without dizziness. Self-possessed, and sure-
footed, she passed the most difficult passages without
fear and without danger. She ascended to the summit of
the first fall by the natural and rough stair-way, and
pursuing her walk, canopied by the over-arching
rocks, and creeping along the shelving shore, she
attained the side of the foaming, deep abyss, into
which the stream rushes at two bold leaps. She stood
for some moments gazing on the torrent, and almost
deafened by its roar, when she was startled by a
footstep close to her. She turned, and saw the
stranger who seemed, that evening, destined to cross
her path at every turn. He bowed respectfully, and
said he had not expected the pleasure of meeting any
one at that extraordinary hour—but he added, ' no
hour could be more fit for a devotee to nature to visit her sanctuary.'

Gertrude thought there was something like a sarcastic smile playing about his lip, as if his reading
of ' a devotee to nature,' was ' a mighty romantic
young lady,' a construction she felt was warranted,
but a light in which she did not quite like to appear.

" Neither did I," she said, returning the stranger's
smile, " think of the possibility of meeting any one
this evening. I came simply for the pleasure of seeing the falls by moon-light—by all other lights I
am familiar with them."

" But no other light can, " replied the stranger,
"be so well adapted to them. Broad day light, and
a party of exclaiming, professed admirers of scene-

ry, convert the most poetic passages into dull
prose."

" Yes," said Gertrude, pleased with a feeling so
exactly corresponding with her own. " Solitude
and moon-light are certainly the best accompani-
ments to fine scenery. They are like the vehicle
of music to the inspirations of the poet."

" And this is fine scenery," said the stranger; " I
have been scrambling along the bank for two miles
above this place, and never have I seen such various and startling beauty. The river has so many abrupt turns, and graceful sweeps—at every
step there is a new picture, as if you had turned another leaf in the book of nature. I have seen three
falls, above this, of less magnitude, and I have been
told they occur, at intervals, for several miles. But
the falls are only one feature. The sides of the
stream are varied and every where beautiful. In
some places richly wooded ; in others, stern, bare,
perpendicular rocks—now sending over their beetling summits a little cascade, that falls at your feet
in diamond drops, and then crested with a hanging
cedar that waves like a warrior's plume—now reced-
ing and sloping, and mantled with moss and fern, or
sending out from their clefts, sturdy trees—sylvan
sentinels on nature's battlements. In one place the
rocks recede and are concave, and the river appears
like an imprisoned lake, or a magician's well,——
there, I confess, I listened for an ' open sessime,'
and thought it possible I might see an enchanted
damsel, walk forth, with her golden pitcher."

" But you saw none," said Gertrude. " Ours
is not the country of enchantments—nature is *merely*

nature here. Neither enriched nor embellished, nor rendered sublime by traditionary tales, nor supernatural graces, or terrors."

"No, thank heaven, no terrors. I was never better pleased than now, with living in a country where a lady may walk forth, at midnight, without fear or danger."

Gertrude felt the awkwardness of her position, the moment it was alluded to, and she rather abruptly asked the stranger, 'if he had ever seen Niagara ?'

' He was ashamed to confess he had not. It was the fashion,' he said, ' to compare Trenton to Niagara, but he thought Trenton must be about as much like Niagara, as a frolicsome child was like to Hercules, or the finite to the infinite.'

"And yet," said Gertrude, "I hear the comparison often made, and Trenton often preferred. She is a younger favorite and has the advantage of youth and novelty over the sublime torrent. She has not been heard of by every body in the four quarters of the globe; nor seen and talked of by half the world. We feel something of the pride of discoverers in vaunting her beauty. She has too, her caprices and changes, and does not show the same face to all. This is one of her peculiar charms. There is such a pleasure in saying, ' Oh what a pity you did not see the falls as we did !' and ' ah,' with a shrug, ' we but just escaped with our lives. There had immense rains fallen, and the passes were all but impassable.' There are no such lucky chances of superiority at Niagara. Like a monarch, Niagara always appears in the same state and magnificence. It pays no visible tribute to the elements ; it is neither materially abated nor augmented by them. Niagara is like the ocean, alone and incomparable in its grandeur." It was apparent that Gertrude had seen Niagara, and the stranger naturally asked her many questions in relation to it. From Niagara he adverted to kindred topics. Not a water-fall, natural bridge, or mountain-resort, was passed by, till the meeting was protracted to the last limit of propriety. There is a peculiar pleasure in meeting with a stranger who discovers at once kindred tastes and feelings with our own. If it be a single sentiment, it is sometimes like a word in the ' correspondencies,' of a certain mystical sect, which may be a key to a whole volume. Acquaintance makes rapid strides in such circumstances ; and it was not singular that the stranger, whose imagination was no doubt stimulated by the time and place of their encounter, should linger in Gertrude's presence. He felt there was no propriety in detaining her any longer, if she intended to prosecute her walk ; nor, much as he desired to do it, could he, after her declaration, that she had come out for a solitary stroll, offer to attend her ; and inwardly praying she might say no, he asked if she meant to proceed farther. She answered—for she was not in the palace of truth, nor dared she follow her inclinations—' yes,' and the stranger, with evident reluctance, bade her good night, and soon disappeared.

Gertrude now proceeded very slowly up the next acclivity. The walk had lost its charms. Her mind was entirely occupied with the stranger, and with conjectures who he could be. 'He did not seem,' she thought, 'to remember our first meeting this evening; his mind must have been intent on his approaching interview with Mrs. Layton. If I had had but one glance at him, I should never have forgotten him.' She pondered over his interview with Mrs. Layton. 'Could he be her husband? No, he was far too young. Could he be Emilie's lover? No, such a lover could never need the interposition of parental authority.' Suddenly, and at the thought she stopped stock still, it occurred to her that he wonderfully resembled the image of Gerald Roscoe, impressed on her mind by her father's often repeated descriptions. She passed the stranger's features in review: his dark complexion, bold expanded forehead, singularly black hair, a stature and form cast in the heroic mould; the prevailing darkness of his face, relieved by a smile that disclosed a set of as white and beautiful teeth as ever decorated a mouth. 'How often has my father said,' thought Gertrude, 'that Gerald's smile was electrifying;' that it was 'like the sun bursting through a cloud—a smile of intelligence, arch, sportive, and good-humored.' 'Could this stranger be described more accurately?'

Gertrude was startled and roused from her reverie by what she fancied to be a strain of music. It seemed wafted over the torrent, and not mingling with its din, as if the breathing of some spirit above her. There was no visible agent. 'Am I deceived by the solitude, the scene, the hour, or is it an unearthly sound?' thought she. She looked timidly

around, and as she listened, the strain sounded
familiar. " It cannot be !" she exclaimed, and yet
impelled by an irresistible impulse, she sprang forward in the direction whence the sound came.
" Should it be he !" she cried fearfully, and hurrying through a tangled path, she came out on a
broad projecting rock, that although a few feet below the summit of the lower fall, commanded a full
view of it.   On that summit stood a figure enveloped
in a white dress, and so shaded by branches, that
hung like banners over the glittering waters, that
it was impossible to say whether the figure were
man or woman ; whether it were human, or some
strange visitant from another world.   While Gertrude gazed fearfully, the person advanced to the
brink of the water, threw the flute into the torrent,
bent over it, and clasped his hands as if in prayer.
" Louis !—Louis Seton ! oh, God of mercy, save
him !" shrieked Gertrude. The scream of agony
reached his ear, and arrested him ; he looked wildly
around.   She reiterated her cries and waved her
handkerchief. He saw her and descended the cliff
towards her so swiftly and recklessly that she covered her eyes in terror, lest she should see him
plunge into the abyss.

As he drew near, she ventured again to look at
him. His cheeks were crimsoned with fever, his
eyes had a supernatural brightness, his fair brow
was as pale as marble, and his long flaxen hair,
which had at all times a sentimental and student-
like air, was in the wildest disorder. He had care-
lessly thrown over his under garments a white dressing-gown, and his whole appearance confirmed .

Gertrude in her first impression, that he was delirious. But when he said, in his usual low-toned gentle voice, "You called me—did you not, Gertrude?" she replied, half reassured, and still half doubtful, "Yes; I feared you were venturing too near the fall, and," she added, with a smile of admirable self-possession, "I thought myself fortunate to meet you just at the very moment I was returning home-ward, and dreading to retrace the way alone."

"Oh, do not go yet! Why go away from this beautiful scene? It is a glimpse of heaven; I will never leave it but for a brighter," he added, in a tone of unwonted decision and confidence; "Sit down on this rock, Gertrude—I did not expect this—this is the first blissful hour of my life. Do not look so terrified—this is the gate of heaven—you shall see how I will throw off the load of life, and leap through it; Oh, it was very good of you, to come out to see this—come, sit down!"

There was something irresistibly appealing, and affecting in his manner, and Gertrude smothered her fears and sat down; "I dreamed," he continued, "an angel would show me the way—it's very strange—I cannot account for it;" he passed his hand over his brow, like one who would disentangle his recollections, "I do not think, Gertrude, it ever occurred to me, that you were to be that angel."

"But I am," said Gertrude, rising, and hoping to govern him, by humoring his wild fancies, "I am, and you are bound to follow whither I lead. Come, we must hasten home, Louis—follow me, I intreat you." He rose and followed, half-singing, and half-screaming.

· This will not do, I am exciting his delirium,' thought Gertrude; and stopping suddenly, she said, with all the composure she could command, " I ought, indeed, to be an angel to flit over these rocks at this unearthly rate. We had best return to our every-day characters, Louis; it is childish to risk our lives, in this foolish way."

Her natural tone and manner, for a moment, restored Seton to himself, and his thoughts reverted to their accustomed channel. " It is then a delusion," he said " yes—yes, life is a delusion—hope a delusion—and yet, who can live without hope? I cannot, and why should I, passively, remain here to suffer? Gertrude, did you see my flute, as it silently floated away? but a moment before, the woods rung with the music, my troubled heart poured into it. Think you, Gertrude, it would be as easy to still that heart, as the poor instrument?"

" But the heart is not yours, Louis," said Gertrude, assuming a playfulness, difficult to affect, while she was in a panic; " you gave me your heart, you know, and you have no right to resume it."

" Yes, I gave it to you, Gertrude, and it was a good gift—a true loving heart—but you would not take it—you could not—you know you said so—but, one thing I tell you, Miss Clarence, you will go forth into the world, you will be sought, and flattered, and you will learn, from bitter experience, the value of a true, faithful heart—no wealth can buy it—wealth! wealth! that was a cruel letter; it was the last drop in the cup. Gertrude, I felt as if

I were going mad, yesterday—but I am well, quite well, now."

Gertrude became more alarmed, at every new in-coherency; and felt her total helplessness, should he again attempt the violence on himself, he had purposed. It struck her, that she might, possibly, lure him onward, by addressing his love of his art, next to his love for her, his strongest passion; without replying, or adverting, to any thing he had said. "Come, Louis!" she exclaimed, "we are wasting time—you promised me, some moon-light sketches of the falls; and, farther on, there is a beautiful view—if we do not hasten, we shall lose the best light for it. She walked at as quick a pace as she dared; and Seton, obedient as a bird to his lady's whistle, followed her. They proceeded on their return, beyond the first fall; and Gertrude meant to lead him on, without alluding again to the view, but his painter's eye, as it rolled from shore to shore, caught the point of sight. "Ah! here it is," he said, " beautiful as a painter's dream—but I have no port-folio, no paper—never mind, I can draw on the impalpable air. I will put you in the fore-ground—you were in the fore-ground of all my pictures—my air-drawn pictures," he added, with a faint smile.

" But I must have a picture, that I can see—here, take my handkerchief—you can make a perpendicu-lar and a horizontal line, and write light and sha-dow, that is enough, you know, for an artist's sketch."

He kissed the handkerchief devoutly, spread it on

his knee, took a pencil from his pocket, and contemplated the scene intently ; the preparation for an ha-habitual occupation, restored for a time, the equilibrium of his mind ; his thoughts returned to their natural channel. " Such scenes as these," he said, " are the despair of the painter."

"Why the despair ? you never fail in your water views. Mrs. Layton said she was afraid to let Argus see your picture of the lake, lest he should try to lap the water."

" Ah, that was sleeping water ; but who can paint this beautiful motion—this sound, the voice of the waterfall—the spray, the most etherial of all material things—the light mist rising, and floating around those over-hanging woods, like the drapery of spirits, made visible to mortal sense ?"

" But you can imitate the most exquisite tints of flowers ; and surely, you can paint these wild geraniums, and blue-bells."

" Yes, I can imitate them ; but in the still picture, will they speak to us as they do now, looking out in wild and tender beauty, from the crevices of these stupendous rocks ? I can paint the vines that richly fringe those beetling crags, I might attempt their expression of security ; but can I give their light fantastic grace, their brightening and deepening hues, as they wave in the gentlest breath of heaven ?"

" Oh, no, certainly not! you cannot make all the elements of nature tributary to your art; you cannot work miracles ; you can but repeat in the picture, one aspect of the scene. You can give the deep amber tint of the water, but not every varying shade it takes from the passing clouds. You can

imitate these wild, broken shores, but not the musical trickling of the drops, as they swell, and fall
from ledge to ledge. A picture is, of course, dumb
nature ; it addresses but one sense ; it is what you
can do, that constitutes the glory of your art ; and it
is a weakness, Louis, to dwell on what you cannot
do."

Gertrude had unwarily touched the wrong key.
Seton sprang to his feet—" a weakness, is it Gertrude ? do *you* reproach me with my weakness ?—
Yes, it is the extreme of weakness ; but I have struggled against it—far, far worse, I have quietly endured it : I will not longer—why should I ? The world
cares not for me ; nor I for the world. I have floated on its dark, troubled surface, like those bubbles
on the stream—they dissolve and are forgotten. So
shall I be."

He spoke with the resolute tone of despair. Gertrude's heart sunk within her ; but calling forth all
her courage, she said, "I agree with you, Louis ;
the world has dark, tiresome passages enough ; but
even the worst of them, like our rugged path here,
may be cheered by a light from above. The light
always shines. Cannot you open your bosom to it?"

" Gertrude !" he replied, with a bitter smile ;
" do not mock me : tell those fretted waters to give
back the image of the heavens, serene and unbrok-
en : bid the stream glide quietly over these sharp
rocks : ask that solitary pine to go and bend among
its fellows. It is far easier to contend with nature,
than with the elements of the soul. I am wearied
with the conflict. I have struggled, and I am subdued. I have had such horrid dreams. My cruel

brother grinning at me—the world's laugh and
scorn ringing in my ears—your voice, louder than
all the rest."

"Do not think of it—it was a dream—nothing
but a dream, Louis."

"Yes it was a dream : and now you speak to
me in your own kind voice—this is reality." He
took her hand and pressed it to his scorchiug lips :
"I have heard the parting spirit had always some
intimation of the future—of good, or evil : this is
good—this is light to my heart : I have no more
fear. Farewell—farewell!" Again and again he
kissed her hand : "it is over now, Gertrude," and
he sprang towards the rushing stream.

Gertrude grasped his arm, and, shivering with
terror, detained him forcibly. "Have you no pity
on me, Louis? do not leave me here alone; attend me round these dreadful rocks; I shall never
get back to my father without your help ; you can
return directly. Come, do not—do not," she continued, imploringly, "refuse me this last kindness ;
come, quickly." She moved forward, and perceiving that he followed, she ran along the broken shore,
sprang from the rolling stones, and leaped from
crag to crag, forgetful of all dangers but one, till
she came to the last projecting rock, where the foot-
hold is extremely narrow, and rendered most perilous by the agitation of the water, which at times
lashes the side of the rock, but five or six feet
below the narrow margin, on which the passenger treads, in a position not quite upright, but
rather inclining over the stream. The hazard of
this passage was extreme. Seton still followed and

was close to her, but the spell that had controlled
him so far, might break at any moment. The in-
coherent sounds he uttered at every step, now
escaping in indistinct murmurs, and then swelling
to shrieks, indicated, too truly, ·the rapid access
of his delirium. Gertrude's courage failed—a nervous sickness came over her—her head turned, her
feet faltered, and she retreated a few steps, and
sunk to the ground.

It was but a momentary weakness ; she ejaculated
a prayer for resolution and strength, and sprang to
her feet again. " I am rested now,' Louis," she
said ; " once round this rock, we are almost home ;
follow me, dear Louis." She advanced to the perilous path, and proceeded around the projecting
cliff, without again faltering.

Seton followed to the front of the rock and there
stopped, and stood fixed and immoveable, as if he
were part of it. His face was towards Gertrude,
but his eye was glazed and turned upwards : it appeared that his senses were paralyzed, and that he
neither saw, heard, nor felt ; for though Gertrude
urged, supplicated, and wrung her hands in agony,
he maintained the same, statue-like stillness, looking like an image carved in the rock, before which
a terror-struck suppliant was standing. Gertrude
dared not advance towards him—his position did
not admit assistance—and the slightest movement,
even though involuntary, might prove fatal. She
cried to Heaven for aid, but while the unavailing
prayer was on her lips, Seton slipped gently from
the rock into the current below. In another breath
his body swept past her. A little lower down, the

current was less impetuous ; a few yards lower still
it was broken by the rocks and tossed in rapids.   He
evidently struggled against the current.   " Oh ! he
tries to save himself," cried Gertrude.   An eddy
seemed to favor his efforts, and impel him towards
the shore.   " Merciful God, help him !" she screamed, and sprang forward, in the hope that she
might herself extend some aid ; but, instantly, a
counter-current swept him off towards the rapids,
and his destruction seemed near and inevitable.
Gertrude gazed after him, speechless, motionless—
as if awaiting the doom of fate.   Suddenly there
was a plash in the water, and a person appeared
approaching the descending body.   " Should he
resist—" cried Gertrude.   But he did not resist.
It was at the calmest and most favorable point in
the whole stream for such an interposition, and perilous as it was, it succeeded ; and Seton, who had
not yet quite lost his consciousness, was drawn in
safety to the rocks.   Gertrude flew to him.   She
knelt beside him, and dried the water from his face
and neck with her shawl.   His preserver was active and efficient.   He supported Seton's head on
his breast, and chafed his hands and arms.

Seton was for a few moments incapable of motion
or articulation, but he looked intelligently at Gertrude, and as if he felt to the heart's core, the joy
and gratitude that lit up her face with an almost
supernatural brightness.   When her first emotion
gave place to a more natural tone of feeling, she
would have fainted—but she never fainted : she
would have wept, but there was still something to
be done.   She attempted to rise, but her limbs trem-

bled to such a degree as to be useless. "I pray
you to make no effort." Gertrude started at the
voice, and, for the first time, looking at Seton's
preserver, she perceived he was the stranger. He
smiled at the sudden recognition apparent on her
countenance. "I have been lingering at the steps
here," he said, as if in reply to her looks, "detained by my good fortune for your service. You are suffering even more than your friend from this accident." And so she appeared, for Seton was stimulated by fever. "You both need more assistance
than I alone can give you. I will go for aid, and
return instantly."

"Oh, not for the world," replied Gertrude, for
she felt the importance to Seton of keeping the adventure a secret, "not for the world," she reiterated.
She perceived the stranger smiled archly at her
earnestness, and she guessed at his interpretation.
' He thinks this, no doubt, an appointed meeting of
lovers, and Louis' fall accidental ; that at least
is a happy mistake.' In one particular she was
determined to rectify his misconception. "I came
here," she continued, "without the slightest expectation of meeting any one. I therefore can
have neither reluctance nor fear to be left alone.
This foolish trembling will be over in a few
moments, and I will then follow you if you will
have the goodness to give your arm to my friend—
it has already done us a service for which we have
no words to thank you."

Seton now for the first time broke silence and
attempted, though confused and embarrassed, to
express his gratitude. "I beg you not to waste

your strength in this way," said the stranger, " I
will take it for granted, that you are infinitely
obliged to me, for a service that cost me nothing
but a little wetting, a circumstance not altogether
disagreeable on a hot evening. I really have not
encountered the slightest danger; but if I may
make a merit of this accidental service," he continued, bowing courteously to Miss Clarence, " I
claim the right to return and escort you, after I
have attended your friend."

" We are so deeply your debtors, that you may
impose your own conditions. I will await you if
necessary—or meet you."

" If necessary! pardon me then, if I put some
constraint on your courtesy. The evening is becoming cool, allow me to wrap my cloak about
you; it shall be fetters and warder till my return."
As he spoke, he took his cloak from the ground
where he had hastily thrown it, and adjusted it
around Miss Clarence. At another time Gertrude
might have felt a girlish and natural diffidence at
receiving such attentions from a stranger; but serious emotions give to these little punctilios their
due insignificance and she received his kindness as
quietly as if it were warranted by old acquaintance.
Seton's unnatural strength was the only indication
of the continuance of his fever. He was tranquil
and it appeared probable from the exertions he had
made for self-preservation that his first immersion in
the water had stimulated his reason. Gertrude
watched him anxiously till he disappeared from her
in ascending the steps, and then she gave utterance to her devout gratitude for his preservation

from death, by an interposition that appeared to her to have been miraculously provided. Accustomed to think and decide independently, she determined to keep poor Seton's sad affair, so far as depended on herself, a profound secret. ' Even my falher, kind and indulgent as he is,' she thought, ' would not deem it quite prudent to retain Louis after this; but have I not solemnly promised to be a sister to him ? and when he most needs a sister's love and care, I will not abandon him.' From Seton her thoughts naturally turned to the stranger. ' How very strange our repeated meetings,' she thought, ' how heroic his rescue of Louis ! and yet (she was constrained to confess it) a common man would have done the same, but not in the same manner. There was a careless grace about him, as if great actions were at least familiar to his imagination.' All her reflections ended in the natural query, ' who can he be ?' Suddenly it occured to her that his cloak might be labelled, and instantly throwing it from her shoulders, she sought and found, neatly wrought in large black letters, *Gerald Roscoe.*

Is it fair farther to expound Gertrude's thoughts ? It must be told, that stimulated by an entire new set of emotions, she rose, threw the cloak from her, adjusted her hair, which she was mortified to find had fallen down, and which, as dame nature had given it neither the canonical heorine wave, or curl, could not but be ungraceful in disorder.

It certainly appeared to her that destiny had maliciously arranged the circumstances of her introduction to the hero of her imagination. How often

in those reveries in which young ladies will indulge
when they weave the plot of a little personal romance—how often had she contrived the particulars of their first meeting—like a skilful painter, and
with pardonable vanity, arranged the lights and
shadows to give the best effect to the picture.   And
now to be first seen by him rambling over perilous
rocks, at the witching time of night, and suspected,
as she knew she must be, of an appointment with a
young man of Seton's appearance, and in such a
fantastical dress, and she such a figure!   She remembered the smile she had detected on Roscoe's
lips, and the thought that she had at least appeared
ridiculous to him, was intolerable.   Then she recollected the Utica scrawl, and was compelled to
admit the conviction that Roscoe had written it.
This wounded her; it touched her feelings where
they were most vulnerable; and, indignant and resentful, she determined to hasten up the steps and
avoid, if possible, speaking with him again.   The
cloak she left on the rock.   She could no more
have touched it than if it had been Hercules' fatal
tunic.   She forgot that a few moments before she
could scarcely support her own weight, ascended the
several flights of steps without halting, and had
reached the very last, when she met Roscoe returning.   She was embarrassed and breathless, and without stopping—without the slightest acknowledgement
of his courtesy, or apology for the trouble she gave
him, " You will find your cloak," she said, " on
the rocks—good night, sir."   But Roscoe did not
appear to notice her abruptness.   " I expected," he
said, turning and offering his arm, which she de-

clined—he mended his phrase, " I hoped to have had the pleasure of finding you there too—I beg you will not walk so rapidly—you have no occasion for anxiety about your friend ; he reached the house without difficulty—and his own room,"—he added, with as Gertrude thought, a very significant emphasis—" his own room *without observation*. I am quite sure of it, for I remained in the entry till I heard his door close." Miss Clarence made no reply, and they walked on a few paces in silence. Roscoe then said, " I am curious to learn how the accident happened. I asked your friend, but he evaded my inquiry—he perhaps felt that his foot ought not to have faltered, where yours trod safely."

Gertrude, in her confusion, and desire to shelter Seton, said, " he was weak from recent illness."

" An imprudent exposure for an invalid !" returned Roscoe, with another of his provoking smiles, " but I honor his self-forgetfulness in so romantic a cause, and only wonder that a prosaic personage like myself has been allowed to appear in the drama, though it be only to turn the wheel of fortune for others, and be dismissed and forgotten, when I have enacted my inglorious part." They had now reached the door-steps, and he added in a lower voice, " I am compelled to return immediately to the village, and proceed thence in the stage-coach —may I presume to ask the names of my new acquaintance ?"

" Oh, no—do not ask them—do not, I entreat you, inquire them—do not ever speak of what has happened to night. The life," she continued, for she had now quite recovered the power of thought and speech, "the life you have preserved would be worthless if there were any exposure."

"Shall I make a vow of secresy?" he asked, bending his knee gracefully to the step, gallantly taking her hand, and speaking in a tone of raillery that Gertrude felt made her pathetic appeal almost ridiculous, "I do make it," he added with mock solemnity, "craving only an exception in favor of one friend, a safe confidante—my mother. I call on the bright moon to witness my vow," and in token of sealing it, his lips approached her hand, but without presuming to touch it. "Now I have pledged the honor of a true knight—do I not deserve a dispensation in my favor?"

While Gertrude hesitated, resolved not to give her name, and feeling that it was almost childish to withhold it, a window-sash above their heads was gently raised, and murmuring a heart-felt 'God bless you,' she escaped into the entry. There she lingered long enough to ascertain that Mrs. Layton was speaking to Roscoe; and then, after listening at Seton's door, and finding all quiet there, she retired to her room to revolve over and over again, and to place in various lights and shadows, the events of the evening.

She had seen Roscoe at last! and in spite of her personal mortification and vexation, she liked him—she could not help it—she rejoiced in her inmost soul, that she was still unknown to him as the dreaded *rich* miss Clarence, and she finally fell asleep with the secret, sweet consciousness, that she had not impressed him as altogether the counter part of '*Miss Eunice Peabody!*'

CHAPTER XV.

" Surtout lorsqu'on a l'air de plaisanter avec le sort, et de comp-
ter sur le bonheur, il se passe quelque chose de redoutable dans le
tissu de notre histoire, et les fatales sœurs viennent y mêler leur fils
noir, et brouiller l'œuvre de nos mains."   CORINNE.

MISS CLARENCE was up at gray dawn, awaiting
intelligence from Seton. She had directed his nurse,
to inform her how he passed the night; and, though
conscious she was better informed than any one else,
she was anxious to learn the effect of his wild sally.
John soon appeared. " Mr. Seton," he said, " lay in
a dead sleep, but was nothing worse. I have not
closed my eyes" continued John, " the whole blessed
night, but one bare minute, and then while I dosed,
as it were, Mr. Louis took the advantage to slip
down stairs, and pump some water on his head, that
was fiery hot, and the poor young gentleman came
back, as wet as a drowned kitten ; I was scared half
out of my wits ; but I put on him dry clothes, and
got him quite comfortable, and I hope Miss Gertrude, nor Mr. Clarence, won't take it amiss that
I was overcome with that wink of sleep."

But Miss Gertrude, though the gentlest of kind
mistresses, did take it very much amiss ; and re-
proved John, with the utmost severity, that the of-
fence, according to his statement of it, (which she
was compelled to receive,) admitted. Those are to
be deeply compassionated, who are obliged to trust

to menials and strangers, for offices, in which affection alone can overcome the weariness of mind and body! Gertrude felt too late that she had rashly undertaken a task she could not execute. ' Oh, were I his sisterindeed !' she thought ' I would never leave him !' She blamed herself for urging his coming to Trenton, and wished nothing more than to get back to Clarenceville, where secluded from observation, she might share the personal care of him with her women ; but the physician, at his morning visit, declared a return impossible—he would not even sanction a removal to a private house, but ordered the patient's room to be made perfectly dark, and prescribed the usual remedies for a brain fever.

Miss Clarence was not exempt from the reserve, fastidiousness it may be, so sedulously cherished in the education of our country-women. But every thing was well proportioned, and well balanced in her mind ; she never sacrificed the greater to the less. The moment she ascertained that Seton's reason was so far alienated, that he would probably be quite unconscious of her presence—and that it could certainly be of no disservice to him, she went to his room, sat at his bed-side, and watched him, as if he were in truth her brother. He was alternately torpid and silent, or violent and raving. The only indication that a spark of reason remained, was in the passiveness with which he received from Gertrude, what he rejected from every other hand.

In the evening there was a slight remission of his fever, and Gertrude went to her own apartment, where Emilie Layton, who had sent her repeated messages during the day, was awaiting her.

The affectionate girl threw herself into Gertrude's
arms—expressed her delight at meeting her in the un-
qualified terms of youthful ecstasy, and her extreme
pity for 'poor Mr. Seton.' After informing her
that her mother was longing to see her, but that she
had been in bed all day, with a violent head-ache,
she was silent, evidently embarrassed, and perplexed. She unclasped and clasped her bracelet twenty
times, twisted every feather of her fan awry, and
at last, throwing her handkerchief over her face,
she said, " dear Gertrude, I am engaged to be married to Mr. Pedrillo."

" Emilie !" exclaimed Gertrude.

Nothing could be more simple and bare, than
the exclamation ; but it was a key-note to Emilie's
ear. " I knew you would think so, Gertrude," she
said, as if replying to a long remonstrance—" I told
mama you would—but it is not so very—*very*
bad ;" and she laid her head on Gertrude's shoulder, and sobbed aloud.

" But my dear, sweet Emilie, if it be bad at all ?"

" Well, I don't know that I can say it is bad at
all—at least, it would not be, if ——"

" If what ? speak out, Emilie."

" Oh ! I had rather speak out to you, than not ; I
am sure my heart will feel the lighter for it. You are
so reasonable, and so judicious, and all that, Gertrude,
that I suppose you have not felt so ; but I expected
to be in love when I married. Ever since I first
thought of it at all, though I can't remember when
that was, I have expected to love, and adore my
husband—I have always said, I would never marry
any man, that I was not willing to die for."

" And 'judicious and reasonable' as you think me, neither would I, Emilie."

" Would not you, Gertrude? would not *you*?—then, it is right—I am sure it is right;" and her beautiful face brightened all over ; but, instantly, a shadow crossed it—as much of a shadow, as can appear on a freshly blown rose, and sighing heavily, she added, " bnt it is no use now—it is all settled."

" Irrevocably ?"

" Irrevocably ; mother says, to recede would be ruinous to us all ; she has not explained to me how, because she cannot bear to make me as miserable as she is. If I can make them all happy,I ought—ought I not, Gortrude ?"

" If yon can, without too great a sacrifice, Emilie."

" It seems to me a great sacrifice ; I do not, and never can love Mr. Pedrillo, and you know, I must never love any body else ; so it is a total sacrifice of my affections ; but that is all. I like Mr. Pedrillo—at least, I should, if he did not want me to love him. Mother says, she is certain, that after I have been married a year, I shall like him better than nine women out of ten like their husbands. He is very kind, and generous to me ; he gave me these splendid bracelets ; but Gertrude, when I put them on I could not help thinking of the natives of Cuba, you know, who thought, poor simpletons, that the Spaniards were only decorating them with beautiful ornaments, when they were fastening manacles on their wrists. I always hated Spaniards—I am sorry Mr. Pedrillo is a Spaniard—I cannot forget it, though he does not look at all Spanish.. Mama says, he is probably

descended from one of the Irish Catholic families
that emigrated to Spain. He is called very handsome, Gertrude," she continued in as plaintive a
voice as if she were counting her griefs ; "he is
very gay when he is pleased ; he has seen a great
deal of the world though he is not very old—not
more than forty."

"Forty ! Emilie ; and you seventeen !"

"So it seemed to me, Gertrude. I told mama
forty seemed to me as old as the hills, but she quite
laughed at me and quoted something from Molière, about his being the better fitted to guide my
youth."

"I presume he is a man of fortune, Emilie ?"

"Oh yes, indeed ; that is the worst of it ; if it
were not for that, I could do as I please."

Gertrude's heart was full of sympathy, tenderness, and compassion for the unresisting victim, but
she hesitated to express her feelings. 'Why should
she increase the reluctance that must be unavailing?
Were it not better to employ her influence over
Emilie to reconcile her to the now inevitable event.'
She tried to look at the affair in the most favorable
point of view, and as there are few substances so
black that they will not reflect some light, so there
are few circumstances in life but that have, as the pro-
sers say, 'their advantages as well as disadvantages.'

"I should certainly have carved out for you a different fate, dear Emilie," she said—"to love, as
well as to be beloved, is always our young dream."

"Yes, indeed ! and is it not hard to awake so
very soon from it ?"

"Yes ; but it might prove an illusion, and you

awake to some blessed realities. You might cease to love, but you can never lose the happiness that springs from a difficult sacrifice to filial sentiment."

"That is true, Gertrude, and I will make the most of it. Mama would have been so wretched—she has so much feeling."

Gertrude recollected the Utica scrawl, and the impassioned intereiew that she had witnessed between Mrs. Layton and Roscoe, and some painful distrusts of that lady crossed her mind. The *feeling* that required all the sacrifice to come from others, appeared to her very questionable. "Do not look so troubled about me, dear Gertrude," continued Emilie, rightly interpreting Gertrude's expression. "I never take any thing very hard. Aunt Mary used to say I was born under a mid-day sun—there were no shadows in my path. If she had but lived!—but there is no use in wishing." Emilie was interrupted by a summons to Gertrude from Seton's physician.

"Stop one moment," said Emilie; "I have not yet told you that Mr. Pedrillo is to be here in a few days, and that mama hopes to be able to see you to-morrow; but she begs you will not speak of this affair to her; 'her nerves,' she says, 'are so torn to pieces,' and—oh! I forgot to mention that I want you to come down stairs to-morrow, there is a Miss Marion here who wishes excessively to see you; and her brother—and indeed, Gertrude, you should come down, for in spite of all I say, every body believes that you must be engaged to Mr. Seton." Gertrude was solicitous to avoid such an interpretation of her devotion to Seton, and she pro-

mised Emilie she would make her appearance on
the following day. But the following day found
her occupied, weary, and heart-sick, and she declined
joining the society below stairs.

Day after day passed, and there was no abatement
of Seton's malady. The scene was sad and monotonous to Gertrude, but there were various incidents
occurring that were destined to affect the fortunes of
those in whom she was interested.

Nothing is more characteristic of our country
than the business-like way in which pleasure is pursued. The very few genuine idlers have not yet
learned grace or ease in their '*idlesse*.' A genuine
idler—a man of entire leisure, is a *rara avis*. The
Duke of Saxe-Weimar was asked by an honest Yankee, ' what business he followed for a living?' The
host of travellers who run away from their offices,
counters, and farms, for a few hot weeks in mid-sum-
mer, hurry from post to post, as if they were in truth
'following the business of travelling for a living.'
Trenton is one of the picturesque stations that must
be visited, but being situated between Niagara and
Saratoga, the chief points of attraction, Trenton is
the game shot on the wing. Most travellers leave
Utica in the morning coach—arrive at Trenton at
mid-day—hurry to ' the steps,' and the brink of the
' great fall'—eat their dinner, and proceed on their
route, in the full complacency of having seen Trenton! Two or three parties remaining there for several days, was a rare phenomenon. The Marions
alluded to by Emilie, were Virginians. The mother,
son, and daughter, comprised all that remained of their
family—a family that, from its earliest existence, had

been among the most distinguished of the ' ancient dominion.' The blood of English nobles ran in their veins, and was not, in their estimation, less honorable for having, in its transmission to them, warmed the hearts of pure republican patriots. They were the very reverse of the character which (we are ashamed to confess) is often ascribed by northern prejudice and bigotry to our southern brethren. Active in body and mind, spirited, gifted, cultivated, kind-hearted, and indulgent to all human kind—even to their slaves—to such a degree, that never was a family better loved or better served by its dependents ; and so far from possessing riches, (which some among us fancy lose their wings when they perch on a southern plantation,) they had an hereditary careless- ness of pecuniary matters, which, combining with the general deterioration of southern property, menaced them with alarming embarrassments.

Augusta Marion had endured severe afflictions, but she did not increase their force by resistance. She had not the usual sweetness and gentleness of deportment that characterizes the manners of the la- dies of the south. On the contrary, she had a start- ling abruptness ; but as it was the natural expression of an impulsive character, of a quick succession and rapid combination of ideas, and as she had a tender heart and good temper, (in spite of now and then a momentary heat and flash,) her manner became ra- ther agreeable, as suited to the individual, and char- acteristic of her. She was sagacious, and her ene- mies said sarcastic ; but if so, her arrows were never poisoned, and never aimed at a reptile that was not noxious.

Randolph Marion, the brother, was the hope, pride, and delight of mother and sister—a man that everybody might love and admire, and own they did so without being asked for a reason, for the reason was apparent. He had nothing in excess, but all gentlemanly points and qualities in full measure. He was not a genius, but talented—not learned, but well informed—not 'too handsome for any thing,' but well-looking enough for any body. He was not a wit, nor the mirror of fashion, nor pink of courtesy; but good-humored and well-bred. In short, he had just that standard of character that attracts the regard of others, without alarming their self-love.

The Marions, or rather we should say Augusta Marion, was Emilie's constant theme during her interviews with Gertrude. 'She was certainly,' she said, 'except her dear Gertrude, the most charming woman in the world, so agreeable and so witty!' Once or twice the name of Randolph Marion escaped her, but without note or comment. 'She had known them both two years before in Philadelphia, and she had always thought Miss Marion most entirely captivating, and so did her aunt Mary.'

Gertrude was delighted to see that Emilie could crop the flowers in her path. Neither of them perceived they grew on the brink of a precipice. Emilie seldom adverted to her engagement. Like death, it was future and inevitable, but its period was not fixed, to her knowledge, and she felt in regard to it, all the relief of uncertainty. Little did she suspect that her mother had promised that the mar-

riage should take place as soon after Pedrillo's appearance at Trenton as he should request.

Mrs. Layton was still secluded in her own apartment, and beguiled Gertrude and Emilie—and
herself too—with exaggerated expressions of sensibility and suffering! 'She could not see Gertrude,'
so said the little twisted pencil-scrawled notes which
she sent her twice and thrice a day, 'an indifferent
person she could meet without emotion; but her
nerves and affections were so interwoven that one
could not be touched without the other vibrating. She
was sustained by the consciousness of performing a
necessary duty, but she had nothing of the martyr
in her composition, and she shrunk from the fagot
and the pile. She thanked heaven, poor Em' had
not the sad inheritance of her sensibility. In a few
days she hoped to see Gertrude—but now her
nerves required solitude and a dark room.'

Of all the mysteries and obliquities of the human
mind, the arts of self-delusion are the most curious.
No doubt Mrs. Layton's imagination figured the
fagot and the pile, but was it the martyr or the cul-
prit that suffered?

"Dear Gertrude," said Emilie, bursting into
her apartment, and looking as bright and fresh as
a sunny morning in June, "we are all going to the
falls this afternoon—do promise you will go with
us." Mr. Clarence, who chanced to enter the room
at the same moment, enforced Emilie's entreaties,
and Gertrude promised to join her in the parlor in
the course of half an hour. Accordingly she went
to the parlor at the appointed time; but finding no

one there, she passed into a small adjoining apartment, and while she was awaiting Emilie she examined a collection of minerals belonging to mine host of the 'rural resort,' a versatile genius, who is well known to have diversified the labors of his calling with occasional lectures on the popular sciences. Directly, two other persons entered the parlor, but as their voices were unknown to her, she remained where she was, secluded from observation.

After some common-place remarks about the weather, the lady said abruptly, " Have you made up your mind, Randolph ?"

" About what, Augusta?"

"Pshaw! don't blush so—upon my honor, I did not allude to Emilie Layton."

" I did not imagine you did, Augusta."

" Oh, not at all ; and you were not thinking of her—were you ?"

" And if I were?"

" If, indeed ! No, no, Randolph, you must not enact the lover there—a beautiful gem she is—but not for your cabinet. Did you ever see such rich hazle eyes, and dark eye-lashes, with such fair hair, and exquisite skin ?—did you ever, Randolph ?"

" Why do you ask me, Augusta?—you know I never did."

" And such dimples and lips—and her fairy Fanella figure—and her exquisite little feet. I do not believe Pauline Borghese's were as pretty, though it was her custom to denude them to the admiring eyes of her visiters—do you, Randolph? Well may you look grave, It was a cross accident that cast her in your way just now, when such

an opportunity of falling eligibly in love is at hand
—when, for once, love and reason might meet
together in good fellowship."

" As they never did meet, Augusta."

" Ah, that is the cant of one and twenty. But
matters are differently arranged with such veterans
as mama and I. You should hear some of our
colloquies. Dear mama! nothing is more amusing
than the struggles of her natural tastes against the
vulgar necessities of this ' bank-note world.' In
your selection of a wife—and mama has no doubt
you can select from the whole sex—she would not
allow the lady's fortune to be even a make-weight
in the scale of your favor ; but the trifling acces-
sory—the little accident of fortune ' removes the
only objection to Randolph's marriage,' so says
mama. ' Removes the objection !' was ever a pecuniary motive more ingeniously stated, and in singleness of heart too. And truly, Randolph, if this
Miss Clarence is the paragon of excellence that
Emilie represents her, the one objection is removed."

" But, Augusta, what if there be in my heart a
thousand and one objections ?"

" To Miss Clarence ?"

" Pshaw! no. What am I to Hecuba, or what
is Hecuba to me ?"

" I understand you—the objections are to mar-
rying any woman, save one ?"

Marion shut the outer door, and then replied,
" Yes, Augusta, save one. From you, my dear
sister, I have no concealments."

Miss Marion made no reply for some moments—
when she did, her voice was changed from raillery to

tender seriousness, "I am sorry, Randolph—heartily sorry—but cannot blame you. All the loves and graces have combined in that pretty creature against your prudence; and then her beauty is so true an index of her sweet, innocent spirit. Well, it can't be helped, and so there's an end of it. No, I do not blame you. On the very verge of the frigid zone of old maidism as I am, there is nothing I so truly sympathize with as a youthful, reckless, true love—a love that hopes, expects, and believes all things—and fears nothing. Randolph, from the time we knew Emilie in Philadelphia, and you used to carry her music-book to school for her, I have had a presentiment of this, and when we met here, I was sure you had turned the critical page in the book of fate."

"And you permitted me to read it without advice or warning. God bless you, my dear Augusta."

Nothing makes a young heart overflow with gratitude like meeting (especially if unexpected) with hearty sympathy in a love affair. Randolph Marion was a pattern of fraternal affection, but never had he felt more tenderly towards his sister than at this moment; and when she proceeded to give him more unequivocal proofs of her sympathy, his feelings were raised to a higher pitch than tenderness.

"Randolph," she said, "I am frank and direct, and must to the point. I like to remove all moveable obstacles. I do not mean to be pathetic; but you know 'there are but two of us,' and between us two but one heart. I have some fortune, thanks to aunt Molly—there are sad rents in our patrimonial estate—take what I have and repair them, and in return, my dear brother, give me in fee simple a

rocking-chair at your fire-side, and that, with a life
estate in your heart, is all I ask."

Marion threw his arms around his sister's neck,
and expressed in a few broken sentences his admiration of her generosity, and his determination not
to accept it.

" It is no sudden impulse of generosity, Randolph, but that which I have long expected and determined to do. Since the event that fatally and for
ever extinguished my hopes, nothing remains for
me but to make others happy ; and that, I suspect,
after all, is the surest way of making myself so."
At this moment the door opened, and Emilie appeared. She perceived the brother and sister were
deeply engaged, and was retreating, but they both
begged her to come in, and she then asked ' if Miss
Clarence were not there ?'

" Heaven forefend !" exclaimed Miss Marion,
resuming her natural tone of gaiety.

" She must have come in here," continued Emilie, " her father told me she was here, and the servant says he saw her come in here."

Poor Gertrude had been on the rack for the last
ten minutes. There had been no point in the conversation from its start, when she could, without extreme embarrassment, make her appearance. As it
had proceeded, she had become as anxious to avoid
observation, as ever a hidden criminal was to escape
detection. She would have jumped out of the window if there had been an open window ; but there
was none—no possible escape—and she had stood,
like a statue, hoping that some kind chance would

call the parties away before she was compelled to
make her egress. Emilie approached the door of
the inner room, and nothing could in any degree
relieve her but an adroit movement. She advanced
from her seclusion.

"Gertrude," exclaimed Emilie, "you are here
after all !"

The Marions looked thunderstruck. There was
tinge enough on Gertrude's cheek to manifest her
full consciousness of the awkward position in which
she stood. Emilie began the usual form of an introduction.

Gertrude interrupted her, then recovering her
self-possession, she said, "An introduction is superfluous, Emilie, you would hand me across the
vestibule—I am already in the inner temple—and
your friends must believe," she continued, turning
to them, her fine countenance animated with the
feelings they had inspired, "your friends must believe that I feel its beauty too much, ever to violate
its sanctity."

Miss Marion obeyed the impulse of her warm
heart and took Gertrude's hand. "We are friends
for ever," she said, "and Randolph is in love, literally at first sight." He certainly looked all admiration. "Do not, my dear Emilie," she continued,
"stare as if we had all of a sudden fallen to talking
Greek—don't ask, even with your eyes, for an explanation. Here is Mr. Clarence looking as if it
were time for us to proceed on our walk." They
did so—and when they came to the steps, Mr.
Clarence turned off, saying that he had arrived at
an age when a man must be excused for preferring

to look down upon a water-fall to the inconvenience
of descending to look up. The ladies accepted his
excuse and promised to join him at the shantee on
the brink of the great fall. Emilie took Marion's
offered arm, without dreaming of the projects that
were agitating his bosom, or the hopes that were
hovering on his lips for expression. She was at
the happy age when the feelings are enjoyed, without being analyzed. She lived in the present bright
hour, careless of the future, for whatever was future
seemed to her, as to a child, distant. When they
reached the flat rocks at the bottom of the steps,
Gertrude was affected by the recollection of the
scene she had witnessed when last there. Miss
Marion observed her unnatural paleness, and im-
puting it to the debility consequent on her fatigue
and anxiety, she insisted on sitting down with her,
and permitting Randolph and Emilie to precede
them. Randolph was nothing loath to this arrangement, and he soon disappeared with his fair companion. The circumstances of Gertrude's introduction to Miss Marion, enabled them to dispense
with the usual preliminaries to acquaintance.
They understood one another, and feeling that they
did so, they interchanged thoughts on various subjects with the familiarity of friends. Miss Marion
did not speak of Emilie, and Gertrude dared not intimate that her destiny was already fixed. They
talked of Mrs. Layton, about whom Miss Marion
was quite curious. She had never seen her, and
had no very favorable impression of her. "I would
fain believe, Miss Clarence," she said, "that she
deserves the admiration you express of her, but I

am certain I should not like her. The happy age of delusion—the luxury of believing all things are what they seem, is past to me. Experience has been to me like the magical unguent with which poor Lelia anointed her eyes, that enabled her mortal vision to penetrate through all disguises into the sins and miseries of fairy land. Mrs. Layton is a woman of fashion—a belle at forty! No, I am sure I shall not like her. Thank Heaven, Emilie has not been long enough in her atmosphere—a malaria it is—to be infected by her." Gertrude interrupted Miss Marion to ask if she knew the gentleman who had just descended the steps, and who after a keen glance at them, eagerly surveyed the only traversable path. "I think I have seen him before," she said, after a moment's consideration. "Oh, yes, that dog I recollect perfectly." She pointed to a beautiful liver-colored little spaniel, with white tips to his feet and ears, and his sides fleckered with spots so white and distinct, that they appeared like wreaths of snow just lightly thrown there. "I remember now, it was on board the steam-boat I met them—the dog is a perfect beauty." The dog, as if conscious of the admiring gaze of the ladies, and like a flattered belle, anxious to show off his commended graces, plunged into the water. The current was stronger than he anticipated, and he seemed in imminent danger of being swept away; but he courageously buffetted the waves, whimpering and keeping his eye fixed on his master, who sprang to the brink of the water, crying, "Bravo! bravo! Triton, my good fellow! bravo!—courage

mon petit!" He looked as if he would plunge in for
his favorite, if it were necessary. But it was not—
Triton came safe to land, and while he was shaking
a shower from his pretty sides, and receiving his
master's caresses, Gertrude anxiously demanded of
Miss Marion if she knew the gentleman's name.
" I do not—I meant to have inquired—it is such a
burden off your mind when you find out a stranger's
name—he is evidently a foreigner."

" A foreigner!" echoed Miss Clarence.

" You start, as if a foreigner were of course a
pirate, or a great bandit." ·

The only foreigner Gertrude thought of, at that
moment, certainly seemed to her to belong to the class
of spoilers. Though Emilie had told her, Pedrillo
did not look like a Spaniard, yet Gertrude's imagination had pictured him with dark eyes ; with a face
of more shade than light, and in every shadow lurking some deep mystery or bad design. The gentleman had large and very light blue eyes, and
a fair, clear complexion, though rather deepening to
the hue of the *bon vivant*, and Gertrude thought at
first sight, (for we would put in a saving clause for
her sagacity,) had rather an open, agreeable expression.

" What does your practised eye," she asked Miss
Marion, " see of the foreigner in that gentleman ?"

" What ! why, in the first place, observe his air—
the *tout-ensemble*—he has nothing of the don't care,
negligent demeanour of our countrymen who, from
living always among their equals, from having no
superiors to obey, nor inferiors to command, get
this easy, indifferent, and careless manner. Our

quiet, plodding, uneventful, comfortable lives, are
stamped on our faces. They are as different from
the Europeans, as the appearance of a tame animal,
from a wild one. After the smooth surface of
youth is broken up, the face bears the record of individual experience. I was struck with this, in looking at David's picture of the coronation. The remarkable men there clustered around their master,
the miracle of the age, looked as if they had lived in
an atmosphere of pure oxygen. I remember turning my eyes from the picture to the sober citizens
who were gazing at it, and thinking that their faces
were as spiritless as shaking Quakers."

"But these are indications to the gifted eye,"
said Gertrude.

"There are others then, more obvious. Just
cast your eye on this gentleman, now his hat is off;
you may, for he does not seem conscious of our existence—that profusion of hair, would be a curiosity
on an American head, over five and twenty; and this
gentleman has some dozen years more than that—and
observe, as he passes his hand over his face, those large,
richly set rings. I never saw an American (I mean, of
course, a man past boyishness and dandyism) with
more than one, and that, some simple token or me-
morial; and finally, see the string of little silver
bells on his dog's collar—an American would not
venture an appendage so pretty and fantastical.
But see, he is coming towards us, and means to
speak—of course he is not an Englishman."

The stranger bowed courteously, and made some
common-place remarks on the scenery. Whether
his accent were foreign, or merely peculiar to the in-

dividual, it was difficult to determine. He compared the falls to those on the Caatskill—the Cohoes,
the falls of the Genesee, Niagara, la Chaudiére, and
Montmorenci. ·This was all American, and Gertrude began to think her companion's sagacity was at
fault ; but in the next breath, he spoke of the falls of
the Clyde, of Tivoli, and Schuffhausen, as if equally
familiar with them. He affected nothing of the
amateur of nature, but appeared the citizen of the
world, who, habitually adapts himself to the taste
of the company in which he happens to fall. The
ladies rose to pursue their walk, and he bowed, and
preceded them at so quick a pace that he was soon
out of sight. Brief as their interview had been,
Gertrude was satisfied that Miss Marion was right
in her conjectures, and instinctively as she shrunk
from it, she believed that she ought to rejoice in Pedrillo's arrival. The sooner poor Marion was awakened from his dream, the better ; and certainly too,
the sooner Emilie was recalled from the labyrinth,
into which she was blindly plunging. But even her
deep interest in her friend was driven from Gertrude's mind, at repassing the rocks on which she
had suffered with Seton the agonies of deadly fear
and despair—some gentler remembrances beamed
athwart her mind.

An abrupt turn in their walk, now again brought
the ladies in view of, and near to the stranger. He
stood partly concealed by a cluster of dwarf-
beeches, his face half averted from them, but still
they could see that his brow was contracted, his lips
compressed, and his eye eagerly fixed on some object ; and instantly Gertrude perceived that object

was Emilie, and she felt assured the stranger was Pedrillo. Emilie stood beyond, and far above them, on the flat surface of a projecting rock. Her Leghorn cottage-hat, tied with pink ribbons, had fallen back, and Randolph was interweaving her beautiful tresses with wild flowers. She appeared as lovely, and both were as happy as spirits of paradise; and Pedrillo seemed to regard them with that oblique and evil eye, that Satan bent on our first parents in their blest abode—that eye of mingled and contending passions, that expresses the ruined soul. Both the ladies stopped, and stood motionless.

All parties were near the great fall. Mr. Clarence was in the porch of the little shantee that overlooks the cascade. Randolph and Emilie had ascended some distance above the basin of the torrent, by the foot-path, that winding around the perpendicular rocks, and mounting the bare sides of those that are less precipitous, affords a safe, and not very difficult ascent to the cautious and agile passenger. As we have said, Emilie and Marion were standing on the platform of a projecting rock, when Pedrillo first discerned them—there they stood, the world forgetting. It was one of those few blissful moments of life, that borrows nothing from memory, and asks nothing from hope. Such moments are too often a prelude to weary hours of sorrow; they were fleeting to Emilie, for recalled to actual existence by a strong and unequivocal expression of Randolph's tenderness, her engagement darted into her mind; she started as if a dagger had pierced her heart, and turned from her lover. As she did so, she saw Pedrillo; she encountered his glance, and she felt to her inmost soul all it conveyed. She uttered a faint exclamation and turned from the rock to ascend the cliff. She left his side, or rather sprang from him so abruptly, that Marion was not aware of her intention till she was some feet in advance of him. . "Be careful, Emilie!" he cried, "Stop! for Heaven's sake, stop—let me precede you. Emilie! Emilie! stop!" he continued, as she, without hearing or heeding him, pressed on. "Just ahead of you, is a most perilous place—for God's sake, stop! Emilie! Emilie! you are below the path!"

Still she heeded not, but pressed on with that fearlessness that sometimes secures from accident. But here there was but one security—but one safe path, and from that she had unconsciously deviated. Mr. Clarence saw from above her imminent peril, and screamed to her to stop. Gertrude and Miss Marion perceived, that one more step, and her fate was inevitable; and in the same breath, they uttered a shriek of terror. Pedrillo, too, in a voice that resounded from shore to shore, shouted ' Beware !' Randolph, only, was silent; almost petrified by the immediate presence of the danger of which he saw the full extent without a hope to rescue her. The panic was now fully communicated to Emilie. The shouts above and below confounded her, without conveying any distinct intimation to her mind. Already her foot was on some loose stones that projected over the edge of the precipice, and only half sustained by the earth in which they were embedded, must be dislodged by the slightest force. She felt them sliding from beneath her feet, and made one more leap forward, but there the support. was still more treacherous—the stones gave way at the first touch of her foot, and she felt herself sinking with them. Instinctively she stretched out her arms, and grasped a bough of hanging cedar that depended over the cliff. Her hold was too weak to sustain the weight of her body, and yet tenacious enough to check her descent. Many feet, sheer down the precipice she went, her hands slipping near to the extremity of the limb where though scarcely as thick as a common sized rope, it yet supported her.

So powerful is the instinct of self-preservation, that the most weak, and timid, and inexperienced, left-alone, without any possibility of help but in the energy of their own efforts, have manifested an amazing power in perceiving and grasping at any means of salvation from destruction. Her friends were gazing in despair. They saw the limb swing back from her released grasp, and believed that all was over. Not Randolph, for he had already descended the precipice with desperate velocity, and from below he saw Emilie, with the heaven inspired instinct that would have guided a kid over a mountain crag, gently release one hand from the bough and grasp some fibrous twigs, that shot out from a fissure in the rock—and just where she needed the support, and where alone it would avail her, there was a cleft in which she placed her feet. One giddy glance she gave to the precipice below, and the foaming abyss that lashed its side, then turned her face, pressed her brow to the rock, and resolutely closed her eyes to shut out the appalling scene. Pedrillo and Marion now ex-

plored the precipice with intense and almost equal
anxiety, to find some mode of rescuing her from the
frightful position, that it was evident she could not
long maintain. At the same moment they perceived a fissure in, or rather a ledge, of the rock, just wide
enough for a possible, though most perilous passage,
from the platform from which Emilie had started to
a place a few feet below, and parallel to that where
she now was. Both at the same instant sprang towards the platform. Pedrillo was nearest and first
attained it, and thus secured himself the precedence
on the narrow ledge. Marion's satisfaction at seeing him rapidly approach Emilie to give her the aid,
which, if it came not soon would come too late, was
strangely mingled with disappointment at thus being
rendered, by the interposition of a stranger, useless
to her for whose safety he would freely have given
his life. But he soon lost every other feeling in the
apprehension that some misstep—some miscalcu-
lated aid, might farther endanger the life, that was
now suspended by a single thread. Once or twice
Emilie half turned her face towards him. It was
as pale as marble ; and even at that distance, it was
evident from a certain relaxation of attitude, that
her strength and courage were sinking away. What,
then, was his astonishment at seeing Pedrillo, after
reaching the extremity of the ledge—the point
where, if at all assistance was to be given, stand for
a moment, survey the abyss, and then return towards the platform. In an instant he reached it.
" Some other mode must be tried," he said, " the
ledge at its extremity is inconceivably narrow—there
is not breadth enough for a bird's claw—my head

became giddy—at the least attempt to aid Miss Layton I must have lost my balance, and we should have been precipitated into the abyss. Follow me, sir," he continued, with the air of one who has a right to command; " there are persons at the shantee who can help us—ropes must be let down—there is no time to be lost."

" Not an instant," said Marion, " and but one way to save her ;" and he passed on to the ledge, with the evident determination ' to do, or die.'

" Oh stop !—my brother—Randolph, stop !" cried Augusta Marion, who, with Gertrude, had attained the platform, and was standing there, both most agitated witnesses of the whole scene.

But Randolph would not heed her; and Gertrude, with a firmness that was a guardian angel in all exigencies, followed Marion saying, " I am sure I can give your brother assistance—I am used to these rocks—be calm, Miss Marion, and do not look at us."

" Noble creature! God help them!" ejaculated the terrified sister, and clasping her hands she sunk on her knees; but her lips did not move—her heart scarcely beat—her whole soul was fixed in one intent breathless interest.

But what was her suffering to that of the father, who stood on the verge of the cliff and saw Gertrude, she in whom all his affections and every hope were concentrated, voluntarily place her life in peril ; and that peril, to his view, aggravated by the distance and depth below him. !

In the mean time, Pedrillo mounted the rocks, intent on his own project of rescuing Emilie. He had not proceeded far, when his little dog, Triton, who seemed to have become aware that danger pervaded the place, sprang yelping after him and before him, as if to arrest his progress. Pedrillo, in his eagerness, stumbled over him and fell; and in his fall he sprained his ankle so as to be utterly disabled, and was obliged to crawl back to the platform, and there endure an irritation of mind that far surpassed the anguish inflicted by his hurt, though that was by no means trifling. His love for Emilie was the strongest and tenderest sentiment of which he was capable, and he was now condemned to remain in utter inaction, and see her beautiful form mutilated, crushed, destroyed ; or, an idea scarcely more tolerable, see her saved from this perdition by the superior devotion and skill of this young stranger rival.

Has Dante described a penal suffering more acute than Pedrillo's ?

Marion, closely followed by Gertrude, soon reached the extremity of the ledge. He seemed not even to perceive the danger from which Pedrillo had retreated. Emilie was not conscious of his approach till he pronounced her name. She then looked towards him with speechless agony. Her deathly paleness, the nervous convulsion of her features, and the tremulous motion of her whole body struck a panic to his heart. His eye turned to Gertrude. "Oh God !" he murmured. His voice and look expressed his utter despair.

"Be calm," she replied, "we can save her—I am sure of it—only be firm. Emilie—Emilie," she added, in an almost cheerful voice, "be resolute for

one minute more, and you will be safe." Again
Emilie turned her head, and still she looked like a
dying victim on the rack. Gertrude did not venture
to raise her eye to her. With the inspiration of heroic
courage and devotion, she bent her whole mind to the
action. Not a thought was spared to fear or danger. "You see," she said to Marion, taking her
hands from the rock and standing upright with a
careless freedom of attitude, "you see I have ample
space for my feet. I stand with as perfect security
here, as on a parlor-floor. Here too, are some
twigs above me, by which I can hold. My position is firm and safe. "You"—she continued, de-
pressing her voice to the lowest audible tone—
"you have a narrow, precarious foot-hold; but by
grasping my hand you may secure your balance.
Now consider how you can get Emilie where we
are."

Gertrude's self-possession and intrepidity inspirited
Marion. "We can save her," he exclaimed, if she
will let us. Do you speak to her—I cannot."

"My dear Emilie," she said, "the danger is
already past, if you will think so. Fix your
eye on us, and mind Mr. Marion's directions."
The poor girl felt already the inspiration of hope.
She did as she was directed, and as she turned her
face towards them, they perceived she was much
less frightfully pale and agitated. Marion gave one
hand to Gertrude, and extending the other, "place
your feet," he said, "Emilie in my hand. It is as
firm as if it were braced with irons—keep your
hands upon the rocks—they will support and balance you. One single yard from this spot, and

you will be in perfect safety." Once Emilie advanced her foot, and withdrew it. "Do not draw back, Emilie," cried Gertrude and Marion in one breath—"do not draw back—fear nothing—keep hold of the twigs till your feet are firmly placed." She did so—they retreated one step. Marion's hand was firm and unbending as adamant—another step—and another, and Marion slowly depressed his hand, and Emilie's feet were on the rock, on the same level with his. Not one word was spoken. He placed his arm around her, and thus sustained her, trembling like an aspen leaf, to the platform, and there she sank on his bosom, and both lost all thought and feeling, save an obscure but most delicious consciousness of safety and love. How long they remained thus they knew not. What mortal art can measure or define such moments? They seem to partake of the immortal essence of the high feeling infused into them—to belong to eternity.

Gertrude had passed the platform, and gone to meet her father, whom she saw approaching. In his arms she was now folded, receiving all the expression he could give to his joy, and pride, and gratitude, and love.

Pedrillo had withdrawn a little from the platform, and though he still stood near Emilie and Marion, they were unconscious of his proximity. With a feeling that she was now all his own, Marion imprinted a kiss on her brow. Pedrillo started forward, "Miss Layton," he exclaimed, in a voice of passion, "have you forgotten?"—He paused. If the rocks had yawned to engulf her, Emilie would not have been more shocked. She became as agitated as when she hung over the abyss. A more dreadful abyss, was present to her imagination. She shrunk away from Marion, and covered her face with her hands.

"What is the meaning of this impertinent intrusion?" demanded Marion.

"Impertinent!" retorted Pedrillo, "and what name do you give, sir, to the advantage you have taken of the accidental service rendered to my affianced wife?"

There was an assurance in Pedrillo's voice and manner that left little to be hoped. Marion turned a look on Emilie that said every thing—he spoke but one word, "Emilie?"

"It is all true," she replied.

"Would to God then we had perished together!"

A check was now put upon the expression of the excited feeling of all parties. Mr. Clarence approached. Emilie's face was covered and leaning on Miss Marion's shoulder, who, half comprehending, and fully pitying her, sustained her in her arms. "My poor little Emilie," said Mr. Clarence, tenderly embracing her, "I do not wonder you cannot get over this dreadful fright. We must get you home to your mother. Where's Marion? Ah, there he goes, running away from our compliments. It was a knightly feat, but he should not withdraw till the ' fair ladye' is in her bower again."

And how to get the ladies to their bower again was the next consideration; but as this was achieved by ordinary means, we shall not detain our readers with the details.

The ladies were all, of course, compelled by Mr. Clarence' tender watchfulness over their health to retire for repose. Gertrude was relieved from a vain attempt to compose her spirits, by an urgent request from Mrs. Layton that she would come to her room. She received her with extravagant demonstrations of joy and tenderness. Flattering as they were, they awakened a passing query in Gertrude's mind why the pleasure that was so fervent had been so long deferred. " My precious Gertrude," began Mrs. Layton, after the first greetings were over, " you may have some faint idea how much I have suffered for the last ten days, from the fact of my not being able to see you. It is hard for one who has Heaven's chartered freedom of mind, to be bound by the stern fatalism of circumstances. I can only allude to certain affairs. If I were at liberty I should open my heart to you, Gertrude, of all persons in the world; but you already know enough from my poor Em' to imagine my relief from having the evil day put off."

" Thank Heaven," exclaimed Gertrude, " it is then put off."

" Of course—Pedrillo is unable to move— what a frightful predicament poor Em' was in, on those rocks; and she tells me, you behaved so sweetly, Gertrude. By the way, dearest, do tell me something of this young Marion who enacted the hero to-day—rather officiously, I think—I am provoked that he should thrust himself forward, and deprive Pedrillo of such an opportunity of rendering Emilie a romantic service." Gertrude in-

ferred from the light tone, in which Mrs. Layton
spoke of the affair, that she was not at all aware of
Emilie's hair-breadth escape, and she described the
frightfulness of her danger, Pedrillo's attention to
his own safety, and Marion's devotion to the single
object of Emilie's preservation. Mrs. Layton listened with great apparent interest, expressed her surprise that Emilie had been so incommunicative,
and concluded by saying, she supposed "the poor
child had been scared out of her wits. She scarcely spoke to me after her return; and said, she should
lie down in her own room, and begged not to be
disturbed—she is taking an honest nap I have no
doubt—she is just like her father—I should not
have slept for a month, after such an affair. Well, it
is fortunate for her, that she has so little imagination.
It will make small difference to her, who enacts the
hero—she is not like you and me, Gertrude; she
never will suffer the sad, sad experience of a heart
of sensibility, its cravings, its yearnings, its unbounded desires, its vain regrets—No, no, Emilie's
life will flow on, as the scripture has it, like still waters in green pastures."

"Oh, Mrs. Layton, I am afraid your expectations are too sanguine. Her childhood has been
serene, but to pursue your figure, the stream that is
destined to frightful precipices, may hold its infant
course through flowery and still pastures."

"It may; but we are misled, by talking figura-
tively. The fact is, I see, (for I am not blinded by
maternal affection,) I see that Emilie is a *mediocre*
character; if she were not, would not her own beauty excite her more? She will just live *even on*, con-

tent with what would be to you and me, perfect
stagnation, ordinary connubial life—it is a safe, but
certainly, not a very alluring destiny. Believe me,
dearest, married life rarely affords much excitement
to the sensibilities, or scope to the imagination."

Gertrude shrunk from expressing her maiden
meditations, on this subject. They were high and
romantic, or, might be called so, by those who are
fond of affixing that doubtful epithet, to the aspira-
tions of those, who modify their hopes by the capabili-
ties of our race, rather than graduate them by its history. Mrs. Layton guessed her thoughts; " My sweet
friend," she said, " I see your mental revoltings from
my views of life. Mine are the result of my peculiar
position; I am not a philosopher, and my opinions
are deduced from individual experience; so, do not
let me cast the shadows of my past, over the
bright field of your future. We will not talk of
shadows; I feel particularly light-hearted. As I
said before, the evil day, which God knows I have
done all I could to avert, is at any rate deferred.
Pedrillo has too much respect for the graces, to go
hobbling to the hymeneal altar. I shall have time
to recruit my spirits; and poor Em', to cultivate a
more tender sentiment for her suitor. Indeed, I
think he ought to excite it; he is uncommonly elegant, and a foreigner; and that is, after all, an advantage *dans les petites affaires du cœur.* The
men of our country, particularly our northern country, are so deficient in all the embellishments—the
mysterious, indescribable little arts, that excite the imagination; they are upright and downright—and
have such a smack of home about them. If they

reach the heart, it is by the turnpike-road of common sense, not by the obscure, devious, mysterious,
but delicious avenue of the imagination. You agree
with me, at least you feel with me, Gertrude?"

"I am listening to you, but I really have no opinion on the subject ; I have seen so little of society,
that I have made few comparisons. My predilection, I confess, is in favour of my own countrymen ;
they may have a less polished exterior, but they
seem to me, to have more independence of manner,
more naturalness, and simplicity."

" Certainly, they have—but less of these prime
qualities than savages—you smile, but you will think
with me, when you have passed a winter in town—
the thing I have set my heart on. By the way,
poor Louis Seton ! Gertrude, a *sentiment* is so necessary to us ; so much is it, as has been said, the 'history of a woman's life,' that, shut up, as you have
been, at Clarenceville, with this ' man of feeling,'
I am amazed you have escaped something more
serious than a passing *tendresse*. Now, no protestations—susceptibility is absolutely essential to an
attractive woman. But come, dearest, one of my
reasons, though the least urgent, for sending for you,
was, to beg you to present me to these Marions. It
is incumbent on me, to make my acknowledgments
to our knight of the rocks."

The ladies proceeded together to the parlor, and
there learned, to Gertrude's mortification, and Mrs.
Layton's well concealed satisfaction, that the Marions had taken their final departure from the ' rural
resort,' half an hour before. A servant gave Miss

Clarence a note from Miss Marion; it ran as follows :

"My dear Miss Clarence—I have forborne to "disturb your repose after your perilous adventure, "to announce our abrupt departure. Accident in-"troduced you into our family cabinet, and as you "are apprised of its secrets, you will not wonder at "poor Randolph's feelings, in consequence of the "disclosures of to-day. My heart pleads for Emi-"lie, but my reason tells me, that it is wisest, "discretest, best, to shun any farther intercourse "with so beautiful a creature, who is so careless of "obligations and consequences. Depend on it, "Miss Clarence, I am right in my opinion of the "mother; and though I grieve to say it, poor Emi-"lie has bad blood in her veins. I am sustaining "the part of a rigid moralist with Randolph, while "my womanish heart is melting within me. I can-"not regard the sweet girl in any other light, than "as a victim—the faults of seventeen are not deli-"berate—but I talk as sternly to Randolph, as if I "were Junius Brutus. In compliance with a kind "invitation from your father, we have promised to "visit Clarenceville, on our return from Niagara.

"'Till then, adieu, my dear Miss Clarence,
"and allow me to be
"your friend and admirer,
"A. MARION."

Pedrillo was on a sofa in the parlor, when the ladies entered; and while Gertrude was reading her note, he and Mrs. Layton were carrying on a sub-dued, but impassioned conference; the result of which was a request from Mrs. Layton, that Miss Clarence would do her the favour to request Emilie, provided she found her awake and sufficiently recovered, to make her appearance in the parlor.

Gertrude found her friend, neither sleeping, nor recovered ; but sitting in a most disconsolate attitude, bending over an open letter, which she had drenched with her tears. " Oh, Gertrude ! she said, " look at this—is it not cruel ?" It was from Marion, and began with the text of all disappointed lovers. " Frailty, thy name is woman ! Must I apply this " condemnation to Emilie Layton? Why have I " lived to find that she, whom my devoted love " invested with perfection, is capable of delibe- " rate coquetry. Am I in my senses ? Could Emilie " Layton, she, who appeared full of all kind and " gentle thoughts, could she, on the eve of mar- " riage with another, trifle with a heart she knew " was all her own ? She has done so—your own " lips Emilie, have confessed the truth—your vows " *are* plighted to another—it is not slander—it is " not a dream—again and again I repeat the first " prayer of my pierced soul, ' would that we had " perished together.' But, my sister waits for me ! " she talks of recovered tranquillity—but what tran- " quillity can be in reversion for him, who bears in " his bosom, a poisoned shaft ? the bitter remem- " brance of her unworthiness, to whom he would " have devoted his existence ; for whom he would " have encountered death itself, without a pang.

" Farewell, Emilie—farewell for ever,

" R. MARION."

Gertrude quite forgot the errand on which she had come to Emilie, in her efforts to console her. "I should care for nothing else in the wide world," said the poor girl, " if Randolph only knew how innocent I have been."

" That he may know in future, Emilie, but at present ———"

" Oh I know I must not vindicate myself—I must suffer, and suffer in silence, and if my heart breaks I must not tell him that I loved him—loved him with far truer love than his ; for I never would have believed any evil of him. I did not know till now— indeed, Gertrude, I did not, that I loved Randolph. I knew that I was always thinking of him, but I did not know *that* was love. I knew that I felt restless away from him, even with you, and happy if I were but near him without speaking, and without hearing his voice; but I did not know *that* was love. Even on that dreadful rock, Gertrude, I felt that I had rather be swallowed up in the abyss than be saved by Pedrillo, when Randolph was so near to me, and yet I did not know *that* was love. But when Mr. Pedrillo claimed me, and Randolph pronounced my name, then the whole truth flashed on me ; and yet I had better die than speak the one true word to Randolph. And with this on my heart I must go to the altar with Mr. Pedrillo—and very soon too —mama hinted that to-day."

" Not soon, Emilie—perhaps never. Mr. Pe- drillo was maimed on the rocks, and he has himself deferred the marriage."

" Thank heaven ! but what reason is there,

Gertrude, to hope this detested marriage may never take place ?"

" Every thing future, Emilie, is uncertain—every thing—but that if you disclose to your mother the actual state of your feelings, she will herself break off this engagement."

" Never—never, Gertrude. Mama has reasons that she does not tell me. She never would have made me write that solemn promise to papa, if it were not *necessary* to perform it. I do not know how I could do it, only that I always have to do every thing mama wishes. Mama was so sure I should like Mr. Pedrillo, and I thought she knew best. I did not hate him then—but now the very thought of him makes me shiver."

Gertrude was well aware that Mrs. Layton would not wish Emilie to show herself to Pedrillo in her present state of mind, and after ministering all possible consolations to her, she undertook to make her apology to her mother. She received it with the best grace possible. Not so Pedrillo. His cup of irritations was full, and one added drop made it overflow. He wrought himself first into a passion, and then into a fever, which produced so violent an inflammation in his wounded limb, that on the following morning the physician gave his professional opinion that the gentleman might be detained at Trenton several weeks. In this state of affairs Mrs. Layton felt her position to be rather awkward, and she and Emilie, after a tender parting with Gertrude, took their departure for New York.

Mr. Clarence and Gertrude were still detained at Trenton for some weeks. Seton's convalescence was slow and imperfect, and his melancholy continued, like an incubus, in spite of all their efforts to alleviate it. When his health was sufficiently restored to bear a removal, Mr. Clarence proposed, that instead of returning to Clarenceville, he should proceed to New York, and there embark for Italy, where in a genial climate, and in the pursuit of his art, he might regain his health and happiness. Mr. Clarence, who seemed always to regard his fortune as a trust for others, assured him that he should place at his disposal a sum that would render his residence abroad, easy and respectable. Seton heard him without reply, but with evident emotion.

On the following morning they were to leave Trenton. Seton did not appear at breakfast. Mr. Clarence went to his room, and found that he had gone, and had left a note addressed to him. It was full of expressions of gratitude and tenderness to Mr. Clarence and Gertrude; but it was most afflicting to see that those sentiments, whose essence seems to be happiness, were so transmuted in his distempered mind, that sweet fountains distilled bitter waters.

"Why," he said, "seek to prolong a burdensome existence? He was a weed driven on the tempestuous waves—the idle sand blown over the desert of life. He cast a blight on every thing about him." The note was written in the deepest despondency, and concluded with a request that no inquiry might be made after him, and a most affecting and eternal farewell.

This request was so far from being complied with, that Mr. Clarence instituted the most assiduous inquiries. He traced him to Utica, but no farther. His family connections knew nothing of him, and Mr. Clarence and Gertrude were driven to the horrible conclusion that he had committed the last act of despair.

END OF VOL. I.